The Lure of an Ancient Fable

✕

Episode 7
Of
The Missing Shield

Copyright

First Edition published in Great Britain, November 2018.
ISBN 978-1-912648-12-2
Cover design by The Chunky Designer, All Rights Reserved
Publisher L. L. Thomsen
Edited by Parkes Editing
Copyright © 2018 by L. L. Thomsen
All Rights Reserved.

For maps, dictionaries, overviews, newsletter link, interviews &
more
Please visit
www.llthomsen.com[1]

To 'Follow' and 'Like'
Please visit
twitter.com/LLThomsen1[2]
facebook.com/themissingshield/[3]
instagram.com/llthomsen/?hl=en[4]

---

1. http://www.llthomsen.com

2. https://twitter.com/LLThomsen1

3. https://www.facebook.com/themissingshield/

4. https://www.instagram.com/llthomsen/?hl=en

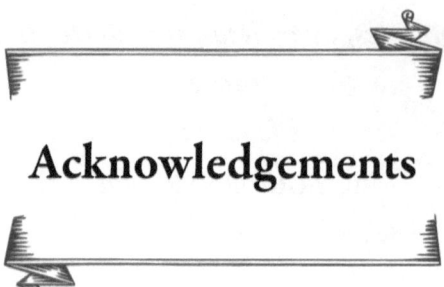

Acknowledgements

To my husband for his patience and everlasting support that helped me realise my goals and dreams. Though not a geek and fantasy lover like myself, your trust and generosity means the world and this work would simply not have been possible without you.

To the brilliant, most inspiring, most important people of all: to the Owl and the Unicorn - my children; my muses - without whom my imagination would undoubtedly still be slumbering in a deep subterranean cavern. Even when dinner is a little late and I spend hours at the computer you still cheer me on – never lose the magic!

And last but not least: to the readers! Thank you for your interest, support and enthusiasm. Thank you for sticking with me and continuing on this journey – as I am a 100% indie author, this means so much more to me than you could ever imagine.

You make the story telling worthwhile!

Head's up From the Author

Hi there and thank you for hopping onboard once more.

As you have probably figured out by now, Solancei and Iambre's homeland of Ostravah is just part of a much large world called Dallancea.

If you are left feeling curious, please pop on over to www.llthomsen.com to browse glossaries, and maps, et cetera. Here you can also check out details of the cast or the other realms of Dallancea. So far you have caught glimpses of the Sabén-Heshep Realm where a break-away fraction of the Elvern people now reside, and you might also recall a brief visit (via Guardian Cahmerhin's mind-link with Guardian Denarlin) to Cahmerhin's home, the Ermaron Realm, where the giants, also named 'The Irnarlai', reside.

Now as The Veil Keepers Quest is a story in development, to avoid spoilers, you will not yet be able to access all the details – sorry to leave you blinded - but keep checking when you come across something new in the books because relevant information and news is constantly being added.

Thank you once again. This story is about to unfold in ways you could not have predicted... ;-)

The Story So Far

> Princess Iambre of Ostravah is on a year-long tour of the fifteen provinces that make up the realm she stands to inherit, but upon arriving in the westerly situated province of Zanzier after self-inflicted delays, she receives a luke-warm reception of local lord, Simarovien Zulavi, ruler and knights Commander. This appears to be just the beginning of a change to her cosy, indulged existence, as a run of bad events follow – including the disturbing disappearance of her closest friend and cousin, Solancei. Things keep going wrong, and she is powerless to affect the situation – something that she is very ill at ease with.

> Furthermore, there is still trouble on the romantic front too. Desperately in love with Bilan Metavo - the captain of her retinue - Iambre has nevertheless been forced to oblige her would-be lover's stout demands that he must be decommissioned to save her honour and his heart - and having finally agreed to oblige, it's with a heavy soul that she knows she must bid him farewell after her ten day stay in Zanzier.

> Though a consummate diplomat and trained in the arts of public self-discipline and etiquette, Iambre is nevertheless pushing her own goodwill to the limit, when forced to deal with Lord Zulavi's derogatory Zanzierian views and hobbling backwards adherence to old rules and honour. As the days pass with no news of her friend's whereabouts, Iambre finds herself more and more at odds with the 'merry' celebrations she is forced to endure in her own name. There is something about the situation that has her instincts on edge and

it floors her enjoyment. However, the truth remains that there is a chance Lord Zulavi could have a hand in the strange disappearance of her life-shield: cousin and childhood friend, Solancei, yet without proof Iambre simply cannot challenge the man.

> As Iambre suffers restless nights and unease behind the scenes, it has meanwhile fallen to Chief of Security, Klaas Eso Mehadja – Solancei's mentor – to investigate the affair surrounding Solancei's disappearance, but as sordid details about an illegal fight and the true nature of Solancei's training – and situation - are gradually revealed, Iambre is roused to experience new feelings of anger and fear. Klaas seems unable to make little head way in her clandestine investigation and Solancei appears to have been swallowed up by the ground. On foreign soil, and without the option to draw on local expertise to solve this missing person's case, will the Chief ever be successful, or will Iambre have to carry on the ploy offered as cover, that Solancei is currently absent duty as she is being chastised for poor conduct and has been 'allocated' temple duty as penance. Iambre is not sure what outcome to expect, but one thing is certain: from wanting to leave Zanzier if given half the chance, she now wishes to stay until Solancei is located. Still, this looks increasingly like an impossible wish, and Iambre fears that she will have no choice but to leave on the scheduled day, whether Solancei has been recovered or not.

> The knot in her stomach is growing, Iambre ponders Zulavi's agenda. She has sought council on the matter from Bilan, but though initially semi-successfully placated by his reasonable theories (something that the Chief has also backed with her own assurances), Iambre is no longer so sure. An opening presents itself to investigate a lead to locate Solancei, and it sets Iambre mind spinning with bold ideas. The Chief, however, denies Iambre any involvement on professional grounds, which leaves the Princess wondering about alternatives. Though it's madness, her gut feeling will not accept no for an answer.

> Knowing nothing about Solancei nor about the truth that sur-
rounds her extra-curricular activities and title, Bilan Metavo is nothing if not surprised when Iambre summons him to her richly
adorned, temporary apartments. Although she has promised to find
a way to call on him one final time before his decommission takes
effect, their previous meeting ended with a nod to bitter-sweet for-
mality - something Bilan did not expect Iambre to overcome. However, his senses have once before told him that something is amiss.
He has tried his best to allay Iambre's ghosts of worry in regards to
Lord Zulavi's personal flaws when in her company, yet Bilan is personally not one bit keen on the commanding knight in charge of
Zanzier. Having had previous experience of Zanzier, he secretly de-
tests Zulavi, but for now he still elects to conceal his true feelings.
Iambre is out of sorts and the last thing he wants is to aggravate her
peace of mind just because of some misplaced personal agenda.

> Of course, the unexpected revelation that Solancei has disappeared
- and during a jackal fight no less - stirs Bilan's loyalty just as Iambre
had hoped and in a way that she is fully prepared to capitalise on.
In honour of the rules that surround Solancei's secret metier as her
Shield, however, Iambre still keeps back the real truth of Solancei's
position and why she has trained in the jackal fights to begin with. It
is not that she does not trust Bilan, but some things are not hers to
reveal.

> Lord Simarovien Zulavi, meanwhile, is busy organising a rebellion
to overthrow the current rule of King and Senate. It is not what he'd
call it, though. Indeed as the Knights Commander sees it, he will
only be making the realm stronger once more, when he claims back
that which was once his - and having allied himself with the strange
Tuxaman scholar and Lord, Visentor Tan'Xaviar, he is utterly certain
of his own success to usurp the power. Of course, there is always
the chance that the bookish Tan'Xaviar cannot remain focussed on
keeping his end of the bargain for long enough for Zulavi to lay his
hands on Iambre and secure her for his queen, but the Tuxaman no-

ble is just too integral in Zulavi's plans, not to take the chance that their odd alliance will hold. It is what he needs to work right now and later he can always adjust and make alterations, should this be deemed necessary.

> Satisfied that his plans are progressing, now Zulavi just has to deal with the feisty prisoner in his dungeon – a task that is both bewitching and frustrating, as he strives to learn her secrets. But Solancei is a Veranto Master and she stands to break every oath she's ever sworn if she gives into Zulavi, so she cannot and will not comply. With only one way forward to break her resistance, Zulavi turns to the poisonous drug Megaa'ron - and the old illegal torture contraption known as 'the rack'.

> Whilst this plays out in the Ostravahn Realm – at the same time in the Elvern Realm known as the Sabén-Heshep, Nefer, the Best-Loved Daughter of Living-God Sheshem'Kufunar and First-Queen Nafretiri, has been taken under the wing of the Guardian Speaker in order to aid his quest in locating any abnormalities in the historical record. The Speaker Sinuhé hopes this could lend the Upper Circle a hint as to how they nearly lost the war against the Mad Ones when last the Veils were recalibrated to protect the Realms. The loss of fellow Guardian and second-in-command, Richarmarlan Envalair, remains a puzzling discrepancy that needs investigating also, but the ancient artefact known as 'the Tapestry', continues to weave the History of all Dallancea without flaw.

> For Nefer, her new apprenticeship was unexpected but also gratifying, but even so the unwavering lack of data-related discrepancies remain both a relief and a burden. Her own visions come to her unaided by any focal point now - and what she foresees, has nothing to do with what the infallible Tapestry predicts – something which has reduced her stellar reputation from 'future high standing seer of the Sabén-Heshep', to something as demeaning as a pariah to be pitied or ignored.

Solancei's Memoirs

The Province of Tarléon.
    Ivanor Fortress.
  Winter of 780 P. C. W.

For twisted morbid fun, I sometimes used to wonder if anyone would miss me the way Ivanor and all its good people seemed to miss my parents after their disturbing deaths?

Would anyone mourn me in that utterly consuming manner that I myself mourned the loss of Taliana? Would Rainan, my father's trusted steward, now unwilling principal seneschal of Tarléon, perhaps shed a quiet tear in private? Or would Trinian - straw-haired, quiet stablehand and occasional fellow-stargazer - regret the loss of his secret, sometimes-unwanted self-appointed groom?

It was an issue I'd ponder with earnest thought for the possible, but because I never knew when to tell myself 'enough', my mind would somehow twist to begin fabricating beyond the realms of plausible. One of my favourite, most cringe-worthy dreams would involve a chance that the handsome Denkard with his quick smiles and caramel-warm gaze, might just fail to swipe the strands of too-long, pale-blonde hair from his eyes when talking to Liance whilst on gate duty, just so that his beau would not notice the new haunting cast of regret in his eye that his Lord's ill-mannered daughter would no longer corner him after mealtimes to press him for a bought of stick-crossing behind the kitchen stores, or to 'assure' him that she'd one day marry him.

I smile now but for a while, I'd sincerely hoped I'd one day marry that guy. My heart had been sweet on the man in the way any urchin would be half in love with the hero of the newest gleeman-tale circulating the province. Denkard was kind and he'd obliged me because I was his Lord's get – but there'd been little more attached to it; he could have been an older brother! When I last returned to Ivanor, he'd long since married Liance, of course. And they have three children, whereas I have-

Well, I don't know what I have anymore. It's of no importance, because this is now and that was then. And then - in the deep crevices of my weak heart - I used to hope that all these people would openly mourn; that they'd care; that my absence would make a difference, but the Tarléonin are unpredictable in such matters. At least, on the surface. And so, perhaps with the exception of Rainan, nobody seemed to mind all that much when suddenly the King's own Chief and Master of Security, Eso Mehadja, turned up to claim me for the road and then the capital!

Mercy, though Rainan's troubled words to the Chief did portray his reluctance to let us travel just before winter, at the end even he seemed relieved to see the back of us.

I, on the other hand, was gutted. And for a while, the young, foolish me wanted nothing more but to see all of Ivanor ripped from the map, the way that winged horror of my dreams had torn my world to shreds! So just like that, Rainan let that ascetic witch take me? *Just like that, everyone fell into line and let me go, even though I had expressed most emphatically that I did not wish to leave?*

Of course, this hateful turn of my imagination was little more than the unkind wish of a terrified younger me, because what I saw as 'forsaking', was in fact the permeating feeling of relief that gripped everyone because unlike me, they knew that Klaas – Chief Mehadja – was going to whisk me away to safety, and this was all that mattered. Well, that... and a Queen's specific orders too.

So funny how perceptions change though, with the compliment of insight.

As it turned out they did not forsake me at all. In fact, as it turned out, they did quite the opposite. In fact, the true reason why the entire fortress could not wait to see the back of me was because my riding the night mare apparently wasn't entirely removed from the reality of what had actually happened – and there was more...

See, years later upon my return, Rainan would show me a dirtied, ripped piece of cloth harvested from the cloak that Taliana had worn at the time of the accident. Across the frayed, torn linen, in broken, poorly-executed lettering, lingered a simple warning that froze the marrow of my bones when I saw it, for in faded, ochre-red words that could only have been drawn with blood, sat just a few words to shake my understanding!

It simply read: Send. Away. Solanc—

A message of barely three words, barely legible – it was nevertheless impossible to misinterpret. And I recognised the snaking sophisticated swirl of the 'S' instantly, the origins of the message suddenly firmly betrayed.

It both horrified and delighted me - but bless her... even in her dying moments, Taliana had lived to shield me; had fought long enough to pass on a communication of dire need; a message of demand to awaken understanding.

I cannot lie. Though I'd seen more than my share of terrifying, impossible things by then, Taliana's final deed shook me up.

There was, of course, no way that Klaas and her men could have reached Tarléon in the time that they did. *Not that fast. No way.*

I knew that Rainan sent word to the Crown as was his duty upon the death of my parents - but this communique would have arrived after Chief Mehadja had already set off and with what I now know, and even without Klaas' outright confirmation of the fact, I surmise that there can be only one reason that will adequately account for the Chief's near-magical arrival in Tarléon.

Queen Ishjah must have had another premonition! A premonition of the kind that would yet again alter my existence - and so she'd already known her sister and brother-in-law dead before it happened; she'd known the true danger to me - and having had no desire to lose me too, must immediately have sent her best and finest to retrieve me like some lost kitten before what killed Lady Mechintha and Lord Vichard, could track me down and turn her grand majesty's own nightmares into reality.

Yes, Ishjah was and is a clever lady.

In the old days, she would have been dubbed 'a witch'.

One of these days, I should perhaps thank her for saving my life. One of these days... after I forgive her.

Solancei

A Night Round Town

BILANDRO METAVO SMOOTHED the foreboding scowl from his face and kept to the lengthening spill of shadows. They were both a curse and a blessing now – he almost didn't know which – but one thing was certain, with the creeping twilight, the scenery would change. And not for the better if he remembered anything!

Of course, the well of shadows served his purpose equally now, as they had done in the past. Under the veil of coming evening, hiding but not hiding, he could be weaving in and out amongst the throng of people who sought the hovels and shelter of their multi-storeyed tenements after a day's toiling in the fields beyond the Snake. *A shadow in the shadows. No one to pay attention to. No one to mind. Here then gone.*

Of course, the shadows were likewise handy camouflage when it came to melting away from the eyes of those who simply moved about before the tavern-hours with a cut-purse, opportunistic purpose as old as the Document of Unity itself. He did not believe his attire would invite that kind of trouble, but you never knew. He was alone. That was sometimes enough. *Expect the unexpected, indeed! Already once this evening, he'd been smacked in the face with surprise, so why not a second or third time?! Why not-*

Calming his ruffled emotions for what seemed the tenth time since leaving the Keep, Bilan exhaled deeply and suppressed a shudder as another rush of the pervasive, inhospitable Zanzierian breeze picked up and pushed down the narrow road with menacing purpose.

Expect the Unexpected...

For a moment, as he considered the figure he'd been following, Bilan did not know if the sudden sense of chill had come on the wind or if it was to do with his foolhardy purpose here. He thought the latter, but pushed the feeling aside. Though an accomplice of sorts, all of this was not of his making, but he'd die just the same if-

But curse the beguiling ways of women and war, Bilan was not yet ready to give up this stupid game, and though the shadows were growing slinky and deep, he judged there enough time yet to let this intended lesson sharpen into form - so no: come wind or discomfort, he would do this!

Pushed aside by a shoulder, the figure ahead stepped off one of the infrequent boards that covered the worst patches of churned up mire underfoot, but they miscalculated and slipped, landing one already-mud cloaked boot in the dark, foul-smelling puddle, they'd tried to avoid. Bilan cracked a smile. *The left boot had a hole in it. The figure didn't pause a beat, which was admirable, but the unfortunate foot would be soaked and cold now! It left him slightly vindicated. Slightly...*

Sliding along, Bilan avoided the same hazard, nimbly staying to the left and hence above the mire even when people pushed on past him, rendering the foothold precarious as the old wood wobbled to the beat of the irregular footfall. Already his smile was long gone again. *Some things you just did not advertise openly in districts like these...*

Watching the figure ahead shake their leaking boot as though they finally could not help but acknowledge the discomfort, Bilan felt slightly sick. It was a refined gesture that didn't belong; if he noticed, others would too, except no one seemed to pay his grey-cloaked mark any attention. He supposed it might be the tanner's stench that served to disenchant any possible interest. The whiff was pungent and he'd observed several people avert their eyes so far.

He smiled. A hard inward smirk. Only criminals or those cursed by the Gods worked as tanners in Zanzier – a convenient bit of knowledge left over from his first visit here some years ago, and it had come in handy tonight. Of course, he hadn't for a moment expected that the tanner's rags would've been accepted, let alone enticed any use, but then again... He was eating a few surprised at the moment, so why not this one too? And besides, for what it was worth, the outfit had thus far proven a godsend. Whether scarred by a criminal past or present illness, the poor of Zanzier did not want to tangle with that, so maybe... maybe...

Bilan mouthed a curse about biting harlots and flees, enough to make an older worn couple ceded space on the board coming up. The crass expression was like a brand on his forehead: indicating his lethal affiliation. It did not matter that Bilan had been years away from any such association. The habits sometimes just surfaced. The couple did not even look at him as they passed; they wanted no trouble. He could have robbed them then and there and they would've thanked him to let them live but-

Ashamed by his slip, Bilan hurried on, folding himself back into the shadows. It was almost disconcerting, but an old, partly-forgotten side of him had sprung back to life a little too easily this evening, and though the better, righteous side of him was just a little too keenly aware -not only of the disagreeable surroundings and the underlying stench of mild sewerage and wet dirt, but also of his own revulsion to be back in a place like this - he was also not too upset to have so easily fallen back into the stride of his youth. It involved the skill necessary to make oneself appear inconspicuous and he needed that here to see how this would pan out: he needed to be just another downcast filth-born rat amongst many going about his business down the narrow run of streets where lack of sanitation, gutters, and paving, appeared to have taken a toll on this neighbourhood for years rather than seasons.

Still, if he might have felt a tiny urge to stick his nose up, Bilan refrained and hunched his shoulders within the threadbare sack that had been converted to constitute an impromptu cloak with a deep, drooping hood that stank of potatoes and ravens' blood.

He should refrain from cussing like a gang-sworn, however. The wrong people might hear, which was why he'd arduously continue to maintain his carefully cultured air of browbeaten dejection, just as he'd continue to ignore the grim neglect surrounding him in this poor quarter of Zanzier City. It was what the local serfs and lowborn did. And then, so must he.

Fortunately, when all was said and done, this was not too arduous a task, particularly courtesy of his unfortunate childhood and youth; mighty shame, on the other hand, that the same couldn't be said about his ability to remain untouched by the persisting bursts of harsh cold wind that seemed determined to invade up and through folds of his mediocre, beggar-worthy clothes.

other flecking body part he could think of – with the issue of her safety. But he would rectify that. *Really soon, he would. Really... because that was an issue!*

Bilan stared at the back of Iambre's covered head and for a moment it all seemed too unreal. *Gods, but there was nothing in what she'd asked him to do that had sounded remotely like something anyone of a sound mind might have sanctioned, but...*

Well, for now, she still didn't know he was shadowing her and for a blink, he fantasised that she needn't find out either.

Yeah and the ice of Ocean's End might melt too, a snide voice injected in the back of his mind.

Still, there was part of him that could not quite believe that he hadn't managed to prevent all of this in the first place, just as he also could not quite believe that he hadn't yet put a stop to this folly now, but there was something very complicated about all of this. Something that... well, something that had his skin run tight with caution; something that warned him that she'd probably never speak to him again if he ruined this for her.

Bilan suppressed a wince. Gods he was an idiot! A loon! *She was going to decommission him. What did it flecking matter whether she ever looked at him again?! She was the Crown Princess and Gods defend him, he should march her straight back to where she belonged. He should...*

Feeling his head muddling up, he straddled the well-placed righteous voice of reason and smothered it. Just for now.

Rats, but just how could he possibly have guessed they'd end up here when she'd called for him this morning? How could he even have thought to guess that his day was going to end with a full-blown, unauthorised trip into the old parts of Zanzier Town and beyond?

Certainly, he reflected, he could never have guessed that she'd been about to make him privy to all that personal information, nor that she was going to require his help in this foolish pursuit and he guessed it had thrown him.

But at least he'd refused her. Or... had at least... tried.

Bilan was inspired to growl at his own convenient ability to believe that this resembled some small victory. *It didn't. For it wasn't.* Yet initially he'd refused to help, and that was important to remember when he considered everything that came after. *Important... yes...*

But Iambre had been flecking serious; his unease had grown, rivalled only by the absolute knowledge that she'd not been bluffing about her own intentions. *She was going to follow the Chief! And all because of Solancei.*

Bilan felt his dislike of the Princess' handmaiden flare anew – he couldn't help it - but no matter his personal views, it hadn't sheltered him from the truth. Iambre had seemed both forthcoming and vague, but not enough to disguise that she'd been riddled with fear. Now he might not care one whit about Solancei Calverhana, nor her bizarre propensity to come and go as she flecking well pleased, but if it hurt Iambre...

With a blast of contempt for the Tarléonin viper tugging at his spirit, Bilan also couldn't help but hate how that grey-eyed noble seemed to have Iambre wrapped good and tight like an Etruian hairdo till it would seem the Heiress was little more than a slave to Calverhana's whims and commands, and yet none of this mattered. *He could say 'no' till he was blue in the face, but as Iambre had talked about her intentions, he'd feared the outcome of her venture was he not prepared to bend his neck and be there to exact a little control. By the time he'd obliged her, Iambre had been in tears, and... well...*

Bilan clenched his fingers around the crispy edge of his cloak, gathering the folds around himself like a shield against the wind and the madness of his own thoughts.

Tears. Bloody tears. He never knew what to do when women did that crying thing! It was like an extra tool that had been specifically designed for them to apply added pressure on any situation; to sway; to deflect. So he'd been stupid; that was the bare-arse truth of it – and there was no one else to blame, apart from – *Arbar'Chi strike her* – Solancei!

Sighing under his breath at the memory, Bilan knew that it had been downhill from then on, but he pushed at the lingering, slightly uneasy river of self-loathing that flowed through him when he admitted to himself yet again, just how Iambre had evidently manipulated him so effortlessly. *But at least-*

Well at least, for what small token it was worth, he now understood the root of Iambre's anxiety when he'd walked her to the banquet on the first eve of their stay. Solancei – *Gods curse her* - had already been gone and the Princess had felt unsettled by the news just received. *Blood and guts, but it was all so very odd!*

As he had done several times today already, Bilan pictured the look upon the Knights Commander's face, were he to learn that the Crown Princess' taxing handmaiden had gone missing during a jackal fight on the man's personal turf. It was inconceivable and it made it all too easy to understand Iambre's fears. *Zulavi must never find out. The noble was an oaf but he was still dangerous! If Iambre was implicated in such scandal, no matter how innocent... no... no Zulavi must remain ignorant. Otherwise, that man would make a meal of Iambre and then some.*

As he must, Bilan had of course assured her of the contrary when she'd asked - but birthright did not necessarily lend a man nobility and Zulavi was no exception. There was something about this supposedly grand leader that Bilan could not put his finger on, but it was something that made him wish for eyes at the back of his head. *Eyes and more!*

As they had also done all day, Bilan's dark thoughts swayed from Zulavi, fluttering full pitter-patter back to Solancei.

That woman was a menace! Gods, but he prayed this would be worth it; he prayed to every deity willing to mettle that Solancei was worth the scores of merit Iambre was willing to accredit her eccentric handmaiden, because if not, or if this went hay way...

He narrowed his eyes against the elements, scrunching up his brows in a way that scored a deep line over his nose. Again rich displeasure filled him.

Handmaiden... handmaiden!? Zulari'Chi the Wise defend him, but could he even call Solancei that with a straight face anymore?

Bilan had thought about this bizarre twist several times since this morning too. *Was he mad or was Iambre?* He'd never even known that Solancei could lift a sword, let alone use one. She was a Duchess for fleck sake; a noble! Those people had people, who had people, to do that kind of thing for them: to fight their fights and guard them; Solancei's wayward behaviour made no sense. None!

Gods, and which flecking handmaiden in history had ever abandoned her mistress to pursue some black sense of personal need to go dancing with danger and dishonour in a filthy jackal fight? None that he'd ever heard of for sure – yet he could see the disaster in the making just the same; could see that if the 'news' spread-

The thoughts only took him back to where they'd begun, his unease still very much peaked.

Ruffled, he vented a little of his pent-up frustration, allowing himself to glare at a fox-eyed pedestrian in black hose splattered to the thigh with dirt. It earned him a most satisfying look of terror as the sleek thief instantly scurried sideways to navigate around the possible trouble as fast as the sludge would let him.

Glaring wasn't swearing, was it? Bilan smiled, though not in pleasure.

The Princess might play him for a fool but few others would. Good to know he could still have that effect on people and his fellow rogues alike!

Momentarily feeling like he used to, he swiped the man from mind with a sideways glance, but the heat that should have carried him on with a swagger of intent, fizzled and died, his inner savagery somehow marred by something too bleak to allow the sensation purchase.

Stepping off the few rotten boards of another improvised sidewalk, Bilan trailed after the Princess' well-wrapped figure, ploughing through a furrow of muck. She was clearly determined to follow her plan for she hobbled on, an unwavering shadow on the heels of her intended target and as relentless in her pursuit as he, in turn, followed her.

Again, he felt inspired to curse her for doing so well and felt a fool. Earlier he hadn't even been able to imagine how this noble lady in front of him could even begin to envisage dressing up as a commoner; nor had he been able to picture just how easily she'd manage to sneak out of the castle without his aid; nor even how she'd forego a night of entertainment in her own honour to trail after a servant.

However, that she'd done just all of that when it had come to the burn did not surprise, though a small part of him had perhaps hoped... *hoped otherwise*. It was certainly a viable excuse to pacify his scorched self-worth to have given in, and still the proverbial expression, 'chew on your bootstraps' seemed a fitting forfeit, providing all of this did not implode all around them to land him a sentence of capital punishment for treasonous conduct against King and Realm.

Solancei. Solancei. Solancei! He wanted to strangle the woman but guessed that for Iambre's sake he'd have to settle for something less agreeable. Didn't mean though that he couldn't ensure that the Tarléonin witch would learn the errors of her ways - *and more* - when she returned. It also didn't mean that he couldn't assure her how he would personally sever her hamstrings or worse, if she as much as stepped one fine foot even half an inch out of line again, and if any of this hurt Iambre...

But despite her flaws and ill-advised participation in illegal sports, Solancei would not leave Iambre, would she?

The thought was little more than a whisper of suggestion in the back of his mind, but it was there alongside everything else just the same – perhaps semi-fuelled by Iambre's feelings earlier. *Gods the Tarléonin might be keeping a schedule of her very own design but she was always around in the periphery, was she not?*

Bilan didn't like his own reasoning, but for all of his personal dislike, for all that he didn't really know much about the Tarléonin Duchess, he did not believe that she would ever willingly leave him and Iambre to their own devices, because so far – for all her uncanny ways and insufferable tongue - she hadn't. *So... could she have left?*

Iambre seemed to think otherwise; had been adamant that her 'handmaiden' would never deliberately have abandoned her. *'Not for such an extended length of time',* she'd told him. *Whatever that had meant?*

Bilan sucked in a breath. Whatever it meant, it was not important either. Even if Iambre had meant nothing more to him than a symbol of the realm's continuity, he could not have helped but to sympathise with her dilemma. He wasn't proud of his decision, no – but he'd agreed to help her, thinking it the lesser of multiple evils.

Naturally, other options had roared for his attention at the time as well... *things he could have done - things he should have done - to stop her, but really...?*

Could he have demanded that she be locked up in her fancy apartment by a contingent of her own soldiers to prevent her from absconding? Could he have stood his high ground and refused to help her? Or could he perhaps even have sought out the Chief to report their conversation?

As he slithered along these streets of Zanzier with these notions of clear-headed regret, the decision seemed obvious – *he should have done something* - but earlier it hadn't been so obvious at all. On the first score, everyone-bar-everyone would have thought him deranged, had he tried to instigate such ludicrous protocol for no better reason than they must heed his word. On the second point, he would have left himself out of her plans then – a thought that still chilled, when he imagined her bypassing him in favour of what-and-whom-he-did-not-know. No, better then to be there! The woman was resourceful and as he'd surmised a score of times already, she would have found other ways by which to bring her plan to fruition and then he would only have served to cut off his own nose and all that.

It had left him with the option of seeking out the Chief, and thinking back, he should of course have intercepted her when leaving the Keep. *That* would have been the opportune time to yank the Princess back from her mad plans, however, that pesky little discovery of Iambre's real intentions to ice him off had done something to his thought processes - which it seemed he was only just walking off.

He guessed it was good luck within bad luck.

Iambre would never have forgiven him the slight; nor the breach in confidentiality, had he hollered for the old pipe's attention in the first place! On the flip side, he supposed that *had* he managed to involve Eso Mehadja, it might have helped to persuade Iambre that she was doing the right thing in decommissioning him after Zanzier, but Gods help him...

Should! Should! Should? Why the fleck was nothing straightforward anymore?

Bilan shook himself within the thin cloak. *For sure, he should do a lot of things. Should indeed! Gods yes! He should keep his nose clean of this; he should rise above his own involuntary alarm that held just a sifter too much intrigue; he should grab Iambre before he lived to regret his finicky sense of misplaced need to allow her this... this indulgence. But he couldn't. Which angered him. Which in turn made him want to stop her even more – except he didn't.*

This had started. And he would finish it. But Gods help him: not before he'd gotten his worth of... *of understanding... and... and perhaps a little vindication also. It was a pitifully useless reason, oddly juvenile even, and yet...*

Why Iambre had decided to burn him he did not know; he could hazard several guesses, of course, but that was rather beside the point. Somewhere between his skewered senses and her disregard, part of him refused to accept that he'd donned this old bit of moth infested fabric and someone else's stinking ancient boots just to be swept from the board as if he didn't matter. Iambre owed him more: she owed him good on the promise she'd made when he'd agreed to help: that she would not attempt this 'foray' without his company; without his protection! *She thought to do this alone? Well, let her – if only for long enough to help her understand a valuable lesson about life!*

Bilan ground his teeth and eyed the cursed woman as she moved in and around amongst the thong as if she'd spent her life in this gutter-stinking part of the realm. The fact that she looked perfectly at ease in her patched-up cloak and ragged skirts did not pass him by and though it was a relief to find her so clever at adapting into the role of a low-life local, he also had to remember that she did not have a clue about the kind of affairs she might run into. *Not a misty night's foggy idea!*

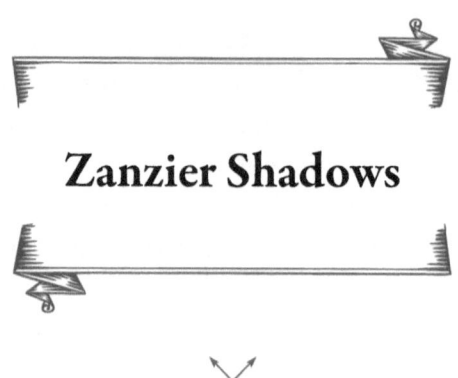

Zanzier Shadows

AS IF TO TAUNT THE fact that both he and Iambre were out of their normal comfort frame, a blustery gust of wind made his cloak billow and Bilan was suddenly just as busy packing down the thin wool as all the other unfortunate locals who looked tired and resigned, though way of habit found them clasping at skirts or tugging to gather and flatten down corners of cloaks with just a sliver more conviction than before. He copied their behaviour as if by reflex. Iambre too. He guessed some actions were just universal no matter family tree or origin.

The weather was nothing, he told himself. He was used to the outdoors and refused to let a little local flutter bother him now. As it went for under open skies, the conditions were not *that* bad and at least it was no longer raining.

Still, it was a thoroughly miserable evening, he conceded; even the rats and cats appeared to have gone underground, yet perhaps he was only feeling waspish because he did not really wish to be here - and because the deeper into Old Zanzier they went, the harder it was for him to suppress the knowledge that he was shitting all over his sworn duty, whilst for reasons he could not pinpoint, still allowing his gut feeling to persevere over that of better judgement.

And just how the fleck was anyone to use such drivel? It raised an odd mix of conflict within him, which made old memories shimmer to life and though many years in the past, they still had power.

Bilan shook his head to remain focused on the present and clasped a hand to the hood of his cowl to prevent it from shifting as another miniature gale pushed against him. It only served to sour his mood further. For sure, he had campaigned in conditions much worse than this - colder, windier, wetter - than anything Zanzier could throw at him, but of course those times he'd not only been infinitely better dressed, he'd also carried the King's blessings and orders, and he most assuredly did not on this occasion!

How much further could he allow this to go on? Nerves warred with unease. He knew these kinds of gutters; knew what came to life as the twilight grew deep, to invite the clandestine darkness of evening closer, ever closer...

When night descended over narrow roads and backyard passages, Iambre could not begin to guess at the rot that would disengage from the darkness to drift to the surface; she could not begin to comprehend-

Bilan thought if he chanced a glance at himself in a looking glass right then, he would most likely look ten years older with the frowns that wouldn't stay off his forehead - but turn it any which way, upside, inside out, this perturbing situation was nothing if not of his own doing. His doing... and Iambre's... and Solancei's... but mostly – in regards to the here and now, it was definitely his doing!

Sucking in a harsh breath when the Princess accidentally clashed shoulders with another random by-passer, Bilan's hand twitched, ready to draw his concealed weapon in a blink. She kept her face down: averted, just as he's instructed earlier, and quickly as that the event was over, both Iambre and the stranger already several steps on their separate ways without word or eye contact.

It made him weak, his spine losing its sharp tension as he remembered to breathe and keep moving. This has already happened a handful of times and Bilan had almost sucked his own teeth into his stomach every time – either for fear that Iambre would react when she was often as not shoved from the path by someone larger or more determined, or else in sureness that someone would catch a glimpse of her unlined features or perhaps detect a whiff of plush perfume that might linger on her skin. Either way, there'd be trouble. He hoped he wouldn't need to kill anyone tonight but if they mobbed her...

Bilan swallowed heavily, allowing relief to slide down his muscles though he outwardly made no changes to his actions or movements.

Expect the Unexpected! *Triviatu al Inhastriviatu.*

The ancient Code of the King's Lancers' circled back, over and over, like a vulture to prey on his already-dead peace of mind. *Triviatu al Inhastriviatu! Expect the Unexpected. He was allowing Iambre del'Dulac Isthalani Actarione to venture deeper into the scummy bowels of Old Zanzier. He was allowing her this!*

He must be mad! He was mad! Why in the flecking seven Wells of Tescaoni was he doing this, again?

Bilan clenched his fists behind the long sleeves of his cloak, suppressing thoughts about the lore attached to the cursed Wells and how any wish would require a price. *Would his ill judgement cost him? Would it cost Iambre? Or would something far more devious occur?* Bilan had never seen the wells of Tescaoni. They did not exist. He had only one wish: to keep Iambre safe, whilst teaching her valuable lesson in keeping one's word, and then leave the Chief to do her business whilst him and Iambre got carried on the wings of luck and fortune back to the Keep without any incident to mar the experience.

Suppressing a shiver, Bilan licked his lips. Okay, so maybe that was more than one wish, but nevertheless! In the lore, it was possible for the magic of the Wells to hear your wishes over miles and leagues, and if the fickle artefacts were in the mood, your ill-considered words might just be granted – hence the adage, 'be careful what you wish for' - but a prayer was surely not the same as a wish? *It couldn't be. And what did it matter, besides? The Wells were not real! The purported place of origin, Gadmaedera, was not on any map – ancient or modern...*

In that moment Bilan thought he was doing a good job of restraining himself but only because Iambre had not seemed fazed by any of the minor 'incidents' so far. Mercy, even with a wet foot she kept herself admirably in check. Chief Eso Mehadja remained blissfully unaware that the Realm's dearest treasure was gliding in hot on her mud-splattered heels, just as Iambre had not realised that Bilan was only a crooked handful of paces behind her own position, and not once had she turned to look back either. There were ways to move and look back without being detected. It required a level of habit and finesse that Iambre didn't possess, but yet he'd fully expected her not to care and it would've made her stick out like a golden circlet on her brow. As she moved so well, he pondered it she might be aware of as much? Recently she'd been erratic, but tonight she showed a level of temperance he'd not seen from her since Etruia before this tour of the Provinces began. *The woman was determined in her pursuit. He was almost ready to forgive the skipping out on him, but-*

Just as he'd almost lulled himself into a false sense of security, memories surged. He was almost thankful, but then not!

Zanzier was not Imkarah but a poor district was a poor district any day of the week, anywhere in the realm - and what surrounded them was really little different from the abysmal living conditions he remembered. What Iambre was making of it, he could only shudder to think, but she did not have his perspective - otherwise she would have waited for him; otherwise she would have changed her mind about all of this.

For a blink, he was assaulted by old apathy and new despair. Once you'd seen one shite-filled, garbage sown back alley or ramshackle, leaning tenement, you'd seen them all. As always he recognized the stench too easily; felt the aura of resignation that seemed to steep the place as though bottled despair came cheap and plentiful. Mercy, as he walked he even recalled the feeling of mud-choked roads dragging at his limbs, whilst his rat-tack wardrobe of eclectic rags and mended clothes gathered a smattering to match, leaving him hoping that there was enough clean water left for drinking?

It had never been a given. On too many occasions, more and more frequently towards the end, his mother had followed her bleeding, soft heart and allowed the urchins from the street to come fill their water skins till nothing remained but the grit-endowed drags. Their well had been deep and it would refill in due time, but...

He cringed, recalling how he'd begrudged the kindness. Half the time he couldn't recall what day it was when he visited 'home' – he'd had little right to claim any of this mother's charity and yet she'd always offered. *Day. And night. Mealtime. Prayer time. Whether he'd been injured, and pissing swear-words; whether cut and bleeding or stashing the most recent bag of loot. Always.*

He hated dirty water. Clothes he could abide, yet sometimes it had almost seemed as if dirt had evolved from fashion rather than filth. Of course the dirt was the least of his concerns now, and in reality, it had been back then. *He remembered that feeling too...*

Cold within from the unbidden memories, Bilan felt suddenly back in the place he'd fought to turn his back on, only it hadn't wanted to turn its back on him, at least not for a long time. His mother's charity had been just. Of course with the money sent them by his father, they could have left the slums behind far sooner than what they'd eventually been forced to do, but she'd been known as the Healer of Lake Side – by the time she might have considered leaving, it was far too late for Bilan and his two brothers, so she stayed - and Gods, perhaps she would've been there yet, if not for the demands of his father's employer, that fat noble, Ihaar Seelen!

Not enough choices, and none to play with at the right time...

Bilan let the uncomfortable feelings slide away beneath disregard, something else he still managed with perfection. By the closed faces, these locals were long-used to sub-standard living too; this was not recent poverty that had befallen the district due to a loss of crops or poor prices or a drop in supply and demand! These people had bigger problems to worry about than a lack of side planks or roads blanketed in mud as thick as lush Carlundulan carpets. Whether farming or fighting, it made no difference when someone else owned your skills – Bilan remembered this too: dear flecking Gods how he recalled it achingly well...

Mood flexing towards the worse, he could do without the nose-to-nose with old times but it was still not as bad as Iambre's pitiful ignorance and the smarting knowledge that after all had been said and done, she'd not considered his reasoning valid enough to keep the promises bestowed in confidence only this morning. *It was the kind of ignorance that got people into trouble. The not 'understanding' that this place would eat you up if giving the Queen of Games even half a chance to turn one's fortune!*

He sniffed. A slight sore throat - the essence of a lingering cold carried over for a few days now - was probably going to be complemented by a runny nose by the end of the night too. It was enough to crank up fatigue, but he wouldn't let it.

Not dissimilar to the Lake Side district of Imkarah, the heart of Old Zanzier was a warren of alleys and passages, some full of cloying stinking heaps of rubbish, others with the gangs and fortune runners that ever-gathered in these areas, both attracted by the cover afforded them by these age-scarred buildings, yet mostly also shackled by greed, misshapen obligations, and shared need. Once affiliated, it made 'escape' neigh on impossible unless it was in fact purchased outright and according to a set fee that was deemed an adequate and fair compensation for the loss of skills and earnings suffered by the gang in question at the time of a person's departure. There'd be 'winners' like that here too! Whether she appeared 'fine' or not, the Old Town was no place for Iambre; he'd told her little of his past - now he wished he'd been more forthcoming, but he'd had his reason...

As the choking hold of the evening seemed to approach so much faster down here amidst the looming, flaking walls of decaying residences, mucky animal pens, and questionable work-shops, Bilan upped his surveillance and vigilance. *Another quarter and he'd call it! He was nearly out of time...*

For a moment managing to focus on the Chief, he wished he knew where the old harridan was headed. In places, the road they trailed would narrow down into nothing - a path two or three paces wide; in others it would gain the normal width of a carriage with a hair ribbon's length to spare on either side, or alternatively Eso Mehadja's path would take them past a parody of something that imitated an itinerant market where people would cluster like beggars round carts or crates to procure what limited produce currently available. From the smell emitted from certain meat trays just passed, he'd be prepared to venture the guess that a vegetarian option might be the healthier choice, but then again: soup and hunger could disguise much.

As if Iambre felt revulsion too, Bilan observed her eying the carts with sideways swipes of her head, as if she could not quite make sense of the meat on offer, but felt intrigued to investigate though she could not pause. *Her golden highness had probably never eaten raw mice before...*

Annoyed that he should even still feel 'annoyed', Bilan shouldered past another man without finesse and managed to duck inside a small recess when Iambre unexpectedly let her eyes flutter over one shoulder. *It was the first time she'd done so. Was she getting uneasy?*

Calming fraying nerves, he aimed not to stand out like a pauper at a ball, but he was as jumpy as sparrows on some high-brow lady's bird table when the cat was about - something that was unlikely to change with the fall of night, and his personal accountability flying ever further from touch.

Ahead, Iambre darted on. The Chief seemed to have changed pace. Bilan instinctively set after, then swore under his breath but the sound was mercifully carried away on the wind. *Blood and guts! Curse this, the Princess could be quick, but she was forgetting to slouch!*

As if his actions might direct her, he deliberately altered pace and re-adjusted to hunch his own shoulders. It was fair knowledge that every poor quarter across the realm birthed an ability in people to spot manners and bearings of authority and wealth; as he remembered, the 'tells' could be small or large: a whiff of soap, a flash of metal, a manicure, a frown of discomfort, a look in the eye... and yes, he'd known what to look out for; he supposed he'd never forgotten, but-

Slightly surprised with himself; slightly split, Bilan realised that he was struggling to keep up his own airs. *Seemed then that the years of exercise and soldiering had drilled him into a different person, sure, but certain things just couldn't be polished off after years of caution and observation. The past was in his blood. He'd rather die than return though...*

Bizarrely afloat, he watched Iambre weave past two scruffy farmers – their clogs and dark homespun heavy with more than gutter dirt after a day of toiling in the fields beyond the Snake. They didn't concern him, nor did the random cut-purse eight paces back, nor the horde of adolescent brats that swept past on occasion, simultaneously hustling and pestering anyone and all for anything of value or fancy. *All except Iambre, it seemed. They knew the smell of death well...*

Innards twisting, stupidly glad Iambre's procured rags had assured her immunity thus far, Bilan shied away from other thoughts of his own youth brought on by the adolescent wave of trouble mongers; shied from thoughts of a half-wit kept in a cage in the catacombs of Imkarah; a half-wit whom the epidemic of lost children would gain joy from raining down pestilence upon whenever given half a chance.

It had always stuck Bilan as sad how Old Three-fingers and Joslano the Younger had encouraged the poor sod to fight like a bear when pitted against the mastiff-hunters recently 'procured' for 'sport'. However, these years later, the absolute truly terrifying thing that had stuck with him was not the fights but how Joslano the Younger would occasionally grab one of the pestering kids by the scruff of the neck and throw the unlucky creature into the brute's cage. The half-wit had been as territorial about his tiny space as a cave-lion, and Bilan could not recall ever seeing any of the children emerge from the madman's rag-covered, filth-caked prison again. What he did recall, though, was the unhinged tone of Joslano the Younger's voice as he'd twitter under his breath in something that always felt like clammy mirth as he secured the metal lock on the screeching child.

He wrenched his mind from the cluttering scenes in his head but the next memory slid in, too fast to stop. *There'd also been the young girl with the scarred arms. He'd almost forgotten her, but-*

He and three others had caught her trying to steal their loot. He thought he'd been about ten autumns old, the others maybe twelve or thirteen but it had made her theirs by forfeit regardless for she could not pay the silver mark compensation that was the customary demand to set matters straight for the attempted slight of stealing from a Feather Hand. Feeling black guilt, he recalled in vicious detail how she'd fought them - *and her fate* - like a wildcat: eye blazing; hissing, biting, scratching...

Of course, she'd been one skinny girl against three lads, so...

Feeling sickened that she should return to his thoughts now, Bilan let bile and self-recrimination mix to raise hateful regret. *She'd had a long blonde braid and no scars when they'd brought her 'down below'. When next he'd seen her, they'd stripped the hair from her skull to sell to the one-eared barber on Hale Street for the fee of 3 silver marks and a fleck; the second time... well-*

Bilan wanted to quench the vivid pictures in his head, but couldn't.

Well, the second time he'd seen her, the first scars had already graced bruised skin: red and raised, gifts of 'Danranar the Deranged's' customary whims - but to this day Bilan didn't think she'd been aware of her own misfortune anymore: her eyes had taken on the same glazed quality as something once seen in a dying rabbit.

As always he shivered to think of it. She'd been humming the same toneless tune under her breath all the while staring into space: *'A fleck is too much but the silver you shall have...'* His father had once song him that song. *Now it gave him the creeps...*

Bilan did not know if she had died or yet lived, but to his mind, he'd killed her just the same, for when she'd butchered that acolyte of Osari'Chi for 'admiring her marks', Old Three-fingers had given her to the temple in recompense and then she'd been gone. *Gone, and for nothing more than a bone recorder and a purse of cheap Carlundulan tobacco that neither he nor the other lads had even pretended to dream they might sell for more than a few gestures of courtesy.*

Old coldness seeping deeper, Bilan had an overwhelming urge to stride up to the Realm's Heiress but forced himself to cool the idea. *'Not yet! Not yet'*, the slighted, bruised part of him whispered, *'not yet...'*

He glared at his boots – old and worn to suit the guise – and wished again that he'd saddled that flecking horse on the back-end of winning that tournament. Obscenely, Solancei Calverhana's prophetic words echoed in his mind. A taunt, perhaps...?

"What Iambre wants, Iambre gets," she'd informed him with a look he'd always thought mirrored pity, though surely he'd imagined things? And fleck... *no matter what, the handmaiden had had a point after all. Iambre had never seemed that way to him before this tour, but lately...?*

The Princess was clever: she knew exactly how to flex: to give this way and that. It was too enticing by far; shame he'd never liked dim-witted women – *mores the pity! –* for here he was... *somehow hoping to teach her never to do this kind of thing to anyone ever again...*

Bilan smothered the reoccurring disbelief that put lines on his face in places there yet should

not be any, but he knew the unbidden state of mind want to stay until this was done. Because he'd been an idiot, he was now paying for it as he skipped across puddles and sidestepped the potential pits of standing water to keep up. Every breath exhaled concern for Iambre; every step raked up memories of times less fortunate; of times-

The wasting images of the past, he could deal with, however: lock away in the vault of pitiful regrets, but against the shuttered eyes of a young girl arose to haunt him - bearing the face of Iambre this time - the Captain could do nothing. *He'd let no one hurt her, nor claim her for sport or any other sick purpose. The past was dead. He'd moved on! He'd made his way out! Not quite as he'd dreamed - but his debt had been paid and he'd escaped Imkarah with little more baggage than cold memories, and – all considering – a surprisingly low number of physical scars. Iambre might be so blissfully naïve about all these horrors, but she would never be a victim. Never!*

As though to question his path, the wind tore at him, jostling his frame slightly, but successfully taking his mind from scars and old debts: Gods' hate, any more prolific and he'd culture that cold of his right into a whooping chesty cough. He did not have time to be ill but sometimes life could be a bitch from the Void! He'd been back here less than a handful of days and already he hated this province all over. *Full marks! That took a lot!*

Rounding a corner on the heels on Iambre, Bilan cussed when he was instantly accompanied by a noisy flurry as the forceful tempest swept forth, sending people stumbling on their feet and raking several lose items off a nearby vendor's cart. A black-haired kid with bare feet and unnaturally gleaming white skin caught his eye when moving in like a sleekly smooth shadow to take advantage when the owner bent to recover his stock. Bilan smiled and it stalled the child for a blink, as though being caught in the act of lifting the bag of dried, salted insects somehow made the theft more illicit.

Then the kid blinked and return him the grin of a much older conspirator: teeth too white, smile too wide, and then it was gone - as were, not one, but three bags of goodies. *Now there was a kid who'd go far.*

Smile fading, he brought his gaze back to Iambre. She was steadying her cowl and hood but the wind had nearly exposed her face. From the set of her shoulders, she finally looked a little harassed. *Soon she'd be a lot more than harassed when he revealed his presence, demanding an explanation. Soon...*

Creeps Closing

The dusk fell deeper. Not much time had passed since Eso upped the pace but at this time of year, it happened faster than high summer. Eso was a little harder to keep up with now too, as though the Chief suddenly had somewhere to be at a certain time and was now pushing to keep her appointment. Bilan feared that Iambre might lose her in a moment's distraction, but the road was gradually widening a little to allow for more traffic ahead and with it came the presence of better shops and even the odd few vendors of old-new clothing that carried such variation in style and quality that it spoke loudly of garments procured off the backs of dead people no longer in need or maybe even from plain simple thievery.

He expected the prices would be backstabbing, yet old habit found him eying a short dark cloak with a hem stitched in red. The cloak was second-hand too and then some, but the material was enviously thick, yet past tonight he'd have no need for it so Bilan left his wish and passing interest behind. *He owned better now. Was used to better now.* Which might perhaps explain his attitude towards the sorry attire he was presently wearing.

Ahead Iambre visibly quivered as the new gusts of wind danced high to swirl her skirts like she'd done a spin to show off the quality lightness of a new dress and suddenly she was busy gathering the expanse of her clothes tightly against her frame, the slightly-frenzied action not enough to ensure her total success, however, as the right side of her skirts flashed wide.

A mournful screech from above nearly stopped her dead. Casting her head back to locate the origin of the sound, Iambre startled minutely.

For a blink, she froze. He saw her gnaw at her bottom lip. Then she honed back in on the Chief, her face once more hidden and her pursuit rekindled.

Bilan needn't look up to know what had her worried. Screeching in dis-cord-tunes to the rhythm of the wind, the suspended hazards made themselves easily known to the people passing below. They hadn't been an issue before as none had been present, but now the unpredictable blusters set every old street-lantern and the odd suspended shop sign merrily clanking and skipping on their careworn chains. *If one fell, it would knock you for six and he stood willing to wager a good month's salary that Iambre had figured this out too!*

With a furtive glance for the rusted, precarious fastenings of signs that looked centuries old, the Captain invariably moved forward with one eye glued to their lively exercise. The plain deterioration of this district left him semi-wondering what had happened to this place.

The houses and shops must once have been in splendid repair - not yet run-down, nor ruined by ill-trade and bad times - because he spied the look of dat-ed, faded affluence left to sag under disrepair, and suspected this had once been a quarter of Zanzier people would've frequented without fear of thieves pos-sessing, first their purse, and then their life!

The cracked plaster of the three-story buildings was now a sullen grey and a sickly ivory- washed-in-dirt to render the effect of neglect complete. Bilan sur-mised that the colours might once have been a bright lemon, perhaps turquoise in places, but it was a hazardous guess in the poor light, his observation based only on the faded lustre near the sheltered protrusions of cracked sills or splin-tered door frames. Sadly, however, the punched-through windows and pealing shutters betrayed the truth that whatever this district had once been, the wealth was long gone through the drains...

Still, regardless of impressions, the neighbourhood was changing and he thought they must gradually be leaving Old Zanzier behind for the painted plaques and faded signs, designed to herald shop names and/or a particular line of goods, served to announce that one was slowly but surely entering a slightly more prosperous area.

At least Bilan prayed it was so. He could not recall this part of Zanzier from his previous visit and he longed to be away; there was just something about the dour, high-pitched sound of unoiled, old hinges that made his hair stand on end!

In truth, perhaps it was simply that he resented that desolate, abandoned feeling that arose in his spirit as the metal protested against the settled state of old age. It was a sound that always got to him...

As if on cue, another recall surfaced. Not a good one, either...

It couldn't be helped, but the screech of rusted hinges put him in mind of the ancient great-gate leading into the grounds of the 'Hallowed' back in Lake Side. The grand ancient gate could have graced the drive of a palace, it's filigree design though tarnished and crippled, still steeped in an old-world splendour that had not belonged to Lake Side. What did belong, however, was the damage sustained over Gods only knew how long. As Bilan recalled, one side was completely immobilised by time and vandalism, and so would not move on its hinges, whereas the other half could be persuaded to open about a third, always emitting such a protesting, indignant screech that few passed the threshold without detection. It had been a terrible wailing sound, and in as far as Bilan had known, no one had ever passed either without a superstitious shiver and a silent prayer; no one. *There'd just been something about that place...*

Curses, but this was yet another stray memory that he'd happily have been without - and yet there it was! And of course he could also almost feel the clammy winter air twisting with the spell of decay rising off the scarred surface of the Hallowed: the temperature never quite cold enough to mask, but never really warm either - and that was before you entered the stone corridors below to stand face-to-face with the dead in their fancy alcoves belonging to families long passed and forgotten.

Bilan shivered, a rat running over his grave. The 'face-to-face' had been literal for by some bewitching kind of unknown sorcery, the faces of the dead had been rendered upon the rough stone with such impossible accuracy that the black lines of their features seemed to move, their eyes following any intruder as he or she passed. Bilan had heard it said the place was millennia old and that what was now buried had once been exposed in grandeur above ground where Magic had been the tool used to recast the dead with such flawless precision that it would ease the sorrow of the living who'd lost their nearest and dearest.

That had been a load of crock, of course!

He'd always considered the stories superstitious nonsense. *And magic?* Mercy, but magic was for books and children!

What, for one, could be powerful enough to bury such a vast area under spans upon spans of rock and dirt? Perhaps an earthquake, sure. But an earthquake would have destroyed everything to rubble, leaving nothing for the future to find...

Bilan pushed the memory of the 'wandering eyes' from mind. Tricks of shadow and light, it had to have been, but it had still been creepy, and it had still served to keep away unwanted guests from the inner halls of the gang's lair.

A lantern sawed on its chain in the present: a violin mistreated by a tone-deaf wanna-be fiddler...

Waking up to the squelching sensation of his boot striking off a board on its own to land ankle deep in a puddle of dark water that splashed up his leg on impact, Bilan dragged himself - and his attention – back to the now.

This foray was becoming less appealing by the heartbeat! He didn't like Solancei... not enough to do this, at least – and evening was closing in.

Passing a wide alley that opened back into what appeared to be a dead-end back-yard, he spotted the first batch of 'pests' who appeared only after dark, and the necessary tug of concern rammed his breath short. Zanzier could not be a rich playground for these gangs – they would not be picky - and though the pests staring back at him were only a handful of raw-boned youths, they appeared as if two-to-a-dozen in their similar-looking, indeterminate clothes and nasty long-knives tugged behind identical, garish sashes. It was a sign, he knew, that they all claimed association to one particular faculty of crime, and their unabashed show of unprotected steel was enough to warrant caution, for touched by the past again, he recognized his former-self in the hard planes of their faces and passive, flat stares.

It was a haunting feeling but from the way in which their heads swivelled with incidental care to size him up, they inspired no lingering urge for him to romanticize an idea of brotherhood now lost, or camaraderie left behind. *These boys represented a sizable threat and to play the game of mice and lion, he kept his head down; not wanting trouble; not able to afford it.*

For a moment, the urge to pick up the pace rode him, but he did not want to give them anything to jump on and just as he'd hoped, his behaviour did not warrant their interest for longer than a split heartbeat before their still-eyes moved on. *No one followed. For now...*

Resisting the urge to release his concealed weapon, Bilan knew he'd need little provocation now. The appearance of the gangs heralded the twilight zone where all and everything could, and most likely would, happen. The edge of danger was closing, the margin for error and forgiveness narrowing. *He was only one man...*

It was sobering, and worrying a hundredfold over the possible scenarios that might yet happen as well as the ways in which Iambre might get hurt, Bilan had to give himself a mental shake.

It almost worked. Almost.

He could look after himself. He carried his ugly but dependable dagger for any such 'mishaps': it had been his truest companion since before he joined up, and as ever, he trusted it was the right kind of weapon to take care of any urgent business if the need arose. *But Iambre was a distraction. He'd stupidly assumed she wouldn't be, but-*

Stomach knotting with sour fear, he almost gave in. Even disguised and without any of her attractive face décor, Iambre was still a pretty, young woman and she could so easily disappear into one of the many passages, never to re-appear. He had warned her, of course; and she'd listened... for about five heart-beats! *Gods curses, he was such a fool!*

"Kira'Cha shield her, Diekima'Chi protect her," he mumbled, the prayer to the two deities repeated a hundredth time, now wishing for Kira'Cha's famed luck to ride Iambre's shadow, whilst also fervently beseeching the double-edged Diekima'Chi to extend his goodwill in favour of Iambre rather than the people who might seek to harm her. *But to intercept her now would be a mistake as it would attract too much attention. He'd have to wait...*

Ahead loomed another group of unhealthy looking youths. He hoped Iambre had said her own prayers - but was that asking too much? The urge to stop her foray grew riveting: a compulsion to demand of her the immediate abandonment of this charade, but the young men were too close and he could not risk attention until they'd both passed the potential threat. A short lean boy in his late teens heckled as she passed; she ignored him. Bilandro's blood ran icy, but the lad's attention was turned by a van-eyed friend, as the others evidently saw profit coming their way in a different form, and before he knew it the gang had retreated back into shadows, the echo of a crisp laugh the final thing to punctuate their slithering departure.

Unable to prevent their activity, Bilan ignored them. At the moment he had nearly caught Iambre up and was having to slow right down to stop himself from overtaking her completely.

A mere a three paces between them, he found it hard to hang back. There was a dark-shaded lookout in a broken-pane window two stories up, one building ahead. *A gang member or a loner?*

Falling back some paces under the premise of scraping mud off the side of a heel, he paused to check where this spy's attention might land, but even a hooded sideways look gave no clear indication, as shadows too deep surrounded the figure.

Would it all turn out to have been for nothing? He wondered, by the time they were done would Solancei already have turned up at the castle? *Or was she gone? And what if tonight left them just as barren of clues as before?*

Considering the situation, he felt inspired to believe Solancei Calverhana had been targeted for the winnings she'd taken – had she indeed won that jackal - but for once his gut-instinct remained quiet. Still, Iambre was certainly convinced Solancei had taken the trophy of 'first- touch', but if so, the Tarléonin Duchess might very well long since have been left face-down in the murky Mesatitan - and with those heavy tides...

It was a disquieting sobering thought, considering his odds with the grey-eyed woman, but to tell Iambre of his fears would've been cruel. *If Solancei was dead, Iambre was better off not knowing. If-*

Ahead Bilan spied the Princess come to an abrupt halt mid-step and in a heartbeat, all thoughts flew his mind. Something about her stiff frame had him on instant alert. *She'd not looked this uneasy before. Was someone or something threatening her?*

Scouting the street, every figure, every face, every dark patch and recess, Bilan reached back into the cloak for the dagger secreted at the small of his back and was already walking briskly towards her as her tight shoulders grew stiff for no apparent reason.

Fleck! Bloody Fleck!

Bilan threw the inward curse at himself. He was gliding up towards her, fast but surreptitiously, eyes never pausing as he searched to locate the supposed danger. *Nothing. He could see nothing.*

He suppressed another foul oath, still looking as he drew up next to her, hand on dagger just shy of pulling it into the open. Without the slightest hitch, Bilan weaved the fingers of his free hand round her wrist, snatching her arm, simultaneously shifting to expand his own survey though he felt her both jump and turn in readiness to fight.

He shushed her, their small altercation not yet causing anyone pause, and gave her arm a yank to keep her moving.

"It's me," he assured in a harsh whisper, eyes still roving, "Just keep walking, Milady, all will be well."

Iambre stiffened, but he felt the fight draining from her limbs. Eyes widening in part-lingering fear, part-incredulous surprise, her gaze roamed across his face. "Bilan? Bilan, what are you-"

"Be quiet and walk with me," Bilan demanded, eyes flying, not really seeing her as he shifted now to link his arm around her waist; casual to the eye, but his body and mind ready to react and shelter.

For a moment Iambre became a wooden marionette, but she had no choice but to follow as he marched her on. *Gods damn it, but he could see no-*

"Bilan, so help me!" Iambre hissed. Recovered too quickly, she demanded, "What in the realm is this? The Chief is a mere ten paces away – do you want me found out?!"

"Sod the Chief, Highness," he hissed back and swung her against the peeling green paint of a window panel belonging to what might best be described as apothecary store with boards nailed into place in lieu of would-be windows and the green branch and leaf of a hedge wizard crudely painted above the door. It looked shut for business but for the soft light escaping between the uneven slats, and Bilan heard the rattle of scales and the breeze of voices within. People were passing from either direction, ignoring them: either thinking them acquainted or else keeping their noses clean of whatever dirty business they imagined between him and Iambre. *This was as good a place as any to make a stand...*

"Bilan!" Iambre hissed at his shoulder, pushing against him with the palm that wasn't still squashed against his side, "What are you doing? I cannot believe you are here! I... How? I mean... what is all this?!"

Ignoring her confused anger for a moment longer, Bilan smiled affably, his eyes passing over all and everything, evaluating and dismissing would-be threats. With still nothing of concern showing itself, he finally relaxed back a little and let up so that Iambre could breathe and she inhaled harshly.

"What I am doing, Highness?" Bilan couldn't hold back the touch of wry anger from his voice then, "Why, I am protecting your royal silken skin. Just like we agreed I would, remember?!"

Hand still in the folds of his cloak, still clasping the hilt of the dagger, Bilan did not look her way and kept his attention on their surroundings, but he heard her paused intake of air all the same and guessed that she was either mad as a goose about to give chase to an intruder or else as chastised as any decent person ought to feel to have broken their word.

"You were scared of something, Milady?" he enquired then, sparing her an answer as he carried on, "What did you see?"

Iambre's chest swelled on another hitched breath. Then, "Scared? Bilan, what do you mean? I was not scared? What in the realm are you doing? Bilan, I was absolutely not scared!"

This time Iambre sounded verily vexed, and Bilan relaxed his guard and let go of the dagger for long enough to finally look at her. Angry, pretty eyes met his.

"Bilan?" Iambre's tone did not alter but her gaze narrowed as she pushed at him again. "Well...?"

With one last look for the road, and the passers-by, and a couple of hard-faced youths strolling past on the far side of the general thoroughfare of churned up filth, Bilan stepped free of her and clasped both her upper arms insistently.

"Iambre, Milady, something had you riled. I've been following you for the better part of a full turn of the hour and nothing has so far found you reacting like you just did. I told you I would help you gain the clothes you required in exchange for me coming along tonight and I am here to guard as promised! Now tell me what you saw."

Iambre stared him in the eye for one beat longer, then she squirmed as if uncomfortable and cast her gaze to her mud-caked boots... *embarrassed?* For a moment she looked up towards something across his shoulder and though it was not as obvious as before, because he touched her, Bilan could feel her stiffen again.

Alert, he half-turned to follow her gaze. Iambre was already shifting her eyes again, but he saw the root of her discomfort none the less, yet it was not as he'd feared. Not at all...

Slightly elated, he barely managed to withhold a grunt of mirth. *A Charmstress! The Princess had walked through mud and past would-be killers without pause, and yet she reacted to the sight of a prostitute as though she'd just been both thoroughly offended and shocked.*

Flustered – *she'd seen him looking* – Iambre licked her lips and didn't know where to rest her eyes as she said, "I was not scared of anything, only... only surprised. And anyway, I left a good hour before our agreed time of meeting and yet here you are. How?"

Suppressing a full smile, though unable to kill it completely, Bilan ignored her question for one of his own, "You find it acceptable to break our agreement; you traipse around this part of Zanzier without care for limb or life, and yet you react the moment you clap eyes on someone like her?"

Bilan nodded towards the Charmer in her scarlet mask, curled hair and bared green hose. The skirts on that one were so short that the red garter of her profession stood out like a stamp on a public crown-declaration and her neckline plummeted so low that Bilan knew the woman would bare the rest, were she invited to bend forward. *She was well-endowed. For Zanzier this was daring.* Still, he suspected it was not this woman's attire that shocked the heiress but rather the metier itself, for as an Etruian noble Iambre was hardly unfamiliar with a showing of legs or bosoms, given the fact that the dry, hot clime of her home province often invited a variety of scantily clad people, both of the rich and poor variety. *Nevertheless, this combination probably took the biscuit, and then some...*

Bilan let go of Iambre's arms but stayed close enough to touch her as her eyes strayed back to the woman in question as though she couldn't quite help herself. Then she tried to look at him instead but she couldn't and suddenly her cheeks carried more colour than before. *Iambre speechless? Seemed he'd 'rescued' her just in time. This was all worth it!*

Bilan's smile widened to a wicked curve, he couldn't help it. "Tell me, Iambre, that it is not the first time you have ever seen a Charmstress?"

"But it's so indecent!" she blustered, ignoring his question. "She flaunts her business openly in the street and her... her... Why would she- ... I mean, how does she not get cold?"

Iambre managed to look at him then, but she did not appear comfortable. *Cold? He'd never considered-*

Bilan looked back at the Charmstress but Iambre punched him in the ribs. "Midnight raffle, Bilan stop staring at her as if she temps you!"

"Huh?"

Iambre punched him in the arm. With horror-laced undertones, she questioned, "Oh dear Gods... she does not, though, does she?"

Bilan looked back hastily and found her gaze fully on him now: berating with a touch of jealous warning. *Nice...*

"No she does not," he assured her, clearing his throat, though without blinking. *What the Charmer was wearing was interesting, sure - but she was not Iambre...*

"No," he repeated, voice turning stern, "And anyway, I am here with you, although you-"

"Milady, what you did is irresponsible; you deliberately sought to waylay my involvement! You deliberately gave me the wrong hour!"

Iambre looked down. "I... there was good reason, please-"

He interrupted, "Save it! I ought to simply drag you back to the castle and hope to all the Gods that no one sees your return!"

Now, Iambre lost most of her colour. "No don't! Please, Bilan... I beg you, don't... this is all right. Look, the Chief is still in sight. We can follow her together as we planned. Please! I will not go back, please..."

Bilan shifted his balance as if to move and Iambre grasped his arm, pleading, "Look, I am sorry I broke our agreement. Truly, my love, I am. But I only sought to keep you out of this mess, that's all. I did not seek to deceive you, nor play you! Please... if this blows up in my face, I do not want you implicated too. Please, Bilan! Please... "

A beseeching look hit him before she turned her head to follow the Chief with her eyes. Bilan was well-aware, but with every heartbeat, the older woman moved further and further away from their position.

"Bilan please... the Chief..." Iambre looked back at him with mounting distress. "It's for Solancei... please, I'm sorry."

He looked away, feeling exasperated. Then-

Bilan's heart flipped, imaginary cold steel floating up his spine. *Fleck! By Inkar'Chi's black heart, not now!*

Seeing two men in patched-up dark cloaks moving steadily towards the two of them, Bilan griped Iambre's forearm and pulled her forward into a walk.

"For now, we will walk. And for now, we will follow the Chief," he told her, resisting the urge to look over his shoulder.

"Understand that I am not doing this for you precious handmaiden,-" he bit out, steering them around a wagon trail drowned by ten inches of standing water, "-I am doing this for you. And for the Realm. And for your Father. But not for Solancei! She does not deserve your loyalty. Not to this extreme. Not to this extent. By her actions, she has endangered you and everyone who-"

"Enough!" Iambre bit back, her tone neither sweet nor pleasant, "I know what you think of Lancei, but I will not hear you speak of her thus! That is not how it is! That is not the truth of it: she is not what you think; this is not her fault!"

"Not her fault?" Tone acerbic, Bilan eyed her askance, "Well, I admit then that I find it hard to see her as you do. In fact, I find it hard to see just how exactly this is not *all* her fault."

Iambre expelled a frustrated sound, "Well it's not! It's... well, it is complicated!"

"I'd say," he snorted, suddenly in a mood to argue the toss, "but I happen to be a pretty good judge character. Complicated it might be but it didn't stop her from planting you in the soup by going to that flecking jackal fight, now did it?"

Bilan looked behind them and gave her arm a discerning yank, which produced a muffled protest as she stumbled against him and righted to match his pace. *Those two men were still behind them. Might be time to catch up to the Chief instead of arguing useless points of view. She liked Solancei; he didn't! Simple!*

"It is complicated, you dolt!-" Iambre flashed at him like a narrow-eyed fury, "-because you don't know everything!"

"Oh really," Bilan deliberately lengthened his stride a notch and was awarded another satisfying sound of displeasure. "Well, if I know so little, why is that then? Tell me Iambre: what exactly is it that I am missing here? Tell me, what *is* the supposed truth then? You defend that woman as though she's a flecking saint! Why? You say it's not like this and it's not like that! Well, what *is* it like then? You tell me!"

"What it's like,-" she spat at him, suddenly provoked to anger, "-is that Lancei is my life-shield! What it's like, is that Eso made her go to that *ruddy* fight, because of me; because of her need to train so that she can be the best and protect me! And, what it's like, is that Eso Mehadja left her alone in that place without someone to watch her back! That's what it's like, Bilan! That's what it's like! Happy?"

Happy? The word echoed with the finality of a deadly curse and yet Bilan could concentrate only on the word 'life-shield'. *Solancei-flecking-razor-tongue-Calverhana-cousin-to-the-Princess... a life-shield?*

Bilan swallowed. *A life-shield gave up everything for their charge. Everything!* His father had been the acting life-shield to Ihaar Seelen, Patrician and Diplomat to the Senate, Gem Trader by appointment to the Royal Family, and Spy - so Bilan would know, because his father had sworn an oath in words and signed in blood, and it had been binding! In fact, such was the bond of a life-shield, that all else took second concern: love or family and even life! And so, his father had indeed served Ihaar Seelen more loyally than his own family, Bilan reflected bitterly. Gods, but he'd barely known the man; his father had rarely left the Patrician's side. That was, at least not until death claimed him in the line of duty!

His father had given his life so that Ihaar Seelen might grow old and fat at Court; his father did his service and died, all the while ignoring that he also left a family behind, so fleck yes, Bilan should know! *And so his father's death had been their ticket out of Lake Side: his and his mother and brothers', for the Patrician had finally paid well for services rendered, but there'd been conditions, and-*

Stupefied, Bilan expelled a breath.

"She is verily your sworn life-shield?" He enquired, stymied by the Princess' revelation.

"Yes,-" Iambre told him, a little winded from trying to keep stride with his quick pace, but her tone held no anger or attitude now, only resignation, "-and since such a long time that I no longer recall the exact date. She is the Chief's prodigy and when time allows, occasionally my handmaiden. Bilan, don't you see... she did this out of duty to me and the Chief, not because she is obstinate and selfish or a trouble-maker, though sure, she can be all of the above on occasions. But not in this case, Bilan. Not this time."

"Hah..." Bilan exhaled. Still stupefied. *Complicated indeed.* Solancei's double role was not common knowledge, in fact, no doubt it was a secret that few had been made privy to and for her to disappear did not bode well. Life-shields had a tendency to know how to look after themselves and land on their feet; if Solancei somehow hadn't, well no wonder Iambre felt so strongly about this!

Bilan looked ahead with a pensive frown. By now they'd nearly caught up with the Chief. *Maybe it was a good thing for multiple reasons...*

"As a life-shield she would not just 'disappear'," Bilan ventured, speaking from memory, "Milady, I am sorry. I have been a fool. An unkind fool."

Bilan offered her a contrite look and she gave him a tired smile. "I should have told you, but the Chief... my father... the rules..."

"Say no more. It was... ah, *is*... above my grade and rank to know about anyway. No doubt it would've stayed that way under other circumstances. I understand the secrecy; the need... but Milady, I hate to say this, but-"

"So don't say it, Bilan. Just don't." Iambre served him a look with a hint of steady dread. "I know your father was a Shield to Senator Seelen. He saved the fat git's life, I know this too. That story is almost as good as the one about you and father. This hero business sort of seems it runs in the family, doesn't it?"

Feeling self-conscious, Bilan frowned at her and she smiled her little secretive smile. "Ah no matter Captain, only my point is that one does not have to hold the title of Shield to act without selfish thought. Like you, Solancei is like that!"

"Iambre..." Bilan began, feeling slightly put out by the reminder and reprimand she'd just served.

Changing the subject slightly, he said, "Gods, and here I was thinking that she was just overprotective because she cannot stand the sight of me in your company..."

Iambre snorted, "Bilan, you say you are doing this for me, but perhaps you might consider doing this for Solancei too?"

Bilan looked at her in surprise. "Iambre, even considering the circumstances, you push my good-will a little too far now. The ruddy woman hates me, keeps warning me about getting too close to you, keeps reminding me with her very presence that I should not even look at you. This-"

"Dolt!" Iambre spoke under her breath, "Bilan, you really don't understand, do you? Solancei does not hate you! As a matter of fact, I believe she likes you well enough! Sure, she doesn't tell me, but I know just the same."

The Princess laughed softly to herself. "Gods, did it never occur to you that the only reason she has continued to dissuade you, is precisely because she likes you enough not to see you make a huge mistake? Bilan, just trust me: if she did not like you she would not care one way or another about what you said or did, she'd simply find a way to remove you, and then your career would be over."

"But-"

Bilan swallowed his natural denial and felt his mind warp at the information she was spewing at him. Part of him realised it made sense, especially in view of the woman's oath.

Feeling humbled, he looked at Iambre and she held his gaze as if to say 'see?'.

"Sorry Milady." Bilan felt a dolt indeed. It was all he could do to place one foot in front of the other and not stop and make some useless gesture to ensure she understood his regret. *Solancei liked him? It was almost a relief to find out: like a sanction almost - not to relent and pursue his feelings for Iambre in earnest, of course - but more in a sense that the best friend of the woman next to him had given him a kind of blessing in disguise; that if things had been different...*

Bilan could have bashed his own head against the nearest bricks. *It was almost a good thing those two men were still trailing them...*

"You will keep the secret?" Iambre prodded, forcing him to blink and think. "You will keep Solancei's title to yourself? Even after all of this?"

Bilan nodded. He heard her doubt. "But of course, Milady. Why would I not?"

Iambre looked sheepish, "Well I kind of blurted this one out, didn't I? And I didn't exactly make you swear beforehand that you'd keep this one to yourself, so..."

A part of him should perhaps have felt offended that she'd think that little of him, but she was in deep with this; perhaps even a little confused. It was a small thing to reassure her.

"Highness, upon my Oath to King and Crown, I swear to you that this will remain a guarded secret: that I will reveal it never - not even on my dying breath. How's that?"

Iambre grimaced as though she'd swallowed something hard and dry but she did not look displeased.

After a blink, she gave his ribs a playful punch of camaraderie, "Oh you do know how to-"

Iambre broke off sharply as they rounded a corner. They were an even ten strides behind Klaasinah Mehadja now, not yet close enough to risk attracting her attention without it being obvious to their surroundings, but still near enough all the same that they could not possibly lose her either, and yet...

Bilan tried not to startle, but just like that, the Chief was suddenly nowhere to be seen.

Rats!

He looked at Iambre. She appeared to read his mind for she looked back at him with round-eyed confusion. Bilan was already surveying their surroundings.

"Where...?" she began but fell quiet. The road was narrow, a near-lane, really. Residential by the looks of the plain terraced buildings rising a sheer three and four stories tall on either side of them. Clotheslines, some hung with washing: sheets, hose, nightshirts, were strung between the buildings high up, the plain-cut items billowing lively across the road above their heads, whilst the vast number of doors and shutter-clad windows appeared too many to count.

Bilan spun around.

Though there were people about, mostly they appeared to be farmers returning home from their day in the fields: their dusty attire and their general lacking aura of danger defining them as easily as the thugs belonging to the gangs. *The flapping movement of sheets was distracting; it made him want to look up when there was no need...*

Instead, the Captain swivelled his head left and right. Lights lit the windows, escaping through shutters and slat-blinds. Cooking smells and others wafted then disappeared only to come back, born anew on gusts of wind; voices and sporadic bits of chatter reached them; the cries of a baby; a scattered burst of laughter; a slamming door; a cat hissing... *But no Eso!*

Bilan scanned the area near and ahead, Iambre mirroring him, but his heart was sinking. *Eso Mehadja was gone! Fleck! He could waste no time!*

Trailing rapidly down the nearest line of wooden boards, Bilan flung them both into a random space between two towering buildings, pulling them deeper without pause so that they were instantly lost in the shadows of the narrow niche. He didn't care if anyone saw. Farmers were not dangerous; the two men behind them were. If he could not reach the Chief for back-up, he could not risk confrontation and would take no chances!

Iambre sighed. "Bilan, being alone with you is nice but this-"

"Hush!" he told her and shifted to lay a finger against her lips even as he kept his gaze trained upon the narrow exit and pushed at his cloak to get at the dagger. Iambre fell quiet against him. She was so close that he could feel the warmth of her body against his own; so close that he could almost feel her quickened heartbeat... *or perhaps it was his own?*

At any other time, he would have welcomed the nearness, but not now, however. Through the narrow opening, he spied the locals press past, somehow managing to walk the planks and avoid the mire but Bilan was blind to anyone not built like a stocky six-foot lean-to cloaked in ragged grey layers of material. *The stench in here was ripe, stripping, but it couldn't be helped. Time seemed to slow...*

Behind him Iambre trembled once, either in fear or from cold, he didn't know which, but he absently ran his free hand down her cheek to comfort, then cupped her chin in brief reassurance and she sighed happily, catching his hand in both of hers to press a kiss against his palm, distracting...

A hulking shadow glided sinuously past the narrow gap, then another, both figures moving in such a manner that Bilan instantly knew them no farmers and his attention sharpened. One cowl swivelled, peering into the darkness as they went, unseen eyes piercing, and for a heartbeat Bilan felt the swipe of the man's attention roll over the both of them but darkness sheltered and the possibility was dismissed. Then the men were gone from view.

Bilan didn't exhale, nor relax. Leaving Iambre in the black depth with a touch to indicate that she should stay put, he ghosted to the exit, chancing a look.

The two bit of muscle had stopped to confer not five paces removed. He could not hear the words but the sharp gestures indicated their frustration well enough. Then one man abruptly pushed open the first doorway, disappearing inside, the peeling green door slamming behind him and leaving the remaining man cursing rudely under his breath as he shifted to fold his arms and take up a guarding stance. *Flecking rats! They intended to search then...*

Bilan drew back and nearly jumped as he backed straight into Iambre's form. She was immediately behind him and he hadn't even heard her approach.

"Bilan I think there is an exit back there?" she whispered. *Excited?*

"Come." Pulling at a fold of his cloak, Iambre tugged at him and he obliged to follow, somewhat speechless. The darkness here remained as thick as molasses and they were wading through something best left unidentified, but then the building bent at a sharp angle indicating a corner and suddenly there was a narrow sliver of light ahead.

Pushing past the Princess, Bilan took charge, bringing them both toward that light, yet halting cautiously as they reached the end. Before them spread another block of housings, but there were few people here and after a single look, Bilan pulled Iambre close and lurched from the hideout, picking the opposite direction of where he calculated the thugs to be. With a look over his shoulder, he assured their safety, then tugged at Iambre, breaking into a rapid pace just shy of running.

"Come along," he told her without preface, "we need to move quickly."

Weaving and wheedling they rounded another handful of corners at fast speed, occasionally splashing through pools or mud or stepping off boards to cross onto the other side of the lanes when Bilan deemed it necessary. At one time Iambre gasped out loud and muttered something under her breath and Bilan thought she must have soaked a boot once more in one of the icy puddles but he did not let up until they stepped into a well-lit square, overflowing with a wealth of market stalls and evening visitors.

In comparison to the relative darkness they'd come from, the square seemed ablaze with light, supplied most generously by eight-foot oil torches placed into the ground at regular intervals as well as lanterns hung from the corners of every open stall or cart. *There were people and voices everywhere, the square was packed enough for them to disappear. Perfect.*

"Ahh, look at that," Iambre exclaimed, brushing past his shoulder to gain a better view. "Bilan... this is marvellous. Did you know?"

Know? Bilan eyed her askance and pulled her back a little to allow two young women and a stern-looking matron passage onto the boards. One of the women had eyes that sparkled as she found his from under a sheer veil and she smiled... *inviting...*

Bilan smiled back but his mind was elsewhere. *This was a good place to get lost. It was also a good place to get their bearings and begin to make their way back!*

"Bilan!" Iambre called; sharply. "You want to go on seducing that trollop or pretend you care for my feelings?!"

"What?" Bilan startled and realised Iambre was giving the woman with the sparkling eyes an evil look. The woman broke eye contact and Iambre smiled sweetly.

"As I was saying,-" she ventured, clasping his arm possessively as she looked around with interest, "-did you know that they had this evening market here? I can see at least three interesting stalls worthy of a second glance, not to mention-"

"Iambre, we are not here to shop," Bilan chided, somewhere between incredulous and frustrated. *They'd lost the Chief... had a couple of thugs on their heels - and she wanted a detour to shop?* "Have you forgotten about Solancei?"

Iambre gave him a desiccating look, "Of course not, Bilan. And, I know you had us running to avoid those men and that was good - but unless I am mistaken, we have now gone and lost the Chief, you are eying up flirts, and I am no closer to my goal than when I left the castle! Maybe I am simply trying to salvage what I might out of this otherwise disastrous night."

With an exasperated sigh, Bilan anchored his hands on his hips. "Firstly, I am not eying up flirts: she was eying up me! Secondly, we are not lost. This is Tyra's Square, which happens to be only four or five blocks removed from the main quays, which in turn means that all we need do, is to go via the riverside, leave up Lightener's Boulevard or Roshar's Run, and I expect we could be back at the main Keep in less than a turn of the hour!"

Iambre sniffed and looked around. "And how can you be so sure?"

"Well for one, the sign across the corner of that building proclaims it so – but I also had the small foresight of looking at the map of Zanzier before coming out. Doesn't make me as insightful as a local, but still... it's beneficial now, isn't it? Perhaps we should get going?"

"Going?" Though she should acquiesce, Iambre looked alarmed. *Gods did she not comprehend that this foray was over?*

Bilan gave a winning smirk. "Yes, you know Milady... *going*... as in: back to the Keep? As in: back to where you are in fact supposed to be? Right now!?"

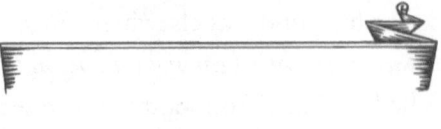

Red Binds the Poison?

IAMBRE HUFFED.

Bilan was aware that she did not appreciate the reminder, but this time it was she who was out of line!

Still... the Princess looked a fine picture and ignoring the controversial perfume coming off her new fashion, he offered her his best smile, suddenly unable to resist.

"If you like Highness, we can pretend you are the trollop I've picked up for the night?" He bent towards her. "I'd have to fix your looks a bit. Make you appear more the Charmstress, less the walking death-sort-a-thing; you have assets; it would work. See, the gate might be shut, but soldiers tend to understand each other. It'd be the easiest way in."

Iambre glared. *Perhaps he'd gone too far? But she was the one who'd brought up the subject, not he!*

"Yes sure, if you like we can pretend just that Captain." The surprising response left Iambre with a mischievous-bordering-on-evil little twist of her mouth, in her eyes a sheen of daring challenge that he could not believe himself ready to trust.

Nevertheless it provoked pause, his jest shaking apart under her unsuspected ability to adjust and raise the gambit. Iambre shook her head, the set of her chin falling into its usual stubborn tilt as she held his gaze with a strange unvoiced promise, yet the light of voluntary confrontation soon faded.

In a sobering tone, she told him, "You may take me back to the castle anyway you like Metavo, but not until I say I am ready to go. This has been a monumental disappointment; I was doing just fine until you came and bundled up matters, so now I wish to do something, and you better not try to dissuade me."

"I... " Bilan wiped the surprise from his face just a heartbeat too late and he knew that she'd seen the imprinted shock of her words when her mien turned knowing.

"Hmm, couldn't quite hear? What was that again, my love?" The cursed woman looked intriguingly guileless as she peered at him as though utterly innocent of all the wily ways he knew her versed in. Hitching up the ragged hemline as though her skirts were dainty silk, the Princess circled round his frame without another word and took a giant step into the turned up mire.

Bilan closed his mouth, eyes narrowing minutely with resigned concern. It was markedly less wet here and the boards to see the customers safely from stall to stall more frequent, but he clearly heard each 'squelch' as she moved towards the safety of a haberdashery display decked out with a rainbow selection of bolted fabrics, tie-string cuts and what to his inexperienced eye looked to be cheap reams of filigree lace and perhaps hair ribbon.

Were other women just like that too, or only Princesses?

As he watched her move from the haberdashery to a store of miniature clayware oil lamps and onto the next, Bilan realised he feared to find out and quenched a sigh. Almost he wished that they hadn't lost Eso. *Almost...*

Wishing for sure that he had the courage to simply leave her smack in the middle of her own stubborn mess – *if only to teach her the lesson he'd meant to* - Bilan folded his hands within the voluminous sleeves of his ragged cloak and resigned himself to simple guard duty instead.

Right then he was not in the mood to look at her fair face, however - and fearing that he might be sulking, yet caring little because he felt entitled, Bilan deliberately hung back, stopping whenever the Princess did, meandering on only when she did. *All this for cursed Solancei del'Isthalani Calverhana, all just because he was trying to please a woman he could never have?*

The irony was almost cauterising. *What the fleck was there not to sulk about?* Before Iambre, he would have looked more than twice at the woman with the sparkling eyes; Gods, he might even have struck up a conversation or he might have persuaded her to reveal onto him her name, but now?

Keeping sure-pace to stay on track with the 'root' of all his problems, Bilan allowed himself to feel a brief spike of annoyance. Iambre somehow managed to keep him on the straight and narrow with nothing more than a casual glance, which was bad. He'd been acting somewhat out of character for a while now and with his often wry reflections upon this very fact, he knew that his abstinence was such that even his men were starting to question if he had hit his head or indeed other vital parts. Sure, it remained nothing but the good-natured cheek of soldiers bored witless from too much travelling and not enough action, but his Second, Lieutenant del'Draventar, was beginning to wonder just a little beyond what uncouth jokes might adequately cover and Bilan suspected he'd soon need to work out how to deflect the ever deeper-scoring questions.

And right there was the trouble with reputations, he mused, rue and wonder comingling. *If you stopped living up to something, if you stopped doing what people viewed as a habitual reflection of your character, life soon became fraught with theories and guesses.*

Bilan frowned at the night, incapable of inventing a satisfactory lie that would suit the future conversations with his friends. There was always 'illness' of course, but he'd bloody rather cut his own throat than release that sort of rumour! His men would never let up then! In fact, they'd wish to know where he'd picked up such slight, so that his sorry misfortune wouldn't befall any of them. *But was he to make up names and locations, now?*

Face ruffled by grim feelings, the Captain kept up the surveillance of the Heiress as she appeared to enjoy herself with restrained enthusiasm. Most of the items were little more than tat: trinkets and brass, cheap temple offerings and yet more second-hand clothing, but Iambre was moving through the hap-hazardous gathering of canvass and carts, temporary wooden scaffolds and ragged assortment of merchants, with an easy lissom sway that belied the disdain she must surely harbour. He observed how it found a few people pausing mid-haggle to look her way, but she didn't seem to notice. *It was a 'tell' she wasn't even aware of now that she'd relaxed, but if* he saw the change, so would others.

Bilan tried to relax the returning tightness in his jaw; the lingering, softly straining ache between his shoulders, but he couldn't quite get there.

The shouting of vendors trying to pry the best deal for their waves, the cursing and the laughing of others, the soft metallic chink of copper scraps exchanging hands, all echoed in the square; riding the air was a mash-up of discord and sound, of people and mild excitement. *Was he wrong or was the press of punters becoming thicker than before?*

Bilan looked around, sighting no trouble, but life was creeping into the night, the thong growing heavier, and by default he moved closer to Iambre. She, in turn, continued to ignore him but it didn't matter. To either side of the bedlam market, make-shift signs proclaimed the often saucy names of after-hours ale houses or certain sordid 'establishments' where innocence was long forgotten. Indeed, Bilan had already spied one whore-house and two seedy-looking smoke houses, from where the noise of merriment flowed from the now open shutters to mingle with the general sounds of the market. Perhaps not knowing their origins, thankfully Iambre seemed oblivious to the invisible clouds of pungent sweet-smelling drugs and illegal tobaccos, but to Bilandro's nose the reek rivalled the sickly smell of decaying bodies and he sincerely hoped that Iambre had no idea what could be bought and sold within ten yards of her toes.

Drawing a shallow breath, Bilan tried to avoid the cloying stink from entering and lingering like a curse in the back of his throat. As he knew it, it was said that some herbs might bend a man to their ways with only one breath; he had never believed such a thing possible, but he still detested the idea almost as much as the stench itself. With poorly hidden disdain he eyed the easily-recognised, glossy-eyed addicts who pushed past oversized door-keepers to gain entry to the smoke parlours beyond.

They were all lost. He pitied their idiocy.

'Smoke once to try it, smoke twice to deny it, smoke thrice to know yourself addicted to the spice' - as far as he was aware, the door-keepers might very well be the sanest people within any of those establishments – and that in spite of them sporting crude markings and clean-shaven heads that seemed to glow with a pink sheen from the trademark soft red lantern-light on either side of the doors they minded.

Bilan looked away.

Ahead, Iambre appeared drawn towards a cluster of people jostling around a portable cart laden with a multitude of colourfully-wrapped parcels. Mildly bemused, Bilan trailed after.

Apparently well-sought after, the tray of ointments and potions looked in hot demand by several women who brandished elbows and shoulders as weapons of choice, clamouring and pushing to gain front row access without concern for the possibilities of ensuing conflict.

For a beat Bilan had second thoughts about Iambre involving herself with such furies, then he deliberately held back, resisting the urge to interfere, leaning his frame instead against a random, nearby canvas-enveloped stall. Folding one shin over the other as he casually crossed his arms over the chest, Bilan sniffed-in sharply to stop his runny nose, sincerely hoping she'd just hurry up. *Gods, whatever she was doing, let her do it – those women acted like fisher-wives and if she earned herself a bruised chin for the trouble... well, then good!*

Shifting his weight again he settled in to wait, though wondering how long it would take the Princess to give over? This was a far cry from sipping honey-laced afternoon tea on an Etruian barge, whilst the songbirds thrilled and the swans swam close to impress with their size and to garner a few crumbs. Iambre could not possibly inset herself into this kind of situation, no matter what her sense of interest told her...

But it was a spectacle to be sure just the same. Equally rude in their eagerness to ensure a dubious purchase before the wares had all gone, the women used small restraint, pointy toes or just mean strength of bulk to muscle-in around the cart and there was something very cut-throat about the scene that Bilan found both amusing and troubling. *Gods but back in Lake Side, men would've paid money to watch this kind of thing unfold; all the women would've needed were slightly shorter skirts to make it a tad more interesting and they would've made a sport of it!*

But of course this was Zanzier. Here, such a thing would be kept under wraps and cover – similar, he guessed, to the jackal fights – but that didn't mean they didn't happen. People might pretend to be different, but essentially they were all the same, the only thing to change: the accents or a personal preference of weaponry. Iambre was way above all of them, though; the most unique person in all the realm; this was usually a splendid thing, except... *except for now.*

Bilan pulled a face: a sawing grimace for a short woman in muck-soiled rags who got her hair viciously pulled by a crone from behind. Gross cuss words emanated accordingly, and someone hissed, perhaps as a result of nails clamping down on their wrist...

His eyes flashed to the peddler of this fair assortment. Handing out her wares as fast as she could pocket the coins thrown into her open palm, the old swarthy woman in charge of the cart smiled with a cunning intelligent gleam in the eye - and no wonder: whatever she was pushing, it must be highly priced and evidently she knew.

Bilan's attention fixed back upon Iambre as she dived into an opening between a fat matron with loose strands of greasy hair and a tall powder-faced Charmstress with lips the colour of old blood. Between the two, the Princess' smooth complexion and celestial nose would have been sure to attract attention anywhere else. *But not here though.*

Heart bounding almost painfully, he sniffed, exhaling a puff of air. He'd let her finish this, but watching the show, consternation still enveloped him – though in fairness: whether it was for his own reaction or for Iambre's nerve, he could not presently have said. Before he could think to wonder how, Iambre was gesturing unexpectedly towards a scarlet parcel the size of a small jewellery box and the Captain could only stare at the scene in near dumbstruck disbelief. She was the Heiress to the Crown – and here she was, apparently haggling over the contents of a trinket box and doing so in heated competition with a rat-faced woman wearing a stripy skirt of the brightest blues and yellows, Bilan had ever seen.

Gods... she was Crown Princess, for Gods' sake! She had no business mixing with these trollops! Did nothing faze that woman?!

Sniffing hard, momentarily distracted by his own condition, Bilan lost the fight with his now freely-running nose.

Pox on it. He thought he'd been on the mend! Fleck!

Bilan absently swiped a sleeve across the nose; tempted, he did not go as far as to blow it on the rags, though it wouldn't have been at all out of place, however, his attention was on the Princess.

Half the women surrounding that old cart looked as if they would not think twice about cutting your throat and the other half looked as if they would just as gladly invite you to try! These were not the kind of women you crossed. And yet, just as the thought went through him, a deal seemed to be struck at the cart for Iambre nodded and handed the vendor some copper marks in return for the square parcel she'd bartered for. 'Rat Face' poked her in the ribs for the 'affront' and Bilan thought her surely about to play the high-lady card then, yet, to his utter amazement, Iambre simply turned sharply on her heel to face the offender nose to nose with a most chilling gaze of invitation.

Bilan froze. He simply hadn't expected this. *Oh, fleck and guts! This was going to go so wrong!*

Trying very hard to compose himself to somehow intercept before this marketplace got turned on its head and someone got chugged in irons for laying a hand on the Princess, Bilan tried to take a step forward, only to realise he could potentially be the one to blow up this situation unless he handled himself with utmost care, but-

Staring at Iambre, all sorts of prayers formed and went without focus, as he could not make a decision. For a blink, the Princess reminded him most uncomfortably of her missing cousin in the way she tilted her chin and in the way the steel in her eyes seemed to promise regrets. From what he now knew, Solancei would probably have decked the woman in the next few breaths, but Iambre did not have such training and shifting surreptitiously Bilan danced onto the balls of his feet in readiness.

Mercy be with him...

For a heartbeat longer the two women eyed each other like a pair of cockerels about to scrap, then something made 'rat face' step back from the Princess and with a display of enough volatile contempt to anger even a corpse, Iambre promptly spat at the feet of the older woman, forcing her to back-up further. *What... the...?*

Bilan knew he'd gasped aloud then. Undecided whether to salute her fierceness or despair of her stupidity, he invariably stepped forward, prepared to stop the catfight that must surely follow no matter what the cost - when instead of the expected outburst, or fistfuls of hair, nothing happened. The slighted woman simply glared morbid rain at Iambre, then turned almost instantly back to peruse the contents of the cart with nothing more than a small shrug, whilst the Princess undulated free of the press of the others, turning her attention towards the next stall. As if it was second thought to her, she tucked her mysterious purchase safely under one arm, gliding on without as much as a glance for him or his sore disposition on the sideline.

With a sniff, Bilan let out his pent-up breath. *Well, what do you know...? Mercy indeed!*

This was an utterly new side of Iambre: one he'd never seen before, and he suddenly wasn't sure why exactly it had been deemed necessary for her to hide behind a life-shield.

But she is the Heiress, he reminded himself, *and a future Queen should never walk without protection; not that this one would!*

Kimonar del'Draventar, however, would be upset if he but knew of Solancei's real purpose, though. *His friend's odd 'affections' for the 'supposed' handmaiden would never be returned; could never be returned; life-shields were married only to their duty and to expect anything more was utterly deluded.*

Bilan felt a rueful smile cross his lips for Kim's dilemma. *Seemed their two fates were nicely mirrored, didn't it?!* Perhaps they could even share cups and commiserate once this farce of a journey was at last an end; yup, they could share cups and weep for the fools they'd been whilst counting their blessings, for life could also always get worse...

A wealth of sour emotion welling up inside, Bilan prepared to continue his strange vigil over 'her royal fierceness', when soft dry laughter sifted from the stall, stalling his intention.

Berating himself that he hadn't even realised that someone was watching him, Bilan flashed the offender within the candlelit square a warning glare. Nothing too worrisome met his weighing glance: only the outline of a podgy woman perched upon a tall three-legged stool, but she boldly met his challenging stare just the same, her weighing eyes shrewdly uncompromising below the days' worth of black, caked kohl. Shrouded in shadows and what appeared to be muted velvets, the woman was an uneasy character to gain the measure of, yet as she shifted her bulk a little left to set the stool creaking, he belatedly noticed the scarlet garter and the drooping neckline. *A Charmstress.*

Brazen as those of her profession was known to be, the woman held his stare with a mien of impeccable candour, the set of her mouth lending to her age a sense of affluent confidence that some might have labelled cavalier.

Leisurely raising a slender reed pipe to contour-enhanced scarlet lips, the Charmer drew a lengthy a puff off the silver-cupped bore, expelling the thin cloud almost instantly around a blossoming sardonic smile.

"So..." the woman's voice was low with a pleasant tint, not Zanzierian, "I see you watch that smooth-faced beau of yours with the certain doleful longing most fools will squander upon only one creature in a lifetime..."

The savvy smile became faded as she tipped forward on the stool, extensive neckline dropping. "Boy, I see you watch that girl but believe you me: that one is not worth it."

Narrowing her eyes towards Iambre, the woman gestured once with the mouthpiece of the reed-necked pipe, then put the smoke to her crimson lips, puffing deeply.

Oddly uneasy, Bilan followed her look and the woman nodded once then as if satisfied that she'd been understood. Exhaling a string of smoke, she let the air clear, then stabbed the pipe in the general direction of Iambre. "You see, my young fellow... that one does not hope for children. You mark my words: as surely as I am an old dog at this game, red cloth binds the poisons. Always. She will bear you only sorrow!"

Frowning in spite better judgement, Bilan cast another glance towards Iambre even as his eyebrows rose in sheer surprise at the fat woman's forthright presumption and bold mettle. Swivelling his eyes back to her shadowed face, he opened his mouth to protest ignorance.

"Lad...you are handsome enough, even with that nose,-" Her smile widened at his cautious pretence. She made a rapid clicking sound with her tongue, the tsk wobbling the generous chin slightly, "-so stay easy. There will be others. I dare say not as pretty, but a face is not all. Oh but come, come now lad; don't look so surprised. You might be in love with the flirt, but she will never have you! Good-looking girls like that end up in the arms of wealthy merchants, not penny-less young dreamers. I've seen it, lad. Red binds the poison, yes – but it needn't leave you all sad. Some revelations are for the better, are they not?"

Uncomfortably touched by her words, Bilan forgot about colds as a chill rolled down his spine. The Charmstress' words rang with an edge of prophetic truth and his expression must have shifted to one of incredulous dismay but the woman only sat back with a most assuring curl of the lip to make her seem almost sympathetic to his troubles.

"My young man, forget her. I have got several girls in them rooms up there,-" the woman gestured towards a three-storied half-timbered building next to one of the smoke-parlours, *not the one he'd noted*, "-several girls I tell you, all ready to please you in all the ways that one over there will not. We are discreet but they will take away your thoughts of that hussy all the same. Why don't you come visit?"

The Charmstress smiled again, offering forth a token in the shape of a hexagonal coin with a hole in the centre, "Here, first time's on me: give it the door-keeper and tell her Madam Rodarah sent you with her compliments."

Bilan stared fixedly at the hand extending the coin, surprised that he should feel so alarmed and offended at the same time. Then he backed away with a silent shake of the head and the woman barked a laugh as she withdrew the token and lifted the pipe to salute him.

"Oh well lad, you don't blame an old fox for trying now, do you? But you remember my words when that one tells you to go poke yourself. Maybe then you will come see me, eh? Here you keep this!" The woman looped the token into the air and Bilan reflexively reached to catch it.

Teeth clacking round her pale pipe, the Madam straightened her garter with curious care, muttering, "Who knows, lad? People come to me and mine for many reasons. If the girls have no interest, I have the various *smokes* too, if you'd prefer – exotic from Tuxama and Shaz; blessed sweet oblivion from Imkarah, cold forgiveness from faraway Tarléon? Still, mark this... you may sample my pleasures by invitation only! That there token has two sides, remember that. I would accept it in either house - and who knows, perhaps by the time you come to your senses you might just find an unimagined desire to lose your memories of that radiant nymph in more ways than one. Whatever your preference, let it never be said that Madam Rodarah does not know how to look after you. Remember... and come to me!"

The woman cocked her pipe at him one last time, then sank back into the hooded darkness of her stall until only the glow of her white pipe revealed her presence.

Bilan shook off ill-feelings, fuelling stray mirth. Who could fault a woman like that for trying her luck? *He'd bet Madam told every unsuspecting fool the same cautionary tale. He'd bet it paid off too, but if he were that desperate he'd rather have opted for 'sparkle-eyes'.*

Feeling touchy in spite of his sensible deductions, the Captain re-centred his attention on Iambre. Whilst the Madam had detained him, the Princess had meandered on and with a last sketchy look for the odd token, Bilan pocketed the thing without further thought, then set out to catch her up. He smiled, the odd episode rapidly gaining a kind of novelty as it replayed in his mind. It was without a doubt the oddest way anyone had ever tried to solicit him but for some reason, the Charmer's words about Iambre had struck a chord and he had to remind himself that the fat witch knew nothing of the Heiress. *Red binds the poison?* Now that was just ludicrous! *How would that old hag possibly know what*

Iambre was buying anyway? It could've been anything from dried flower petals to itching powder – who knew what or why? *And as to the medicinal benefits hinted at...*

Bilan shouldered his way past a young couple, not caring if his step landed on board or mud as a sad coldness began to sieve into him. *Iambre had beseeched him to give her 'memories' – was this somehow part of what she was planning?*

By now, they both knew just how good she was at getting what she wanted - and just how rubbish he was at saying 'no'. *Now if that 'poison' was somehow what he suspected it to be - courtesy of the old Charmstress - how was he to carry on without getting them both burnt?*

It was yet another question for him to ponder but since they were both here, right now, he could at the very least ask Iambre exactly what that parcel contained and he found himself walking faster then, in order to reach her.

Ahead of him, she was crossing the main thoroughfare again, braving the sludge with her head bent and skirts hitched-up and for a moment he feared she was deliberately trying to lose him, but as she reached the sideboards, she halted to cast around a searching look as she shook out her shirts.

Bilan looked up the facade behind her and knew a moment of private agony. *Well forsooth! Of course, of all the places, she'd stop right there, wouldn't she?! If she realised...*

Bilan cringed. The pleasure house's cracked-plaster and pre-Chaos War architecture raised a toast to the fact that the building was respectably ancient, but this was only at a single glance or until you noticed the signs, and Bilan could verily feel the old Charmer's eye boring into his neck. Scrolled paintwork and faded wines proclaimed 'The Dreamer's Delight' a place of 'privacy, excitement and good taste', although Bilan had to wonder. Two doors led the way inside: one marked 'Dreamweaver's Lounge', the other 'Dancers of Zanzier' – however, as inviting as the names might sound, each entrance was guarded by a huge Kheltian woman: top knot and pelts and knives on display like full regalia - as though they'd only just stepped forth out of some story of legendary beasts and yore. Barely tamed human guard dogs they looked, and Bilan carried no doubts that they knew how to enforce the idea of ' by invite only'.

"Ah there you are," Iambre smiled, breaking his thoughts and reaching for him with her free hand as he caught up to her. "So are we going to find Chief Eso, then?"

ıief?" Bilan looked at her sharply, his perusal of the house and ıckly forgotten, "Ah... I do hope that is a very poorly-chosen jest?"

ıe stiffened but kept her gaze steady. Bilan closed his eyes for one long mc ent. Then he squared his shoulders. *Tricksy it might be but this time it would be a resounding 'no'!*

He drew her out of the path of people, steering her towards the Kheltians but it couldn't be helped. "Iambre, what we have to do is make our way back to the Keep. I must insist. This is not a safe place to be without more guards – it may seem that way – but it is not. The Chief is long gone now. I don't know where the Golden Ball is – and I do not intend to ask either. It is not our business, we tried, but now I need to see you safe. Let Solancei be Eso Mehadja's priority, because right now you are mine, you understand?"

Iambre pulled a face. Almost he thought her about to argue and steeled himself for a verbal fight but then she grimaced and looked away, blinking several times before she returned him her attention.

"Bilan, I am scared," she burst out, lip quivering slightly. "What if I never see her again? Gods but if the Knights Commander has somehow got something to do with this, what are we to do?"

The Knights Commander? Well, what do you know? This was another bit of news and for a moment he felt disturbed. *Were there more layers to this than the mind would first believe?* It astounded, but of all the things she'd confided so far, bizarrely this sounded the least shocking to his ear.

Unable to comment without sounding insincere, Bilan drew her close, thrilled in spite of everything to have the brief freedom to do so and she melted into him as he brushed her forehead with his lips. *Yes, sure he'd wanted to know more, but-*

Bilan shook himself. *She felt cold, they'd better go.*

"I know she is not well, Bilan," Iambre spoke against his shoulder, startling him, "I can feel it in my core: something is wrong and I have to help her."

"You are friends," he allowed, "it is only right that you should care – but we cannot do anything more today. I am sure Chief Eso will do her utmost to see you united."

He pulled away and looked at her, started to say something but was brought up short by the sudden clamour of raised shouts. The sounds of trouble drew his eye: a cloaked figure had entered the square from one of the many narrow exit routes and was running for all he was worth straight across it, slipping and sliding but never falling, dodging puddles and people like he had the hounds of Osari'Chi snapping at his heels and Bilan had to applaud the sprinter's efforts even as a stab of concern fixed him. Behind the man came a group of six or seven armed men in loud pursuit and though they fared little better on the unforgiving surface, Bilan suddenly knew a stab of icy fear they might catch up the person they hunted. It was irrational, but he couldn't help it though it puzzled. The runner was wrapped in a plain brown cloak and hood of a decidedly common cut – nothing to indicate status, high or low; from their vantage, Bilan could not make out the man's face, nor his true height or other features, yet all the same there was something oddly familiar about the way the runner moved. Something disconcerting even.

Unease deepened. The running man had given no sign that this was his intention and yet he looked to be steering straight towards the two of them.

"Come along." Bilan drew Iambre with him.

Her attention now also on the ruckus, she followed without argument. The runner had already flung himself onto the boards by the market and was passing the old Charmstress stall, making better progress now that his feet were back on steady ground and Bilan pulled Iambre slowly sideways, hoping to avoid calling too much attention to the fact that they appeared to find themselves right in the runner's path! They could, of course, turn and run but low-key was the deal tonight. *Low key...*

"Bilan?" Iambre quested, her voice uncertain. She too had seen the runner's trajectory and though she kept an admirable control of herself, Bilan could feel her mounting unease.

"Steady," he cautioned her as they drew alongside the blonde Kheltian guarding the Dreamweaver's Lounge, "Steady."

Bilan eyed the tall, broad woman in her black-lacquered leather armour but she looked a statue, the only thing moving, her light-coloured eyes and the fall of black feathers from her top-knot as the breeze played across the length of her hair.

Some people thought them coarse of feature. He thought them statuesque, and this one was no exception. Her attention was on the escalating pursuit too, her sharp eyes bright as a falcon's, though her emotions remained veiled.

It was not her duty so she would not defend them from trouble and Bilan whispered to Iambre, "Just keep moving; we do not want to get involved. Just keep moving. This is just a coincidence, in five steps we'll turn down that lane there and then we'll follow the path right to the quays, yes?"

Iambre breathed-in hard. "Yes, but that man-"

"Coincidence!" he reiterated with a look for the unfolding chase and though uncertainty had him by the throat, he drew her on. The unknown man was steering through the filth: like a guiding needle of a compass pointing straight towards them, and Bilan could feel Iambre quiver. *In a few heartbeats, he'd either run them over or...*

Bilan reached for the dagger as the runner stumbled onto the scattering of boards, deep cowl flapping low, his breath falling hard and jagged, and the pursuers yelling even louder, cursing him to stop and be accounted... *the three paces between them seemed both too far and yet too close!*

With a rush of air, the cloaked runner sped past, close enough for their own garments to stir and though Bilan didn't see exactly what happened, as they passed each other, the man appeared to look straight at Iambre for one split blink: long enough for the Princess to suddenly blanch as if taken ill

"Your Grace should tell him what that box is for," the stranger urged over one shoulder, the breathy voice hoarse but clear, "You know he will be terribly hag-ridden until you do!"

In response, Iambre issued a strangled sound and faltered as though she was about to keel over, but though the small hairs seemed to stand up along his arms, Bilan chose to ignore the runner in favour of extricating himself and Iambre from the situation before the armed men could reach their position. One hand on the dagger, one hand bearing up the Princess, he just about had time to see the runner stumble through the Dreamweaver's door, elbowing himself half-way past the blond Kheltian yet pacifying the possible affront by throwing her a handful of half-silver marks, followed by an uncomfortably-familiar, six-sided token of invite.

It seemed enough. With an agreeable grunt, the Kheltian let the man disappear inside. Shouts of enraged anger arose from the pursuers, the first amongst the more agile streaking past he and Iambre then, instantly attempting to follow where the runner had gone, only to be halted by not one, but two, stone-faced Kheltians in demand of the necessary token.

As anyone might have predicted, harsh arguments and hard threats ensued; Kheltian sickle-bladed axes came out, the door guardians taking no chances as the ruckus threatened to become a brawl. But let them have their fisticuffs. It would take the attention from him and the Princess!

Bilan pulled Iambre with him to relative safety, rounding the intended corner with long, rapid strides. *And a good thing too,* he thought, *she felt leaden...*

"Bilan, what... what..." Iambre choked, then gasped and stuttered, "By the rat and bone, Bilan, what the fleck was that? Who... Who was... I don't... Bilan, I..."

Daggers Away!

AS IF CONTROLLED BY someone else, Bilan ignored her half-formed words and feverish look to drag her along though he did sympathise. Her face pale as death, they could not risk stopping, but seemed that teaching her the intended lesson was not nearly as rewarding as imagined.

The runners blatant 'Your Grace' more than bothered: they drilled shards of pointy dragon silver into his core, leaving him soaked in strange dread. *How the fleck could this random person have known? How could he have recognised her?*

Warding off a superstitious chill, Bilan shrugged. *The man must have spotted her purchase as he passed, but there was no way he could have known about Iambre's identity. Not unless he'd followed her from the Keep too – which was impossible! - and the cheek of his random comment...!*

Bilan shook himself again, unable to fit the pieces. *He had not been followed when he left the castle, he was ready to swear on any God and all-*

Had the runner been simple a thief, caught mid-move? It seemed plausible, in the view of the heated pursuit, but-

Knowing he'd never get the answer to this disturbing puzzle, Bilan turned to Iambre.

"Milady, I appreciate you might feel upset but that thing back there had nothing to do with us," he assured her as much as himself, looking at her sideways as he hastened them on without much attention to the gleeful fact that the mush underfoot had now receded in favour of proper cobbles. "Probably all just some dispute over money or someone's doe. Don't worry. These things happen all the time."

"Do they?" she quacked in a peculiar tone, offering a strange look.

"Absolutely. Just relax. I can feel the wind getting stronger so we must be on the direct path towards the quays. We'll be there in a blink if we do not dawdle and then we'll be at the Keep before you know it." Bilan squeezed her hand in encouragement, then forced a smile as he observed, "Gods Iambre, but I rather think there's been enough excitement in one night - you look as though you've seen a spirit."

Iambre shuddered. Clutching her crimson parcel as though it contained a hoard of newly-mined Centinae gems and had been left fearful of their imminent theft, she blanched for a moment, then swallowed hard. He still wanted to ask about the contents but now was not the time.

"A spirit, you say?" she remarked, voice still peculiar, "Well, perhaps I have at that."

Pinpricks flooded down Bilan's back, for a blink filling him with new disquiet. Suddenly very reluctant to pursue the issue, he shivered, dispelling with the sense of more mice scurrying across his grave in favour of the here and now.

To waylay the odd atmosphere that seemed to have taken a grip of them, he cast about for something to say that would distract. One item sprang to mind...

"So you know that Lieutenant Kimonar del'Draventar is really taken with Lady Solancei?" Though he had not meant to speak of his friend without consent on the matter, Bilan still thought it an acceptable trade. *If this caused trouble, he could deal later...*

Iambre gave him a weak smile. "Bilan my love, I think the entire retinue is aware of that fact."

Bilan forced himself to tease. "Ah well yes... but does Solancei know?"

Iambre gave him a wry look and Bilan shrugged, offering her an innocent wink. *This was good: her colouring was returning...*

"What's your point?" she asked, her tone revealing a kernel of mild curiosity.

"Does there have to be one?" he retorted innocently, then relented as she elbowed him, "Well okay... it's only that he's a noble... and she's a noble... you know... I mean would you ever consider...?"

Iambre's lingering tightness broke with her smile. "Ah yes, I see what you are trying to say here. Hmm... interesting. I guess... I mean, I ponder the idea of releasing her from her charge all the time, but the rules, and the risks, and my parents, and..."

Pulling a face to distort the smile, she gestured with her hand to indicate the reeling number of unspoken obstacles. Clutching his elbow, she grimaced softly as if another thought had stirred.

"Still... in any event, I'm afraid Lancei would not take kindly to such things being discussed behind her back, nor would she ever be forced into any kind of situation she was not happy with." *Pause. Then....* "Bilan, I fear for such a match to work, she would have to return the regard in kind, otherwise..."

Iambre shrugged, seemingly a little uncomfortable suddenly, "I guess what I am telling you is that I am just not sure that she likes him, like... *enough?*"

Bilan had also wondered about this in the quiet, but the reality would not please Kimonar. *Not one bit...*

Aloud he said, "I have already done much to dissuade him, but I think he might be willing to... well, you know... help her see things differently? I mean, please, don't take this the wrong way, but for a noble, he was never shy of accepting a challenge. Still... those oaths? They change everything, of course, but del'Draventar is... "

Bilan paused, searching out words. Then he shrugged. "Well, actually I guess he noticed how she keeps herself apart. Unlike that Ina, and even Palea, she never makes eyes at any of the men, and he... well dear Gods, I have told him... I mean...I have encouraged him to forget her, but still..."

Iambre smiled again. "Bilan, what will be, will be."

Rubbing a hand across his face, the Captain washed off the negative uncertainty that had brought the creases back. "That might be so, but-"

He sighed. "Gods Iambre, do you think you might speak with her or something? The man talks of her like she's the sun and the moon and the air."

Slowing their pace, Iambre turned to him, a sheen of interest glowing in her eye, though she also radiated a sense of... *of subtle relief?*

"So he speaks of her, how?" she asked. Face half-shaded by the cowl, the extent of her emotions were hard to read but her tone held a note of intrigue, comingled with a tattered hint of hope. She hadn't said anything much for him to pass on to Kimonar in encouragement, but still... for now, he almost didn't care.

Body flooding with relief, he noted that she no longer appeared scared and pale, and so he chuckled with relief as he said, "How does he speak of her, you ask? Well... let me see if I might recall now... "

Having rolled his eyes and not paid particular attention, he failed to remember his friend's exact words of course, but it was commonly something to
the effect of, 'Solancei's beautiful eyes comparing to the colour of slate washed
up on a beach after a tempestuous night' or 'the inviting curve of her lips tempting a parched man as only a full glass of the sweetest wine could'. There'd been
other things too, though: stuff about the nubile curve of her ass and how the
way she walked put all Jethar'Chi's trained dancers to shame for the images she
stirred in his imagination, and so on, and so forth.

Bilan grimaced softly. Kimonar was of the sort who could wind out poetic
nonsense without breaking a sweat and the women loved it, but there was also
no doubt about the message when it came to Solancei and Bilan wasn't about
to tell the Princess that his friend and fellow Guards-Man carried thoughts of
that kind in his head.

Instead, he said, "Kim is- ...I mean Lieutenant del'Draventar... he speaks
of her as though he intends to write her a sonata or something; as though he
would kill armies for her, and he speaks of her *'beautiful eyes', her pleasing accent...*"

Petering off, Bilan shook his head. *If Kimonar had been feeling bored and in
need of a diversion, he couldn't have chosen a better path than the pursuit of Solancei Calverhana but he was a noble – and nobles did silly things.*

"I knew it!" Iambre exclaimed, half-halting to clasp his sleeve, "You know,
I told her before that she has pretty eyes but she won't listen: keeps telling me
that I am daft and to quit jesting, but I am right, aren't I?"

"I guess..." Bilan allowed, still not won over, but the Princess looked heart-
ened.

"Well fair enough then," she nodded, "I'm her friend but perhaps if someone with a flair for words were to tell her there is more to life than serving me?"

"Well Lieutenant del'Draventar has that all right," Bilan mused. *Fleck, the
jest he kept throwing at his friend went something along the lines that Kim could
not help himself! That because he'd been 'exposed' to the 'polluting' fumes of the
marshes near his Northern stronghold of Alahbro since childhood, it had clearly
addled his mind without recourse!*

Bilan quenched a smile. *Well, it was either that or common lunacy, for what
else might account for all that verbal nonsense that sometimes sprouted from his*

friend's mind and tongue? But perhaps it was just a ploy – for sure, the doves all loved it, and then some!

"Anyway Milady, I will not speak to him about any of this nor will I reveal any of your secrets but perhaps it might be wise to summon the man for a brief talk? I would not presume to go telling you what to do, nor to offer you any kind of advice such as it might be, but with the Lady Solancei sworn to you, and Kim- ... I mean, Lieutenant del'Draventar not knowing...?"

Iambre glanced at him, her forehead crinkled by a pensive frown, but her front teeth now releasing her lower lip. "Bilan... you hardly presume! And what you say makes sound common sense, but allow me to speak with Lancei first. Perhaps she might indeed consider... well... you know? In any event, I-

"I guess the thing is I'd certainly want Lancei to be happy. However, for this to work, Lieutenant del'Draventar would have to be patient, because although I'd release Lancei in a blink to see a marriage torque around her neck, I would certainly wish it an event to please, not haunt her."

Bilan nodded. "But of course. I understand."

Iambre sighed, "Whatever might be, I fear that I would need to be Queen first too - the Chief and my Father will never sanction this otherwise! In verity, at this point in time, I imagine they'd simply brush-off the demand as a mere whim of mine not to be taken seriously, so I would need my Word and Will to carry true, irrefutable weight."

Bilan nodded again. He understood, but Gods... *for this, Kim might either thank him or kill him; Solancei had not given his Second-in-Command even a whisker of encouragement thus far and in return, perhaps he'd already given up on the idea? Perhaps... perhaps Kim was no longer even... keen?*

Bilan subdued a wince. *Yes, Kim might very well kill him – or at the very least return him a sore jaw for this 'favour', but... well, that trouble was for later and stranger matches had been made and survived.*

He smiled to himself. At least he didn't think that Kim would mind the idea of a wife who was able to best him in almost any type of one-to-one combat, but you never knew... nobles were funny.

The smile faded. There was still also one other crucial thing to recall: namely, that for this to work in the first place, they'd have to get Solancei back. It seemed a tangled mess of knives all right, and yet whatever became of it, at least his ploy had worked: Iambre was no longer wickedly pale, for she had been offered something other to think about. *Something other than the fact that they had effectively failed this evening and that there was now nothing for it but to return to the castle.*

To the right a shadow moved, inserting itself across their path. Lost in his thoughts, Bilan was a blink in registering the change, then took another to understand.

"Let the girl go or it will end poorly for you!" The shocking ultimatum was delivered, just as a second shadow clasped a hold of Iambre from opposite. It drew them apart before Bilan could react and Iambre exclaimed a frightened sound of surprise as she stumbled and was dragged sideways, seemingly stunned that someone was laying a hand on her.

Fear steeping his heart, Bilan thought of self-defence second and of protecting Iambre first as he quested madly towards her. He had all but a split blink to wonder if that man was one of the same two that had followed them earlier - *the cloak and size seemed to offer up a match* – then someone attacked him from behind, splintering his thoughts and foiling his pursuit of Iambre as he too was dragged off-balance and dragged away from her.

Seeing him in trouble, the princess' eyes flared wide. Her spirit coming to life - assuring him at that moment that even if he'd perhaps often believe otherwise, her affections did indeed run deep - she wailed loudly, wiggling to free herself. Yet the man was stronger and remained in control, now clasping a hold of her other shoulder, easily pacifying her actions, though she continued to twist and snarl like a wildcat.

Pushing through the undulating ripples of fear that seemed to have drained his ability to move, it took Bilan two long heartbeats to recover – enough time for the two of them to get dragged further apart by their assailants; enough time to harden resolve to stone. Then habit kicked off and to the sounds of Iambre's distressing, indignant yelps of 'no' and 'unhand me', Bilan's left hand closed around the leather-wrapped handle of his dagger. It slid free unhindered, him instantly flipping the blade in his palm and aiming the nine-inch serrated metal backward as he stopped fighting the man who clung like a shadow to his person.

Sensing the shift and somehow alert to the threat, the assailant reacted: an attempted counter move, yet knowing he'd be faster: the fact that he was left-handed always a feather in his cap, the Captain shifted his trajectory in the final moment, evading and altering his grip slightly as he cut out, stabbing down...

The diamond-sharp blade did not disappoint: connecting lower than originally intended - but with the view that if that other bastard hurt Iambre, he wanted this one to stay alive for long enough to regret their misguided attack!

The man he was wrestling was strong, his grip like claws of iron, yet the Dragon Silver rode two-thirds of its length into the man's thigh muscle as though slicing soft wax. The action was smooth: there was no resistance... *here... we... go...*

The injury registered with the man about the moment his leg gave out and as he stiffened, the grunt of disbelief turned an oath of pain just as Bilan had the satisfaction of feeling the formerly strong hands unclamp their hold.

Laying in strength, suffering blunted sympathy for the permanent damage he'd wreak, he twisted his wrist right, ripping muscle and sinew as he tore the blade free, springing instantly for guy number three who seemed to slide into his path as though made of air and grace, rising out of the night like he'd come through a doorway directly from the Void itself

Bilan didn't care if the new guy had come directly from a gobble of spittle ejected from the Gods themselves. Feinting with the dagger so that the man was forced to swerve, he clenched his empty hand into a fist...

The man looked up with a game grin, but sharp surprise flickered, twisting his dusky features. *He'd evaded the steel, but he wouldn't miss the blow coming straight at his nose!*

Knuckles flaring with blistering pain, the crunch as Bilan's punch caught the man squarely in the face was nevertheless most satisfying, particularly as the man fell down like a wet rag, knocked out cold and hence unable to cause further trouble for a while. *It left only one...*

Hand throbbing, but refusing to shake it out, Bilan stalked after the brute who held Iambre. The cloaked man had continued to widen the distance and didn't stop, his eyes stuck on Bilan like blistering obsidian chips, weighing, watching...

"She will come with me now if you value your life," Bilandro grated at the stranger, trying to search out an opening that wouldn't harm her.

The man only laughed softly under his breath. With a broad Zanzier twang, he said, "That's a decent right hand you have on you there, brother; a mean knife too - but it will not help you!"

Bilan observed the man look askance for a blink as if distracted - a heart-beat at the most – but it was a good a chance as he'd be likely to receive. Looping forward, too late did he see the bluff as the man drew Iambre sharply left rather than risk entanglement, and suddenly things were happening fast.

The Princess yelped as the strain on her wrist must have intensified: Bilan saw the cloud of anger roll across her face and she kicked out sharply then, catching her attacker's shin beautifully with her heel, driving a curse from the brute who flung her wide, either losing or releasing his clasp to send her tumbling to her backside, cloak and skirts flaring.

Horrified Bilan sidled half a step towards aiding her, then halted sharply and danced back. Iambre's rude assailant was suddenly armed: two slender blades the length of Bilan's forearms, slicing the air to create a deadly barrier.

Blinking Bilan cussed inwardly. *Black metal!* He had trouble seeing the weapons against the darkness of night and the man's black attire. It meant that the twin knives had been deliberately fire-darkened to rend the edges barely visible: perfect for a nightly job like this. It was an assassin's trick; Bilan recognised the need for caution because this level of demure elegance would come with a price. *A price promising silk cutting sharpness and purpose...*

With experience-instilled weariness, he retreated another pace, resisting the urge to hasten attack but the man feinted towards him anyway, swiping both blades simultaneously up and into his personal space, the ferocity of movements leaving him no choice but to retreat back towards the man he'd just stabbed. A rapid glance at Iambre told him that she was okay, if no longer calm as she clambered back to her feet with new darker patches of wet filth adorning the length of her hip and thigh.

It was an observation done in a blink, his attention never really leaving the aggressor pursuing him. *If the creep was good, he'd-*

Something yanked a hold of his right leg, shaking his balance, nearly tipping him arse over heel - but the fingers lacked strength, slipped purchase, and he heard mumbled curses from below as he managed to sway from the daggers coming at him like dark strips of lightning. With his luck holding, he spun tightly, evading another fall of the singing blades, somehow landing a kick to the gut of the man he'd stabbed.

Ignoring the grunts of pain so that he could dance clear of further contact and gather his wits, Bilan watched the man for flaws. *Iambre! He must get to Iambre!*

For a blink he allowed himself to look up to orientate himself. *Iambre was to the right. Taking one halting step forward – towards him – then another. He saw her intend...*

Anxiety stole the breath from his lungs.

"No!" he barked at her, deflecting one descending blade from its intended path with the hidden steel cuff on his right wrist, at the same time locking the other one down with the square cross-guard of his own dagger - he and the assailant momentarily clashing, grappling with what seemed equal-measure spirits for control over the first knife. Fear that she could be caught between the two of them shook him. *She mustn't come near! She mustn't!*

Maybe it made him stronger than usual; the man was good, but Bilan twisted his shoulder, punched the man's arm with his elbow and used the blink of space to lock his hand around the assailant's wrist, tightening the hold as he spun them around, pulling, using the inertia to drag the other man along, straight into a backward roll.

As they went down, action not thought ruled, yet as he spied Iambre take another uncertain step towards them, he fought not to lose his faculties. The man with the stab-wound was on the move too, half upright, one hand clasping his thigh to staunch the blood as he half-hobbled, half-dragged his torn leg - but he was going to reach the Princess before Bilan could disassociate from the oath who was fighting to open him up, one dagger or both! *This would be over the moment they put a weapon to her heart! Time... he needed time! And space!*

With the world disappearing backwards and the man he was throwing growling heartily in his ear as they went, Bilan rolled on his shoulder, threw off the assailant, and gained a knee. He heard a crash of crates as the other man landed in someone's neatly-stacked livelihood.

"Bree, run!" he yelled, no longer taken with caution, "Run now! The way I told you! Go back! Run!"

The foul woman startled to a halt. Rather than oblige, for a moment her wild eyes looked into his: utterly shocked. Bilan gritted his teeth. *For a wonder she looked torn...*

"Flecking run or Anchan'Chi will have a new Bride!" he cursed at her with enough wrath to send her scrambling, only she gave him a tight little nod, then spun from the reach of the stabbed man who promptly collapsed, hand closing on the open air where her skirts had been.

For a moment Bilan rolled his eyes to the heavens, thanking every God he knew the name of, then he watched her go, semi light-headed from a mixture of emotions rarely felt. *He had to trust that she was not going to find it difficult locating the quays.* They could be no more than two or so blocks removed and the streets were already tilting slightly, steering the pedestrian as much as the enforced tangy breeze that had become more marked only after they'd left the old district and begun their descent towards the river. *Iambre would find it easily enough! She just had to keep her head down and not engage anyone in conversation! She would be fine! She would be all right! She would-*

Bilan heard the crunch of feet as the man with the blades came at him again, but he turned and twisted, avoiding contact so that he could watch the last flash of Iambre's mottled cloak as she raced along the gently bending road until the curve took her from sight.

It seemed to infuriate the stranger...

"You flecking son of a rat! You will rot in chains for this!" the foreign man rasped, pushing forward like a furie to land Bilan a ringing blow to the temple with the butt of one knife.

Staggering, head reeling, he somehow still managed to slink from a debilitating cut that followed. *A double heartbeat earlier and it would've taken him down!*

Bilan grunted in pain, retreating further, still drawing the other blade master. *Rotting in chains? Well, that was quite possibly true, but at least he'd not be alone, and if he did only one last thing right...!*

Barring his teeth through the blood flowing off a split lip where the assailant's fist had accidentally caught him during their close up, the Captain smiled without mirth, "You speak of rotting in chains, mate? Well... you and me both, then! You and me, both!"

The man swore aloud, pouncing as though truly goaded by the words but Bilan deflected, ducked and kicked out to swipe the back of the man's knees, successfully downing him. Yet the fiend moved like a snake even as he fell, slithering sideways, adjusting: one brawny shoulder crashing into the Captain to send him likewise to the floor.

One black-blade weapon shot forth to impale and disembowel...

Bilan rolled, shifting right, unable to avoid the clash yet timing the man's move to suit. He had to end this on top, or else...!

Time.

Reversing the hold on his blade with a smooth gesture as the two of them drew together, Bilan tossed the dagger, switching it from left hand to right with a lithe move perfected through sad need many years ago, and the attacker's fingers closed around his left wrist... *too late to intercept.*

To.

The assailant grunted with surprise, pushing to fling his bulk against Bilan to send him off kilter, but the oaf had miscalculated and Bilan spun his weapon...

Kill.

Dagger descending, Bilan twisted an inch, exposing the man's neck...

"Stop! So help me the Gods, you blithering imbeciles! Stop!"

The shout sundered the night, smarting like the crack of a whip across the empty road's traffic-worn cobbles, raising instant notions of demand and obedience.

Bilan felt his own eyes widen in shocked surprise as recognition stabbed him, his harsh breathing halting on a burning exhale. In one slewed heartbeat the world went cold, but the painfully familiar voice had already sheered through his single-minded intent with crystalline command. *Mercy...*

The coldness expanded: frost trailing into his veins. *Somehow he reacted. Somehow.* Yet only sheer discipline combined with the habit of alternating feints made it possible for him to change his weapon's deadly trajectory just a blink before the kill. Hand and arm jarring as the dagger found purchase, impacting not in flesh but on the hard paving, it almost cost him the grip.

Deaf to the aggressive 'chink' and grind as the dagger crashed into the ground raising sparks mere hairs from the other man's neck, he shifted to look up.

Fleck. Fleck. Fleck. Pox and bloody swords! Fleck!

The blade all but forgotten in his hand, he did not care that the other man was pushing to scoot away from him faster than a two-inch bolt released from a crossbow. *Bilan knew himself dead meat now! Fleck and bloody guts!*

"Captain Metavo! Kraie Meranson! I will flay the skin off your ugly backsides; get on your feet! Now! Or I will string you by the guts for all to see right in the capital central square!"

Immobilised, heart pumping, he let Iambre's assailant go with wooden reluctance, but it seemed the man was not one bit bothered about finishing him off now either.

Mercy, but it was just as well, really. He didn't know how it was possible, but Chief Eso Mehadja was somehow here, staring them down with fury and impatience written all over her stance and it made everything else truly irrelevant. Everything!

Insides shrivelling, Bilan pushed past shock and belatedly shot to his feet, blade now abandoned. The man he'd been fighting was a veritable ox, he realised, but he was no slower to obey and now they both stood there: silenced, breathing heavily but somehow with bated breath, his opponent slightly doubled over as if he'd been winded during the fight. *Strangely, they no longer felt as much enemies, as they felt accomplices...*

Rapidly wiping the blood from his lips, Bilan straightened to attention almost at the same time as the other man made a semblance to follow suit.

"It's hardly better, but it'll do!" Eso took them and the scenery in, her eyes black as night, and her smarting voice brimming with contained wrath. Bleakly wondering how in the flecking abyss he might live to tell this tale to any grandchildren he might once have thought to sire, Bilan simply knew both he and the ox were about to experience a spectacular fall from grace.

His eyes riveted to the Chief as she let up and stalked towards them like an avenging spirit made flesh, he prayed Iambre would for once just follow instructions and that she'd make it safely back to the Keep. Had he'd but know that the chief-

Bilan swallowed consternation. He and the ox – probably even 'peg-leg' and 'knocked-out' guy - were all in the soup here; good and truly about to drown, and he could not question the certainty of his conviction, because they'd all lost Iambre to the night and the Chief remained livid. *Flecking livid...*

and seemingly about to spit brimstones too as she looked about to let an imaginary axe fall on their necks...

Solancei's Memoirs

The Province of Tarléon.
Ivanor Fortress.
Winter of 780 P. C. W.

The morning came too soon.

Soured by a sorry night's rest and a gnawing sense of premonition that I should most certainly attempt to make myself scarce whilst that peculiar small lady was in residence at Ivanor, I snuck out of the kitchen-side door a little after first light. Armed with a still-steaming cinnamon loaf, extra-slices of fat-rimmed smoked ham pilfered from under the nose of near-sighted cook, Shaylor, I considered my own nutritional welfare taken well in hand.

It conveniently ticked off the first part of my plan.

It was my idea to now set up lair on the second level of the old hayloft where I already had a secret den of sorts. Here I'd be snug as a bug in a rug within my burrow of straw and old linens, even if it was perhaps the wrong time of year to camp out like this, but with the infallible optimism of a child, I also figured that a little discomfort might be worth it since it obviously wasn't going to be a permanent situation.

In my head I'd surmised that I could raid the kitchen every night after hours in effort to avoid any of the visitors and if I swung left round the corner by the smithy, I could perhaps beg Mistress Luni – our champion brewer - to part with a stoppered flacon of undiluted mistlar root to sweeten the snow I would scoop from the roof to serve as my source of hydration. It was a pretty sweet plan. My schooling, such as it had been, had been remiss ever since the accident. Rainan would be busy with his noble guests and never miss me. I figured I could re-surface once they'd gone and then life might slowly begin to resemble what it had been before... before all of this!

Lost in thoughts of roosting with the pigeons and perhaps a couple of snow owls, I focussed on breaking a piece of soft bread from the loaf and had just stuffed my mouth full as I rounded the smithy as intended, only to look up and halt on the spot.

Leaning casually against the old red brick of the workshop, stood the very woman I was trying to avoid, her arms folded at ease within sable fur mittens, her feet encased in a pair of heavily tooled boots that would insulate against the cold all day long, even without the wicker on the ground to alleviate discomfort. She saw me and didn't even startle. *She'd been expecting me.*

I forgot to chew as our eyes met. The cinnamon loaf grew chill and heavy in my gloved hand, the food in my mouth suddenly too gooey to swallow.

"You are later than I expected," the short, ascetic woman declared, eyeing me up and down as if to gain my measure in more than stature.

I simply stared. Her eyes were hazel, her stature short, but I sensed in her a wiry strength that guaranteed she'd have me hooked by the skin of my neck before I could think to flee more than ten steps. The few parts of her skin that were exposed carried a ruddy, golden brown cast, as though her complexion had weathered during her recent travelling. I noted it sat the bones of her face smoothly yet with the mild traces of lines that offered her features a maturity to match the sombre steel in her gaze.

"So..." The woman's fine eyebrows took shelter beneath the bangs that cut straight across her wide forehead as she swung her eyes from my form to roll across the dirty snow and cracked cobbles to ride high up the main Tower.

I followed her gaze; uncomfortable.

For a moment fearing that she'd want to chastise me for something – *maybe for planning this rude get-away* - and perhaps sought put me on the top of that pinnacle just like my parents had been wont to do, I quivered but resigned myself to the inevitable.

"So?" I repeated, finally swallowing my load. *Had that word held an edge of challenge?* It hadn't been my intention, but-

The woman's dark eyes swooped down on me, keen as a raptor about to rip into its catch with a beak that would tear flesh from bones.

"You know what happened to your parents? To Lady Scavino?" The brutal questions held questions within, and something else I could not decipher. *What did she want?*

I quivered again, now suddenly cold. It was an odd thing to ask me. That woman was odd. I could have sworn the noble lady had been about to say something else, but...

I nodded. Of course I knew what had happened. "They are dead."

The hazel eyes widened a fraction, some emotion pulling at the woman's waxen moderate lips. In a dry clipped tone, she said, "Indeed."

I eyed the tower again. If she plonked me up there and I was really penitent, I might be down before the wind picked up too much. It was quiet for now, the skies promising a clear day, but on the horizon, I'd spotted a front earlier. It could have been a trick of the grey morning but I thought it not. At least, on the tower I'd be able to see for certain...

"Did it scare you? The manner of their passing?"

I wanted to lie, but in truth, for all the fright-born comments and accidental eavesdropping I'd experienced, I actually really didn't know exactly what had happened still. *I had my night-time mares and some daytime peculiar thoughts, but beyond that...*

"I am not scared of what I don't know," I told her half-truthfully, but feeling wistful, I watched her hazel eyes grow pensive. The cinnamon bread had turned cold. With regret, I felt it ossifying in my cramped hold.

"I'm glad I'm not, though," I hastened to inject, "Dead, I mean."

Confused by my own words, I wondered if I should have stayed in bed. *They were certainly true, but-*

The woman seemed bemused by my comment, but she also smiled. Not a kind smile like Taliana's, but more of a knowing grimace as if I'd just shared some kind of secret and she liked the fact that I'd made her privy.

I coughed, inspired to fill the stretching silence. "I mean, alive is better than dead, is it not?" This time the noble lady did smile with more sentiment. "Indeed."

It was one of the few genuine-relaxed smiles I'd ever seen Klaas crack. Staring at the tower again, she inclined her chin. "You think they ever truly landed dragons on top of that pinnacle? It seems a farfetched tale."

"Dragons?" This was one of the weirdest conversations I'd ever had. One where I got the feeling more was said and evaluated in the presence of pauses and lingering silences than in what was actually spoken aloud. "There is no such thing as dragons."

The small woman looked at me. "And yet the Dragon is part of the Tarléonin heraldry, is it not? You do not believe the stories, then?"

I shifted my feet. *The stories...* well, they were many and bold in their claims, but in reality? Yes, I might be a child, but seeing is believing and I'd never seen a dragon - not even a small one, though I must reiterate that I should dearly have loved to, and that, my friends, is something which now fills me with a grand sense of irony!

"Stories are for kids and toothless grannies," I told the fur-clad woman, "and I am neither."

She raised a brow. Perhaps I was too forward, but she did ask. I didn't know this woman's purpose here. Her accent was strange: both stern and mellow, with a whip slash of authority that made my stomach lurch in equal parts fear of displeasing her and icy self-targeted disdain that I should allow this tiny noble lady to stir such a wealth of concerns where none had previously existed.

Feeling rebellious, over-tired from lack of sleep, and cranky for having my plans rumbled (I clearly could not go to the stables now, as the woman would know), I decided I had had enough. *The woman did not look cold at all, but my feet were growing numb...*

Glaring at the tower, I jumped straight to the chase, "So are you going to lock me up there, or not?"

The lady turned her face towards me, subtle but unvarnished surprise pulling at her features, but only for a blink.

"So are you going to lock me up there, or not, My Lady?" she corrected with steely emphasis on the omitted title, continuing, "In Etruia, that is the proper address to any woman of the Senate or any woman of noble blood or married into it. However, since I am also so much more than a lady, you may address me as Chief, understood? And no – I am most assuredly not going to lock you in the tower. Why in everything holy would I want to do that? Your manners are lacking but I guess the rules are slack in this barren wasteland so I'm sure the Queen will forgive you. You are young and as we travel, you'll learn in good time for our arrival."

All thoughts draining from my mind, I blinked. Cold air seemed to press into my lungs. For a beat I couldn't breathe. *Travelling? I wasn't travelling anywhere? I had horses to groom, daggers to polish and-*

Taking a step back, I felt the moment my imaginary hacked went up in earnest.

"I will not be travelling anywhere," I assured her with a flinty stare to match the rebellious streak that seemed to roll through me at the thought of this person just coming here and making stupid strange statements and judgements.

"Oh my little dragon, but you will," the lady chief argued, her voice calm but promising the truth of it just the same. "We will take a week to get our provisions together and to plot our journey back, but come sunrise eight days from now, we are returning to Etruia. We came for you. I would suggest you spend the remainder of your time here as you must, but whatever is not loaded in those saddle bags on the eve of our departure, will remain here."

"The fleck it will!" I cussed obscenely like gnarled Sargeant Hylinn would, making my feelings clear, because it was very important to me that this woman understood me right. My unenviable streak of contrary blood rising, I challenged, "Who do you think you are? Does Rainan know of your mad ideas? He will not allow this. I will run away."

The spiel would've sounded better if it had come from a woman of self-assured standing and mind, not a stupid wilful child whose voice was turning shrill and brittle with emotion. I cringe, thinking back: this was one argument of many I was never going to win, but I guess then and there was the birth of our love-hate, tug-of-war. Had the woman not suspected trouble from me upon arrival, I imagine she certainly saw the truth at that moment, but she also didn't give an inch. On the contrary...

Had I just gone too far? I thought, perhaps yes; no, not 'perhaps'; definitely!

The Chief's eyes flashed with a new darkness that made me cede a step as she turned fully towards me. Leaning slightly forward, planting both mitts on her thighs, she bore into me with presence and tone, "I see now why I'd lock you in that tower you so fear, but I shan't because that is not my way, yet make no mistake about my charity here, little dragon. I am Chief Klaasinah Eso Mehadja, Councillor to King and Senate in all matters of Crown and Realm Security, and I have been sent by Her Royal Highness, Queen Ishjah herself, to bring you back to civilization, so that's what I'll do. You saw my seal of authority last night and be warned: run from me and you will not be able to sit for the first two weeks of our journey and you'll wish I'd left you to grow icicles up on that roof! Are we in accord?!"

Anger and fear twirling around my core, I bit my lip. Eye to eye with the Chief, she shouldn't have instilled such a fearful sense of resignation in me - she was just one tiny woman - but I confess, she felt six feet tall to me. And though my natural obstinacy still swelled and crashed unchecked for long moments then, she had somehow already bound me in the same way that the landmass of a beach would always stop and purge the power from the violent waves of an ocean hitting those shores.

Straightening, Klaasinah Eso Mehadja, prepared to take her leave, yet as she passed by me, barely two feet taller than me, she reached out to squeeze my left shoulder as though in comfort.

Pausing for a blink mid-step she said, "You look like your mother. Don't let anyone tell you otherwise. And you need to breathe. Focus on your centre and on the breath to even out the aches of your fears and the assault of your feelings. I know you can do something like this already, but it's unrefined and the energy you require, wearing and wasteful. Focus on your core;

on your presence in the now. It will calm you and aid your sleep. Once you can detach yourself, I will teach you more."

And with one final squeeze, she was gone, gliding from my presence like a breath of wind kissing your cheek one moment only to be gone the next.

For a while I remained rooted to the spot, then I pulled myself out of the strange slump that I appeared to have cultured. Abandoning my original destination for a new one, I went in search of Rainan.

It seemed I had some packing to attend to. But I was not convinced I should give in without a fight. A week was a long time and I had things to do.

Solancei

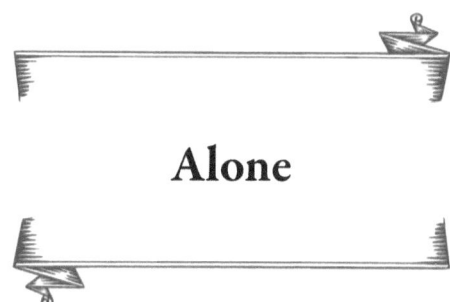

Alone

L eaving Bilan, Iambre sobbed under her breath and bolted. Skirts hoisted high, not one whit bothered about modesty or appearances, she fled the violence as though her very life depended on her making that get-away. *And perhaps it did? Perhaps it would do? But dear Gods, Bilan...*

Fighting the repeating urge to moan out loud in agony at the thought of 'what' she'd left him with; with the danger; the violence; the fear; she already hated how she'd so easily complied with his command. *He'd told her to run, but-*

She squashed the feeling. She ran. How far, she couldn't have accounted for. At some point the narrow streets levelled out though, presenting her with the dark vista of the Lower Quays.

Hot from the exertion, Iambre shivered, the evening chill of the open domesticated terrain cooling her down faster than iced tea on an Etruian summer's afternoon, but she slowed the pace regardless. *To take stock... of everything!*

She didn't like it. After the cramped lanes and press of people, the waterfront seemed a snaking, deserted expanse of treacherous darkness: a monochrome portrait of shadows and greys, of obscure silhouettes and labour-worn cobbles, heeling to the gentle curve of the riverfront as far as her eyes could reach.

It made the knowledge that she must press on hard to fathom, yet if she didn't...

Well, the alternative bore scant comparison. She could attempt to find an alternate route back to the castle, but did not fancy her luck; she might get lost, or Gods-help-her, even get accosted by similar type scoundrels as those Bilan had stayed back to defend her against, and-

A new surge of panic sent her lightheaded.

She'd landed herself in a terrible mess. Gods, she could not believe that Bilan had followed her, nor that he might now lie injured or worse because of her! This was all wrong now. Her folly was grave, yet unless she kept going, her fears of the unknown would wrestle away what control she'd retained, and then-

In distress, she pressed a hand to her forehead, walking faster than she normally would've dared on such a murky path where there was no guarantee her next step would not find a pothole, or – *Gods forbid* - something of a dead animal variety. Overwrought by the events, her senses seemed supernaturally poised to take-in every small sound or foreign flicker of movement, whether it'd be imagined within deep shadows or perceived from the corner of an eye. Though not that tall, forbidding warehouses and harbour trade-offices sat like a row of squat forgotten monoliths to her right - in-like the day of her arrival, mostly shut for the night: rendered dark and spooky - whilst the strange and unfamiliar movement of the ships moored to her left, set her balance off kilter with their bobbing lanterns and long hulls tiptoeing at anchorage.

She licked her lips – an uncomfortable gesture that would have translated the measure of her unease true, had anyone at Court been present. Never one for an over-active imagination, there was a quirky slash to suddenly finding her current thought-pattern so easily guilty of supplanted anything real, just to paint danger and doom. It was not like her; walking through old Zanzier had not bothered: there'd been the illusion of safety in the presence of other people, yet now...

With the attack, with Bilan gone, she acknowledged the idiocy of comforting illusions. *They no longer worked!*

Sucking back a harsh breath, forcing herself to put steel in her backbone when really her bones felt mellow, she applied a trick of her mother's design, occupying thoughts and attention with the idea of normality.

It was equivalent to Lancei's breathing exercises. It offered calm. It made the surroundings lose their threatening aspect just enough for her to perceive of a place, not dangerous, but ripe with commerce and life. It was the idea of the flipside to the quays after dark. The notion of daytime noise and spectacles, of foreign wonders and costly cargo, and it bolstered.

During hours of sun, the tar-black waters of the river would be aquamarine with a tint of grey depth. Commerce would fill the atmosphere, an array of people passing through: vendors, commissioners, traders and tradesmen, sailors, custom officers, porters...

Running her eyes along the solid facades of the now-barred trade syndicate offices and rising warehouses, she pictured the iron-enforced doors and portal-like gates open to business: men and animals busy drawing sliding panels wide to accommodate the shifting and storing of goods being loaded and unloaded, shipped-out or signed-in. There'd be seafarers seeking passage, captains procuring new commissions; clerks, able seamen, ballast-heavers, ale drapers and ewers, runners, carpenters, and unskilled workmen; ships would cast off to the ripe orders of quartermasters seeking favourable tides, whilst others would be drawing in - those not of local origin probably dropping anchor off-shore to await the Quay Master's word as to which birth they might occupy and when. *That was real. That... and not her vivid imagination that had her running scared of the dark.*

Still... argument would not deny she was alone now. She 'felt' the menacing eyes of dark-shaded assailants following her, and she could not draw past what had happened, nor could she ignore the lonely feeling of exposure now riding between her shoulder blades in the wake of both Eso and Bilan-

A loud burst of male laughter stilted her thoughts. She whipped her head towards the sound, her attention landing on the nearest ship, and for a blink the breath stilled in her chest before she managed to relax. Snippets of conversation reached her. More laughter. Shadows shifting against the developing night sky, then gliding from view.

She sighed. Sounds distorted. She was still alone on the quay. A rising attack of blustery wind carried further sound from her ears, leaving only the notion of a dancing lantern atop a tall mast and a slight edgy sensation in the pit of her belly, as the vessel she viewed bobbed and danced at its mooring as though it was somehow disjointed from the very reality she'd been trying to build.

Forcing the sensation, she calmed down. The stench of mossy brine and brackish saltwater assaulted on a waft of hesitant breeze that seemed to sneak past her, the air momentarily growing still as though capable of drawing a breath, then extending soft tendrils to rustle along the edges of her garments. *Well, that was also all too real. And indeed most pungent!*

She sniffed again, clearing her nostrils and the smell was gone, erased by a new ravishing wind that seemed fresh and hard as it dragged a hundred invisible fingers across her cloak, forcing her borrowed skirts to balloon sideways. It left her quivering within the rags. Unsurprisingly, Zanzier had proven as eclectic as any other large town or city when it came to presenting a new visitor with its very own array of smells, and it had certainly been a pervasive part of her experience tonight, yet the wind made it both easier and harder to find immunity. *The Keep sat high. Up there it had been little more than an underlying fix in the air, but down here...* one moment she stood ready to swear she'd smelled steak, then it was tar amalgamating something belonging to the bowels of the earth - then wood smoke wiped it clear, only for the fishy brine to overrule. *'Pungent' was perhaps too kind...?*

Her forehead sawed into a frown of mild disgust. She was aware that she reeked like a death house but she'd been prepared to take that and live it for the sake of her quest tonight. Now she had cold wet feet, mud where no one but Bilan had touched in a long time and to know it had all been for nothing? To now fear for both Bilan and Solancei?

Iambre clenched her hands into fists, squeezing her eyes tight on the tears that threatened. If she could distract herself it worked better, and the air worked wonders.

She sniffed. After the open widths of the Wilderness, the spell of autumn rains within this large city, had not done the place any favours; though she could no longer really smell herself, the general feel of what hit her senses was at best what she'd describe as 'north of interesting' and she cultured the notion to stay in the moment; to not think...

Still... a sneaky voice whispered in her ear, *a few days more, and you might no longer notice – similar to the immunity you seem to develop against the smell of raw incense after just a quarter spent in any temple.*

Again an undertone of decaying foundations and fishy brine wafted in and out, sending her stomach twirling in revolt but she would not let it touch her, and to escape she breathed in deeply through her mouth and felt a touch of the anxiety leave on the brute exhale.

She'd never been aware that ships would carry a slight stink too: not overwhelming like what she got on the air, and not the same punch in the guts as what came crawling off the water, but something more subtle: something slightly rank, with a prevailing bouquet of tar, topped by what she presumed might be the scent of wet rope, edged with the notion of damp wood.

She wondered if one could ever grow accustomed to the ship stench similarly to the city smell and it struck her again, just how absurdly she'd behaved. *This was a world away from the tidy Etruian barges with their softly-gleaming oiled decks and enamel-inlaid floral incense burners attached like decorative baubles to the traditional crooks at the raised sterns, either in the shape of leaping trout or attending kingfishers.*

The vessels here were functional; commercial; there was no incense, no pleasure rides to be had on a hot afternoon, and - unlike the barges - these ships hugged the harbour front, moored like tight pearls on a string, riding too high out of the water for anyone below to catch even a glimpse of the decks beyond the bulwarks.

She hoped it meant the people on board would not be able to see her either unless they came to peer, or - *Gods forbid* - pee, over the rail!

'Absurd'? Gods but that word barely covered, either!

She gnawed at her lip. The same old horizon was still there in the dark... just harder to see...

Mind eclipsing with uncomfortable flights of fancy, mostly of Bilan lying dead or cut open, bleeding, drowning in his own blood as Riselta had once told her was a thing of 'actual possibility, not story spinning', she wrestled her eyes from the curving pale hull of a near-by two-master, feeling beyond sick.

Her mother's trick would only cover so far. She needed something other. Her mind was breeding Ghouls and Demonai, but she couldn't give in to convenient pretence just to shut out a mistake. *She'd been too stupid; too hasty; and now Bilan-*

She shivered and ripped her attention from the darkness in her mind, fixing instead upon the ships again. Some rested dark as night, void of light and life, others carried those lanterns suspended from masts or great curving iron brackets attached to the aft hull. *Bilan was good. He was alright. Luck was on her side. Ina had assured...*

She suppressed an involuntary shiver. The occasional torch left blazing by a lowered landing plank seemed no godly sign of welcome or sanctuary, yet they taunted with the possibility, playing havoc with her faith. *If she called out she might find help. If she was brave enough. But she might also only find more trouble, and then where would they be?!*

Turning her gaze to the cobbles, concerned by the idea of exposure, she began to walk a little faster, the fear of many faces ever-gnawing at her heels. She did not want to be spotted on her own in this place, yet all the same a part of her almost hoped that someone would. *Yet if she daren't reveal herself, why would this change if offered opportunity?*

Iambre crewed her lip harder, feeling less than proud. Further ways ahead, she sighted a tall gap in the wall of buildings, seemingly wide enough to take a full-size wagon, though at present the distance made her guesswork little more than a random estimate. It was certainly hard to miss, however. The gate was flanked by a pair of huge braziers what looked attached directly to the stonework, their live-fire flickering enticingly even from where she stood – obviously beckoning travellers arriving from the waterfront to enter the city and taste its straight-laced offerings.

It would be one of the paths Bilan had mentioned. It had to be. She too had looked at a map beforehand, and it just about seemed right - though she could of course not yet be sure of the route beyond: the multiple warehouses ever-sheltering further view, even if one did get the sense of the two rolling hills that characterised the better part of Zanzier rising beyond.

She looked back to the ships with a weak sense of relief and a strong sense of despair. *The Keep was up there. Some of it was just visible.* She could be back within the safety of Zanzier Castle earlier than an hour from now - perhaps less, if lucky. *As to how she might get back in though...?*

She shook her head angrily. She'd run blindly from the danger she wouldn't even have been in, had she only been wiser in the first place. *Stupid... so stupid!*

As though on a whim, something quivered within, raising new stupid tears. *How many blunders was a future sovereign allowed to make? Too late now to admit that Bilan been right; that Eso had been right! Gods, but where was the luck in that?*

A painful notion that she needed help reared up, but the waterfront remained frustratingly empty of people. *Even if brave, there was no one to hail, no one to press for succour...*

It left the streets ahead, yet when she got there...?

Perhaps part of her reluctance in attracting attention lay with the fact that in reality she feared it slim chance someone actually rallying to help. And if they did, where to go back to? *Relocating the spot they'd been attacked would be all but impossible, and Bilan would still...*

She refused to finish the thought. It didn't matter. The earth would move for her. It had to! Of course, she would need to give up her identity then. The 'mess' would get 'boggy', but this was all on her. *Her responsibility! People made mistakes... and they fixed them.* Yet though she'd never before been faced with doubt that anyone might ever question her station - in this outfit, 'whiffing' of gutter perfume and without a single piece of finery to her name...?

For sure, just this once, her authority might well be questioned, and who would believe her? *'But I am the Heiress! And I demand your aid!'*

Iambre shook her head mentally. No, even she could see the problem! *By the time she'd manage to straighten matters, it'd all be too late. Much, much too late...*

Her belly twisted – no stench needed. *Already she was worrying herself grey over Lancei. Why had Bilan followed her? And had he not...!*

Over and over, she relived the force of her assailant throwing her off. Over and over, she saw Bilan retreat before those nasty-thing thin blades meant to do more than raise respect. She was no soldier, but she'd verily tasted the renegade's intent in the air. *He'd been huge.... strong... fast...*

Iambre tripped, the wind slapping her skirts wide then wrapping them between her legs, the ragged hem catching. Chocking on her own alarm, she flung out her left hand to avert disaster, her nails clawing at the coils of some near-by musty-smelling hemp piled high, but averting disaster. A curse she didn't recognise escaped her: abruptly loud, then stolen away on a gust. *It was a good save. A quick reaction that even Lancei might have been proud to-*

Iambre paled, her weak sense of achievement crumbling.

There was nothing here to be proud of. Lancei would be furious; would rain down verbal shame on her for placing herself in such a compromising situation in the first place! The disguise, the sneaking, the 'let's-completely-disregard-Bilan's-warnings', and worst of all: the fact that she'd decided to take action in the first place...? *As her Shield, Lancei would have her guts; but as her friend...*

For the first time since raising this mad idea whilst cradling a broken china cup, she realised how she'd effectively elected to spit in the face of Lancei's Oaths by pursuing this foolish whim. *It was not good. Lancei might just not stop with the guts - she'd make her life grim, capitalize shamelessly!*

Suddenly not caring, Iambre's sense of shimmering despair raced deeper, the highway to regret glowing red – though for too many reasons now. *She had done wrong, but how could she have acted differently when her heart knew so much fear?! If she did not get back to the Keep, the entire province would be turned upside down in efforts to locate her, but for Solancei-*

Had her cousin been what she was supposed to have been: a Duchess of refined taste and learning, this would have been different, but then one might also have argued that had Lancei not been her Shield, circumstances would never have found her cousin gone and missing either! Still, now because of a stupid oath, Solancei was not so privileged and the conflict Iambre felt when thinking of her friend, was not as armoured by ideas of safety and future sovereignty, as it perhaps should've been.

Could she simply sit back with wine and mithara and merriment whilst her friend wasn't with her to enjoy the dubious honour? *But of course not!* It was what the Chief had wanted; what everyone wanted, so she was ashamed of her own conduct, yes – but even as she pushed on – *a new stitch in her side hobbling* – even as she thought of Bilan with icy fear chilling her marrow - she also knew she must be cursed, for in this matter, she could not have done differently!

Feeling pained by the inconsolable conflict within, there was an urge to stop; to cover her face and cry, but she didn't even waste a hiccup. Her rapid walk had the breath sawing in her lungs once more, her mouth running dry with too much fear to swallow, but whether she could have done this another way - or not at all - her golden confidence seemed tarnished bras now. *She'd never help Bilan in time; most likely not Lancei either. Noble and Stupid. But mostly stupid...*

From somewhere high-above some screeching night bird's call seemed to mock her; from the edge of the quays came fine, subtle sounds: the soft rush of water lapping and plopping against the nearby hulls, over and over, in rhythms made unpredictable by nature's tune; like the excited gossip and prattle of invisible sea world creatures,

She looked towards the brazier light. There was a similar feature further down the quays. It hadn't been there before – maybe it had just been lit?

Loathing the truth but beaten enough to stand by the understanding that the only way she might help anyone now, would be by getting herself back to the place she belonged without further incident, she lamented the harsh ache in the back of her throat and in the centre of her chest where rapid breaths had rubbed her sore.

This was not what she'd envisioned; not what she'd hoped for. She must abandon this ill-conceived foray before more consequences could ripple down, *yet* the guilty part that wouldn't apologise seemed less enthusiastic. As ever the case, shame was like a parasite, though. *Consuming. Poisoning.*

She had to go. *That too was the right thing now.*

She looked to the ships with a sigh. Another time the smells might not have seemed too bad. Another time she would have liked to come back here in daylight and walk amongst the hustle and bustle and witness life in more detail. *Another time...*

A capricious breath of wind sent her old skirts flaring in line with nearby-warehouse canvas signs, and Iambre gathered her wayward cloak close to the invigorated creek of timber, as the line of vessels danced the necessary jig with the river - on-board lanterns bouncing like enlarged drunken fireflies against the night-time sky. *Back to the Keep. One foot, one step, then another. Back to the Keep.* The braziers were closer now, the glow growing, drawing her with every step like some backwards fascination with a strange monster she could not trust, though she must. *Looking at the ships she could pretend she still had options, looking at river she had not quite failed yet...*

She ignored the creeping sense of latent panic. *Nothing. She could do nothing...*

Immediately ahead, a three-master rode low in the water. To escape the inner voice of punishing humility, she made her eyes observe because it seemed easier on her constitution than the mental flogging she was otherwise want to undertake with every other step. In her mind, she imagined the vessel must be bearing cargo and forced herself to remain distracted by the idea. She imagined it a rare instance if goods were not unloaded immediately, and since the harbour was not adrift with work-hands and blazing torches, she suspected it was all set to sail, yet might have been left wind-bound.

Though probably just another illusion, she let her imagination play with the idea.

Wind bound? If such be the case, she knew the inconvenience was already costly. Some vessels were privately owned, but most merchants paid homage to a trade syndicate too: a wise alliance when it worked, a costly one when matters went awry. Or so she'd been informed. *Loaded ship or no, however, only fools braved capricious winds like this, and if they'd missed the evening tide...? Had she not read somewhere that Zanzier quays could be treacherous?*

Unsure where the latter thought had come from, Iambre tilted her head.

She supposed this a nice ship. A plaque surrounded by the flicking tails of a carved banner near the jutting bowsprit proclaimed it 'The Morning Glory' - a fitting name, considering the ship's pale hull and the carved sun positioned like a figurehead with spikes of stylized rays, cleverly involving the bowsprit itself in the design.

If she had a ship she could escape: take Bilan and Lancei and-

Feeling suddenly dizzy with the idiocy, she did not allow *that* particular idea to blossom. Perhaps the unkind combination of fear and exertion was to blame? Certainly, if she should ever consider that running from it all might be required, she'd need a vessel with a little more... *panache.*

She half-smiled at her own fancy but in her mind's eye, she saw Bilan yet again whip towards her, blood-wetted blade in hand, face set in lines so fierce, she'd barely recognized him. He'd wanted her to escape and never look back then, but where duty beckoned, he'd never allow her to run from obligations. *Gods, but she hoped he'd run from those men, though!*

Out of nowhere, the dizzying feeling meandered back, intensifying, reminding her of the way she felt when she could not breathe, yet that was not her problem right now. Her breath came even, still – the warning clusters of blistering stars never materialising.

Intent on undermining the sensation, sure stress was playing havoc, her eyes deliberately drifted to the next ship. The hull looked black in comparison to The Morning Glory and of a differing configuration entirely. Not for adventure, she judged as she walked alongside it, the heady sensation still developing within to spite her efforts. *Bilan had to be all right. There was nothing more to it. He was a soldier; could look after himself. And he must be fine!*

Because she would have to tell him 'sorry'.

A-ruddy-gain!

So yes... he'd have to be fine! And as for Lancei...

Dizziness retreating, Iambre ghosted past the black hull. The lights of Zanzier still beckoned her to do the right thing. *Not far.... not long...*

Strangely lulled, she ambled on.

The next mooring lay empty, reminding her of a gap left behind by a missing tooth.

She shivered, disturbed as the wind picked up between strides, the folds of her attire almost tripping her up a second time so that she was forced to gather her skirts and bend her neck into the stiff wind as she hurried to reach the sheltering outline of the next ship.

Eyes watering, the strength of the wind left her dizzy. Snatched from her lungs, her breath shortened for a blink as the weather seemed an enemy too bold to go against and she feared it meant to rip in through her skin and bones - then the air calmed, courtesy of the vessel that arose like the stout presence of the foothills of Oriana's Mountain near the Etruian capital, all dark substance but a protection against the elements just the same.

Curiously drained, she halted, gasping. Her head seemed funny; not quite willing to cooperate with her line of thoughts as she ran the edge of a ragged sleeve across her eyes, momentarily beset by a spinning sensation. It vanished as it had come, leaving her belly slightly unsettled. A hint of delectable cloves and spice drifted in the wind... or maybe she was just imagining things. She sniffed but it was gone...

Left shivering, cold, for a blink she was absorbed with wondering if she truly was going down with a fever of some kind. It would most assuredly not be good...

The dark spice in the air seemed to return, teasing her with an idea of something... something irresistible...

Iambre haltingly raised her eyes. An urge to do so gripped her; pressed her.

The hull of the ship was a solid, smooth presence, truly just like any other vessel, only slowly did she become aware of it now: like she were a heavy sleeper coming to out of a mellow dream...

She blinked.

Looking at the ship, a jolt seemed to jab through her: invigorating...

A shot of excitement followed, stripping her of breath. Then a sense of wonder settled over her.

This was far from just another ship!

The Lure of an Ancient Fable

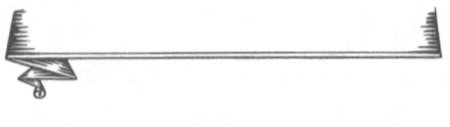

STARING AT THE DOCKED three-master, Iambre wondered how she could've been so blind before? How she could not have noticed? The hull was in fact not just a plain indecipherable dark mass like she'd first thought. Looking at it she realised it was red; not just any red either, but the rich warm red that in sunlight would look brighter than plumb burgundy wine poured from a flacon of finest Tuxaman lead crystal but also not quite as garish as the intense colour of fresh blood.

The ship was long too, perhaps thirty-five pace or more, but though it was indeed large, the red hull appeared of a certain sleek design rarely seen, the golden scrollwork enhancing the carvings along the outer hull and balustrade bulwark, elaborate and elegant with an old-fashioned slant to the words spotted, so that she could not decipher what was hewn into the side like some mystical script that cast the vessel an aura of age and mystery.

Abandoning her purpose for a moment, Iambre couldn't help it. She loved the sense of calm that begun to permeate her as she gradually relaxed. It was such a relief.

Allowing herself these moments to admire the ship, her earlier fears drained to the back of her mind. She was still wary, but she was coping better. Much, much better...

Her eye grazed the huge lantern suspended on a brace attached to the main mast, the light of an uncommonly golden hue that helped the appeal: alluring, calling, leaving her strangely hot with elation as the world slowed down to match.

Without realising she was moving, she drifted forward. Somewhere on board, someone played a slow mournful tune on a fiddle with more than passing skill though it was barely audible above the gentle hollow slush of water lapping against the hull. It mesmerised, and as the wind picked up to send the vessel bobbing hard, her dizziness seemed to return. The salty pong from the river seemed to fade, the darkly rich notion of some alluring, luscious scent came back but the smell was indefinable, tingling not only her nose but tightening her senses and eliciting emotions too.

She could get lost in that scent; live forever in one breath, yet this was what she'd been looking for. This... no matter how... no matter consequence: a certainty that her actions could be condoned!

Relaxing truly for the first time in a long while, Iambre couldn't fathom her luck. Standing here, somehow everything seemed to join up in perfect unity: from the softly spoken creak of timber, to the countless ropes thumping and pulling, to the persistent gusts of wind that caught and occasionally cracked the fine pennant streamer atop the main mast as though it were a bull-whip. *She'd been right. All along she'd been justified! And now she could go... go wherever she wished!*

The anxiety of the last few days forgotten, for a moment the golden lantern light was all she saw. Drawn, she moved – *moth to a flame* – towards the vessel. As the Gods bore witness, she needed no maritime expertise to know that this ship would be a swift one. Indeed, it was quite possibly even an ice-runner, and for some reason that failed to solidify in her mind, a vessel perfectly matched for adventure too.

Iambre smiled, as she ambled along. *Was this the Luck Ina had been guaranteed? An ice runner...?*

Her smile widened of its own volition as she rolled her eyes away from the gold - endorsing speculation on how rapidly this ship might reach Tarléon, even as her gaze dipped momentarily low to appreciate the fine flow of the hull. The elegant, symmetrical lines pulled her naturally towards the bow - almost not aware she felt her feet shift to perform a natural retreat so that she might consider the figurehead too. It wasn't that it mattered, but she was in a most peculiar frame of mind: somehow reluctant to leave the vessel behind though she knew she must. Paying that much attention to a silly ship didn't matter, yet as she beheld the avatar, suddenly it very much did!

A spark ignited.

In a sudden rush, the earlier woozy feeling re-embraced her. Obscenely, she'd nearly not seen this, had nearly not noticed what was right before her eyes. *The figurehead was an Eikyr.*

A heart-thumping burst of delight followed, settling over her like awe.

An Eikyr! An actual Eikyr - as in the horse-like being out of myth; as in the creature that could never be tamed, nor owned, nor commanded by magic; as in the very steed of legendary heroes!

Right here, right now, it was towering above her and the quayside, leaping out of the ship's sweeping prow as though it had been caught and frozen in the very moment it rend the wood apart to pursue freedom. *It was a piece of art and then some...*

Mouth forming an astounded 'o', she chuffed down a sharp lungful of air. For a marvel, the creature was of a perfect likeness, bringing life to otherwise sketchy drawings seen only in books. This here might be a creature of petrified flesh, not carved wood...

A sense of perfection rustled through her. *It was all there: the armoured-scale legs and neck, the curving scythe-like edge of the deadly steel-touched hoofs pawing the air to split an enemy horde from its path, and the horns...!*

Iambre stared at the near-equine head. The bold signature horns, rising from the poll behind flattened ears, were cast in a sinuous curve like the flaring arms of a lyre, but terminating in deadly spear points – sharper-looking than she'd ever seen in the books. The golden mane along the proudly arched crest was flowing wild; long; the intelligent triangular eyes that looked out on the world were narrow with focus, mean like those on a predator stirred to fight, and below the flared red-tinted angular nostrils, the teeth that could never have belonged to a common horse were barred in challenge. Mercy, it was a silly fancy of course, but almost she could hear the intended snort or derision floating on the wind of her imagination; almost she could imagine the earth-shattering effect as the hooves came thundering down to impact with the force of a striking dragon.

Out of nowhere, the warm, fulfilling feeling returned inside her - like gluhwine on a nippy Kheltian winter's night, soon filling her with hazy content. *She'd never seen anything like this.* For sure, the illustrated fables lacked a level of detail never dreamt of until this moment: like the kite-shaped red-golden scales that seemed plucked from a real creature and nailed in place by meticulous craftsmanship, the hues growing subtly from dark at the base, towards a lighter effect at the barbed tips.

Like the ship, it was a thing beyond beautiful. An actual extension of the vessel itself! The longer she beheld it, the less it seemed a figurehead and in the obscurity of moon- and lantern-light Iambre knew a sudden strange sense of intimidation, the towering figure a dwarfing presence perfectly proportioned to the vessel it championed.

On a whim, she got the urge to touch the Eikyr, but of course she couldn't, and she was suddenly saddened. *It was perfect. So perfect. Too perfect...*

Her smile faded, melancholy draining it. She probably shouldn't, but she allowed herself to imagine what it might have been like to stand here with Lancei and her heart quivered.

Her friend would have admired the art too. Lancei's interest would've been slightly less enthusiastic no doubt, simply because between the two of them, Lancei had always been the harder one to impress, but still...

The illusion of gluhwine-warmth evaporated, and heavy regret arose, supplementing a sudden bitter-sweet feeling. In childhood, this creature had been their favourite fabulous monster - easily surpassing the dangerous Draken'Dah or even the majestic Griffin. Of course, given the symbol on her family arms, Lancei's preference had ever been challenged by the Dragon too, but this... this...

As myths would have it, only true heroes could ride the Eikyr – a thing that had appealed to them both immensely. However, perversely, as history recalled, the rebellious Thain Phudor – *so very much not the hero of the Chaos Wars!* – had been rumoured to ride an Eikyr also, hence clearly discrediting that bit of glorified writing.

Still, as it sat though, Iambre recalled her father ever commenting that even if the traitor Thain had eventually lost his mad quest, as well as his head, his supporters had certainly made a brilliant move when they'd linked their leader with the pristine Eikyr as part of their propaganda, for the realm would forever wonder, not only if the Eikyr might actually exist, but also if Phudor had perhaps possibly been wronged.

Well, the usurper was long since turned to compost in whatever shallow grave they'd afforded him – right or wronged. In fact, by now it was wholly inconsequential whether the mythical creature had carried heroes, or villains, or none of the above. The rather embarrassing memory of a forgotten childhood incident popped to mind – as vivid suddenly, as the dear belief she'd once nurtured of silly romantic connotations.

Lost for a moment, Iambre cringed. *Gods, she'd happily forgotten about this little thing, but now it came back with haunting clarity, the fact that she was staring at an Eikyr in real life, no doubt the culprit.*

She winced a little.

Mercy, not only had she believed the Eikyr real - she'd also nurtured a rather unhealthy, if stout belief, that she was destined to have a great adventure wherein one of the heroes-of-past would come rushing forth to rescue her from evil and doom on his trusty Eikyr! Gods! And how Lancei had ripped her for that! Repeatedly!

Iambre looked at the figurehead's massive silver-flecked hooves, wishing she could just swipe that memory from existence, particularly because she'd also been adamant that she and her 'brave hero' would then do the usual stuff that people in that kind of stories did, whereupon they'd all live happily ever after. *Gods rot, how Lancei had ripped her indeed...*

Pushing the embarrassment from mind, somehow the memory did not dwindle however, and with the ship's figurehead roaring silently before her, Iambre knew a double stab to the heart as she recalled too easily a young, fierce Solancei swinging a practice sword longer than her own arm whilst proclaiming 'Princess Air-Head' a fool for believing such rubbish. *Gods be good...*

Lingering between fond sadness and a glimmer of sustained humiliation, Iambre's feelings swelled. *The unfortunate event didn't bear thinking of. Really, it didn't.*

Her own childish emotions had been overwrought to snapping by the time their tiff escalated: Solancei skipping around her, darting in and out like an excited puppy, but with purpose – on, and on, and on, until she'd finally picked her moment to poke Iambre's bottom with the dull sword, whilst mocking her doubly for dreaming of a boring, dull marriage to a dusty old hero who'd surely be sprouting grey whiskers by now!

Iambre exhaled hard. Goaded, she'd yelped indignantly, her angry but impotent swipe at Lancei as much a joke as her beliefs, for Solancei had simply jumped from the intended harm, informing her friend that *she* would not be willing to settle for anything so stupid!

'If you want the geriatric hero that badly, then you're welcome to him,-' Lancei had declared, mocking disdain already finely honed despite their young age, *'- but there is no amount of wealth or pledges that would ever find me marrying an old git! Never!'*

And there...! The remembered words of dispute between two girls lost in fables and dreams made Iambre feel hollow.

'Hero or not,-' Lancei had continued to proclaim, *'-know that I'd pick the Eikyr over old whiskers any day and forever!'* - to which Iambre (hurt like only a child could be at her friend's apparent ridicule for her perfect romantic vision) had stuck her tongue out, then told her rather callously *'that this was a good thing too, for no one would ever want to marry someone like Lancei anyway!'*

And well...

The ghost of a would-be smile momentarily shifted the shadows within her. As expected, the ensuing 'fight' had been epic, proving that Lancei was not all sword and breeches after all, and for some reason, it turned her mind to Bilan's words about Lieutenant del'Draventar. Back then Solancei had been willing to pull Iambre's hair out to make a point about her prospects of attracting a 'suitor' - and that was how the Queen's first lady-in-waiting had caught them: pulling at each other's hair and screeching like a pair of gulls.

But that was then...

Iambre shook her head. Solancei had changed. That business with Lazrin Sandborn had seen to that. And it was wholly feasible that her friend no longer harboured any interest in attracting that kind of feelings from anyone, that was clear too.

Gods, and she hadn't let on to Bilan - but since a long time now, Solancei's conduct had followed a philosophy where she held clear that *'a Shield should do well to never mix complicated emotions and first loyalties for the two did never align'.*

Iambre resisted a sigh.

Even without the circumstantial complications, in fairness, that did not speak well of del'Draventar's overall chances, but how to explain that?

Iambre watched the Eikyr bob up and down, and felt a hollow tuck at her innards for the way things might have been, yet she'd promised Bilan she'd raise the question about del'Draventar and so she would: plant a seed of possibility in her friend's mind, at least - even if the outcome could be predicted to within a margin of a single per cent.

So... no hero for her, and no Eikyr for Lancei. What a let-down for the girls they'd been: their destinies set, their eternal summer-dreams long obsolete. It seemed a sad thing. A sad regretful thing indeed, but it was a fact that they'd both had to grow up at some point – even if it should perhaps not have felt so wrong. *And she hadn't lied to Bilan. She didn't really need a life-shield; at least not if said Shield was Lancei because if her friend should ever die in the line of duty protecting her, Iambre knew herself only too well and such an event would render her heartbroken. However, should she offer Lancei 'permission' to return del'Draventar's attraction in earnest, would her friend then perhaps not consider her options?*

Staring mutely at the Eikyr, motionless yet in motion, the forgotten free-dom of simple childhood surging, she couldn't help but wonder if she was go-ing to lose both her best friend, as well as the man she loved, to witless duties and stubborn demands? *She did not want to go back to the castle. She knew she had to. For Bilan. And for Lancei. Rats, yes even for herself. But Gods...*

"So tell me here, precious, what are your feelings about the Insandar?"

The question came out of nowhere. Soft, accented words that felt like fur on naked skin, but with a hint of incidental breeze to belie the notion that more might have been implied.

"W-what?" Iambre quacked, for some reason feeling like a thief caught mid-act stealing.

Almost startled into the river, her whole body aflutter with surprise to hear somebody address her, she tilted her head sharply to locate the speaker, simulta-neously dancing backwards a good few paces from the avatar, both in effort to disassociate herself from interest as well as in readiness to defend her loitering.

The world spun...

Swaying, for a moment the whooshing rush in her head seemed to deafen as her eyes found and zeroed-in on a male figure balancing like some impossible acrobat on the bowsprit above. Then her mind wiped blank, all functional co-operation between limbs and thoughts evaporating.

It lasted all night; it lasted a blink... then the image above her clicked into place and her emotions caught up just as her already-pounding heart skipped a beat to perform a bona fide somersault before she regained the proper measure of control. A hundred words and none came to her, yet her mouth did not work. Something within her had already spun her head up-side-down, and possibly in-side-out; for a moment she was gone from time and place, perhaps never existing...

It made a part of her recognise the urge to reach for the straw hat on her head that denoted her a fool and half-wit to the world. She did not wear one of course. Because she was none of the above. Yet surely someone ought to give her one for the tongue-tied oaf she'd become from one breath to the next.

She didn't know why it seemed so unfair, but that darkly-hoarse voice had an owner all-right. Oh yes indeed...

Blinded

M*ercy...*
Mercy. Mercy. Mercy!

Belatedly realising she was gaping, Iambre clapped her mouth shut with a staccato sound that was reminiscent of the sharp click her jewellery box would make when one of her handmaidens dropped back the carved-metal lid to seal away her deposited valuables after a long day's wear.

She swallowed hard, the small action taking forever. *My... but to say that the man currently peering down at her was merely 'attractive' was like sinning against Silicia'Cha by proclaiming that She might possibly not be the one true Goddess of Beauty!*

The sailor was handsome. *Beguiling-forget-your-own-name-handsome! And his choice of clothing was... well... limited!*

She swallowed again, the act of breathing strangely complicated suddenly.

Above, calmly regarding her as though he was awaiting some kind of response, the man on the bowsprit looked patience incarnate – *handsome patience incarnate!* - and Iambre wracked her empty mind for words she might once have possessed, only find her once-fine rhetoric well and truly gone. *Had the world stopped moving? Or was that just her?* Her own stupefied reaction annoyed her. She was better than this; not some-

Embarrassed to the core, an uncharacteristic, playful giggle escaped her.

Instant shock washed over her. She heard the flirty edge attached to the sound and took a blink to avert her eyes as though she'd just walked through a door to find her heart's desire stripped out of his outer vestments.

It was mortifying. Her cheeks warmed.

Clenching her eyes tightly shut, she had no choice but to eat her embarrassment, but also found she could not erase the sailor's half-naked image from the insides of her mind. *Shirt... he should wear a shirt! Definitely wear a-*

Biting her lip, she cut her own mad thought short. Her mind was covered in syrup. She ought to say something but couldn't quite think what, nor did she even really recall what he'd asked her in the first place. She'd never imagined that sailors would have such splendid physiques, nor wash-board stomachs, nor eyes to rival sapphires to-

Cursing herself for a loon, she tilted her neck and landed her gaze squarely upon the face of the tall sailor still innocently studying her with a glimmer of curiosity from his elevated vantage point. She tried to gather her faculties, but for a fact, she could be forgiven the gawk, couldn't she?

He'd called her 'precious'. Stupidly she was flattered. *'What are your feelings about the...?'* The what? The... the *'inxandarh'*, was it? Belatedly she recalled the words, but she was flustered and they made no meaning.

Fearing she'd lose what little faculties she'd managed to recover - *should she look at him again* - she let his accented question roll within her mind, focussing inwards rather than outward, and the pressure in her head seemed to lessen then. She was unable to place the origins of the underlying pleasant lilt she'd heard, but it was certainly nowhere near the flat Zanzierian nor did it harbour even a hint of clipped Etruian either - but had she perchance heard a touch of soft Esardan?

For certain, the man's slightly melodic tilt of vowels did remind her of Ina, but for an underlying harshness that brought old Kheltian to the mix too.

"Well then?" the sailor prompted, drawing her eyes to his with the simple words, and she died a little. Lifting dark-golden eyebrows to mirror question, his penetrating too-ruddy-blue eyes somehow seemed to peer beneath her rags and skin to ready her flustered heart and mind, saturating parts of her with slow promises of what was yet to come and-

And like before, it stopped her thoughts dead. In their stead, a shamefully delightful twist of fluttering butterflies invaded her belly. Reason evaded, yet...

Head whirring, she tried to gain perspective. The feelings within were delicious, but... but...

Gathering some mediocre strands of herself together, she wondered how she should feel so swept off her feet? *For a fact she'd... she'd only ever felt that way when looking at... at whats-his-name? At that...? At that Lance Captain from her retine. But this... this was so much more! Just exactly what was one supposed to do with this?*

Above her, balancing one naked foot before the other upon the long bowsprit, the sailor adjusted minutely, his easy hold on the rigging relaxed even with a shifting ship beneath him. Smooth with the move, he ventured forth a few steps until he was nearer the middle of the wooden spar, directly over the water, and Iambre prayed the subtle sigh did not escape the insides of her head via her mouth as she feared it might just have done! *The sailor was ruggedly fine. Not a prissy noble, not an unwashed barbarian either, but something else, and though her eyes seemed to burn, she couldn't get enough – even blinking interrupted!*

Shifting with the ship, the lines of flat muscles along the man's arms, chest and stomach flexed naturally. It was an enticingly mesmerising display and very obviously hard to ignore, given the fact that the man was wearing nothing but a wide, heavily-adorned golden arm ring just above the right elbow and a pair of tight stripy breeches, laced indecently low on his perfect, narrow hips. *What had she just thought about a shirt, again? Shirts were boring!*

Wanting to run for her life but feeling also trapped and betrayed by these new strong emotions, Iambre licked wind-chapped lips. She wanted to shift her eyes but couldn't. It flickered through her mind that his near-hairless sun-burnished chest would not have been out of place on a temple rendition of a deity - except maybe that the deity wouldn't have been wearing too-tight black and white breeches, which would have been a crying shame, of course.

On the back of that, a tally of several other complimentary observations flickered through her mind like a runaway stallion taking unkindly to a new rider, and with a rush of heat she belatedly flung her eyes back onto his face from whence they'd so cleanly wandered.

It made her senses reel - but in a delightfully crooked way where forbidden promises lived too close to ignore.

Angular, even features, a distinguished aquiline nose, clean-shaven dimpled chin and knowing eyes. Mercy, he was handsome, yes - she wouldn't mind a few promises off him! Not even if his slightly wind-tussled hair brushed well past his shoulders, rakishly long...

Taken aback by her lurid thoughts, Iambre pushed away at the feeling cooking within her. She was just about aware the man had spoken something again, but-

Just say something! Anything! Remember this man does not hold your heart; remember there's someone else!

But her mind had zeroed out. To keep the sailor in sight she had to crane her neck uncomfortably, but bizarrely it seemed worth the discomfort. Torchlight from somewhere flickered across the man's face; he seemed so totally at ease - as though he and the ship could not help but move as one, his every tiny adjustment as natural and unrealised as a seasoned rider manoeuvring his steed in and around an agility course. *Grace and balance, a cat on a fence would have looked less comfortable and the Pantheon help her... she really should look away; should really walk away, and in this very instance too, but her feet were bound and her eyes...*

Across the lean muscles of his naked torso and arms, the tanned skin looked the colour of darkly burnished bronze. *Which she loved.* Yet she loved even more how the sadly sparse light could not disguise the healthy golden sheen of his dishevelled hair. It carried a warmth that seemed to match the armband. It made her want to run her hands through the strands...

Gods have mercy, but he might well let you do that too, she realised, *he is smiling at you in a way that people do not usually dare!*

Heart leaping to spite her better judgement, Iambre swallowed excitement. *By Endar'Cha, Goddess of Dreams and Vision, sailing was wasted on this man. He was too attractive: too perfect even, and...*

Feeling a tendril of frustration, her words failed!

Knowing she must have hit her head on something, still she was unable to direct her gaze away from his muscled chest for long enough to start feeling guilty. *She wanted to touch him; wanted to run her hands down all that naked hard flesh, and-*

Iambre blinked hard and wrenched her eyes back to the sailor's face, only to stare into his deep eyes. Like earlier, they were strangely assessing – as though he might see straight past her ungainly, scraggy robes to what lay beneath, yet for a blink, she could've sworn the judgement was not for her looks.

It was disconcerting, voiding offence. Emotions rolled, some familiar, some foreign. She couldn't move; didn't want to. She tried to breathe normally, tried drawing in a shuttering breath, but under the intensity of this man's stare, such a simple thing proved harder suddenly than breathing under water. *But it was fine. All was going to be fine...*

Like the fine sands draining into the bottom of an hourglass, time slowly fell behind. She had a need to get to safety; to leave this parade of peacocks and insincerity behind in favour of the adventures she'd always read about. *And this ship... this man...*

The world narrowed, yet Iambre began to smile. *In the centre of her new life there were just the two of them. On this ship, she could leave... just go... forget all. And she wanted to; if there was a sense of wrongness attached, she drowned it under selfish desire. Because she wanted to! The quays, the ships, the harbour, her own purpose... did it not make sense to stop the sacrifice of more dreams?!*

Slightly dizzy from a mixture of shallow breaths and unrealised worship, Iambre felt suddenly weak in the knees as the constant swirl of fluttering butterflies increased their happy activity inside her midriff. *That earlier gorgeous smell of darkness and spice was back; how could she have missed it?*

The gold on the sailor's arm flashing, above her the man moved slightly, the small action causing his tightly-packed stomach muscles to roll under the spell of light, and no longer bothered if she was gaping or not, Iambre had the brief urge to ask if he was a God descended, but verily, the words just did not breach her lips.

She frowned. The sailor looked pleased however, so maybe she had spoken aloud after all, for he smiled at her again: a slow sensual smile of white teeth - *the smile of a lover, the welcoming home of a soul-mate* - and Iambre simply knew that she was meant to go to him then, if only to-

At this exact point, something odd scratched at her mind, sending small ripples across her perfect moment, *distorting... ruining...*

Sudden irritation spiked, growing stronger, until she was unexpectedly able to make out an impression of her own rankled feelings and subsequent protests against this... *this treatment?*

Like someone had slammed a door to a wondrous world in her face, the beautiful smells cut off. She felt cheated, but-

Butterflies evaporating, wherewithal returned like a rush of pressure in the air. It slammed into her like a wave of serenity, clearing out the thick syrup the seemed to cloak her mind. For a moment she shattered, then reassembled. *Colder. Wiser. Sad.*

Left only the crushing reality - the imaginary trellis of detachment she'd momentarily but successfully erected against consequence and care, broke apart like an old moth-had tapestry turning to ancient dust under the touch of a careless hand.

For a blink, it left her shaken and she heard her own inner voice lift up in wild reproach over this crude indiscretion. *How she could possibly have convinced herself of such disregard, not only of her duties but most importantly, of the people she loved?! She did not even know this sailor for dear Gods' sake, and here she was...?!*

Confusion hit her like a blow of blunted maze. Shaking her head, coming to as if out of deep sleep, she felt the wind drift past her thin layers of clothing, shivering the bones within her skin. *This was not her! Ogling some random sailor?! She had things to do! Places to be!*

Shocked by her own conduct, concern permeated her like a fast poison, jolting her squarely back onto the quayside. *Mercy, she was acting like a strumpet in heat. And for a man she'd never met, no less! What... what must he not be thinking?!*

Burning with shame, she managed to tear her gaze free of his, all of a sudden uncertain; nowhere to put her eyes. In her head, a sense of hazy dysfunction tugged at her self-worth. It shouldn't have been an effort but it seemed overly complicated to focus on the ship's crimson hull rather than on the sailor himself. *Endar'Cha, the Goddess of Dreams, must be testing her somehow, but why? Or could it be that Jethar'Chi had momentarily blinded her with lust to prevent her from doing something else?*

It made little difference. All the man had done was to ask her a question and here she was... losing her manners and all good sense! Choices were simple: either she could bolt without further interaction, but that would be rude, not to mention, very odd. On the other hand, she could embrace composure, brave speaking an apology for her half-wit behaviour, which in turn also just might make her seem less the flirt. Furthermore, and rather importantly, the latter option would also help her recover just a semblance of her deflated self-esteem. Which she sorely needed!

How could she do this and not look a fool, though? The man was a walking recommendation for anyone with eyes to take a second look – or in her case: a third or a fourth!

For a moment, Iambre fought the urge to flee, but Lancei would rip her for that too, and-

The idea put an edge of horror to her present situation, just a heartbeat before guilt collided. *Lancei! Midnight raffle, how had she forgotten?! Solancei was still out there! And Bilan!*

The sailor's hot eyes rested on the top of her head though – that had been no random fantasy - and at the idea, a small shudder vibrated through her. She had to recover herself. If not for any other reason, then at least to prove her own sanity intact. *What had he asked her? Something about liking someone? Gods be good, this was embarrassing!*

Bracing herself, Iambre looked up, words of reason ready, yet the very moment she re-locked eyes with the man, all intentions swept cleanly from her mind. *Unwavering deep-blue, his gaze met hers and she felt her carefully chosen words wilt.*

For a blink time flexed again, leaving her insides spinning as though she'd just been twisting

like a top. Then something seemed to snag; an echo of a feeling: of what was right. *Sailing away on a random ship was not! Leaving without Bilan or Solancei was not! This... this was not what she wanted, and yet this sailor...*

Unexpectedly, Iambre felt a sliver of fear race through her. On an intake of a rushed breath she realised that if he beckoned for her to do so, she'd go to him - even if she would have to launch herself from the quayside and climb the pegs set into the side of the vessel like an impromptu ladder. It petrified her. She could not do such a thing; she couldn't-

In that very moment, the sailor chose to wink at her. *Actually, wink.*

A bizarrely good-natured, semi-tongue-in-cheek gesture that did not seem to fit into the loaded situation, it sent a ripple of discomfort through her body. *Wha-?*

A near-physical severance of something she could not have substantiated, followed. Ice permeated her, then leaving, rendering her unexpectedly weak.

Swaying on her feet, feeling sick to the stomach suddenly, the Princess swallowed hard. A cold gush of air swept past her, cooling her blood further. The evening was freezing. *She was freezing. It was dark. Too dark...*

Stomach twirling, Iambre slowly peeled her eyes off the man on the bowsprit. The fuzz in her head was gone; her words were back, as was her resolve, encasing her priorities like a perimeter.

Moments ago lost to her, thoughts of Bilan slipped back into her mind: and invisible spirit gaining corporeal form once more, and she clung to the knowledge; to the familiar; to the real. *Bilan! She loved Bilan – and no matter the eye-turning fancy avatar, befuddled imagination or lean muscles, that sailor up there was most assuredly not he!*

Relief snapped through her. She remembered Bilan's black eyes and easy grin. It left her doubly mortified. She had no clue how in the realm she had come so near to losing her mind; how she'd so indiscriminately gawked at a common sailor as though she were one of those Charmers.

Tentatively she backed away a little further from the ship. *She did not do this without apprehension, but this she must do!*

Iambre raked in a resolute breath.

Readying speech, fortifying her stance, she looked up...

Slow in the head?

Nothing happened. Absolutely nothing. No rush of emotions. No silly ideas rising. No strange syrup congealing her thoughts.

Iambre filled her lungs, cutting relief sliding past the breath.

Well fine, so she was assuredly still flustered, but that was all - and it was of course wholly to be expected, wasn't it? After all, she did gawk before...

Cautiously trusting her own feelings, the relief expanded. Of course it hit her that the ruddy sailor *really* was very handsome and she supposed she found him instantly attractive – *that she hadn't imagined!* - but what he now inspired, arose in a muted, manageable fashion that had little to do with the way her feelings had seemed to stampede only moments before. And besides: the light concealed as much as it highlighted, muting what had seemed crystal clear before. For one, the true shade of his skin was hard to make out. Furthermore, his hair though certainly on the blonde side, did not appear 'luminous', and his features though mildly handsome, were nevertheless also hard to determine the details of and certainly not divine. Mercy, and *however had she even decided that his eyes were a beautiful blue?*

Under the cover of darkness, their colour was indistinguishable and could in truth turn out to be as murky as the waters under the ship's hull, for it was impossible to see from her vantage point.

Concerned with her state of mind, yet happy she seemed herself once more, she ascribed whatever she'd just gone through as a blip of some kind, perhaps related to the stress she'd been building, and she was more than pleased to find his face completely devoid of the suggestion she'd dreamed up with such passion. The sailor was handsome, yes – and far too naked for decency, sure - but he was simply looking at her now, one eyebrow lifted in patient query, as he lingered on his perch, moving gently with the action of the ship.

"I... ah... I...? Do I like what?" Iambre belatedly – *much too belatedly!* – managed to inquire, grossly aware of her own embarrassment as she massaged her temples with shaking fingers, more than a little ill at ease. Unable ignore her own glowing cheeks, she hoped the sailor wouldn't notice.

Thinking to explain herself, yet only waving her hand nervously, she heard herself mutter, "Eh... I... it's just that... I... I failed to... you know..."

Iambre faltered and saw the sailor shift uncomfortably in response before suddenly cocking his head as though in consideration. Then his eyes lost the pensive crinkle, his face splitting in an easy smile that appeared to convey subtle relief.

'Ahh, I see,' he began, as though he truly did. "I am sorry, Jewel, but of course, I see. Forgive me. I did not realise you were a little slow in the head; I mean: you are so pretty that I was distracted from the idea of a dull mind behind the beauty."

The man chuckled under his breath, the subtle mirth directed at himself, not her.

Shocked at his crude assumption, however, Iambre frowned at him, again rendered speechless, though for clear reasons now. *Slow in the head? He thought her dull-witted? Never mind she'd just imagined him thinking that very thing about her! Slow...?!*

Before she could pounce though, he reigned in the mirth. "My mistake, Jewel, my mistake. Slow or not, I would have you know now that I am not like some people who'd shun your 'type', so if you'd like me to, I'll repeat? Shall I speak slowly though, or...?"

The sailor's voice petered off. His face carried an earnest openness as he smiled at her in that careful way people had when seeking to win trust, yet Iambre noted the light in his eyes already dismissive, and she guessed he was awaiting an answer purely out of politeness for the awkward situation.

She couldn't quite seem to care, however. *Slow in the head? Jewel?*

Without realising it, she'd clenched her mouth shut before she could drop her jaw again - this time for an entirely different reason than before, of course. *Repeat himself? For her benefit?!* That alluring, dark voice suited him, matching his good looks perfectly, melting her just a little – *curse the man!* – but where moments ago she might have been prepared to elope with the guy, she was now simply thoroughly annoyed. *Pleasant voice or no, she was not going to stand for such talk. Why the rude oaf! In all her life, she'd never been called 'slow'!*

With a scowl – *definitely not a pout!* – she chose her usual battle stance, shoulders back, chin up. Arms folding across the chest with deliberate attention to exaggerate the sentiment of her mood, she summoned to her voice, cool semi-sweet derision. "Speaks a half-wit, makes a half-wit! I am not slow; nor a loon; nor deaf; so have a care how you frame assumptions and kill the presumptuous endearment too! As it happens, you merely startled me – I was lost in thought when you so rudely interrupted and I will not-"

Iambre cut herself short, suddenly unable to carry on without verbally exploding - a feeling that was stroked from embers to flame, when the sailor chose that very moment to look out across the quays as though bored with everything. Iambre shut her mouth with another click, but he appeared not to notice and when he spoke it was to the air over her head - in what she perceived to be a droll kind of absent regard for what she'd been saying.

"So I simply noticed that you appeared to like my ship earlier and I thought that perhaps you would have liked to come on board?" He shrugged, a subtle move of moon-lit shoulders, continuing, "You know? To see the ship? Maybe earn your eve's worth of silver marks, maybe more?"

Silver marks? Iambre sucked in a giant breath of surprise. *Was he saying what she thought he was saying?*

Forgetting about everything that had come before, she spluttered indignantly and the sound made him look back down on her then, quite as if he'd just recalled her presence.

Almost as if - in spite of his words - she were a just a random afterthought after all, the sailor nonchalantly flicked her a dismissive look.

"You really are most pretty you know," he offered, his deep eyes randomly assessing. "You get some better clothes than those rags and you will be popular with the lads – yes, even the ladies – of this quarter. Like I said Jewel, I will not mind if you are not 'all there' in the head. My offer to board stands and I am able to make it worth your while too."

The sailor smiled – *a very good smile, damn him* – and Iambre swallowed, simply speechless as his words sank in. *He really did have a nice torso too! He would not be accustomed to hearing the word 'no' very often – and Gods... he really, truly, was propositioning her. Her!*

Iambre gulped down a breath as though the air was too thick. A burst of indignation inflamed her.

Midnight raffle! But he was not that handsome! Full of himself? Definitely! And such, was a thoroughly unattractive trait in her books!

Squaring her shoulders and straightening the spine with new purpose, she stepped back, encasing him with a glare of narrowed eyes.

She would tell him what to do and where to stick his flaming ship and rude suggestions-

"Ouch Precious, no need to knife me with those lovely eyes of yours!" the sailor interrupted, raising his free hand as though to appease and avert further conflict, "Now clearly, you are most assuredly not slow in the head, my mistake again! But if perchance you are also not a casual flirt looking for a little work, then... ".

With an oddly solemn bow from the waist, the sailor swept low, the gold of his wide arm-piece winking softly at the shadows and leaving Iambre no room for any kind of reply, before he turned nimbly to retreat with surefooted ease back down the bowsprit.

Iambre's mouth fell open, but she watched him go; speechless. How was it possible to swagger whilst performing such a balancing act? It annoyed her as much as his abrupt termination of interest, yet her treasonous eyes couldn't stop watching him take his leave.

Lining his spine like a jagged silver tattoo, an echo of a sun-bleached scar ran from beneath the longish hair at his shoulder blades to disappear behind the waistband of those stripy breeches, and it caught her eye, raising misplaced fascination; *distracting...*

Split by soft concern and insulted ego, she battled herself to gain some equilibrium. She knew that some clever and awfully tart reprimand had to linger just beyond her ability to formulate whilst also preserving the feeling that she had any kind of dignity left intact, but if it did, the words would not come to her. It made no sense but looking at his golden back with the offending scar, Iambre felt itchy... ill at ease... oddly protective. *Not a blink ago, he'd not only insulted her intelligence, but he'd also tried to proposition her - and yet, looking at that scar...*

Again she shook herself. *No! This was not how she was going to leave this! Not a chance!*

"Hey, you! Captain Breeches!"

As she'd hoped, the sailor paused between steps, his frame freezing for half a beat before he twisted subtly to peer back over a shoulder, but... *Captain Breeches? What? Where had that come from now? That was something Lancei might say! What in the Void was she thinking?*

She had his attention again though and not wishing to squander the opportunity, not willing to research the verbal drat just come out of her mouth, Iambre cleared her throat.

"I am not... well, I am not a blanket warmer! And... and you assume much up there... up there on your... lofty perch! Too much! And... and on such a crude note, you just... leave?!"

Iambre tilted her head defiantly. The man had the indecency to smile as though bemused by a naïve child, yet the would-be good-will was of a negative character, threatening abuse. It should a have cut her to the quick: made her bristle... but it did not.

"My dear girl, it's been a fair long while since I last found myself fortunate enough to make assumptions about anything," he told her with a dark candour that made her squirm.

In his eyes, she saw both a shimmer of concern and the morsel of salubrious dismissal of someone who knew a world of secrets she'd never even understand and thereby couldn't help but be predisposed to consider himself superior.

The smile gained width, but the humour was elsewhere as he issued a short mirthless sound that might have held an edge of irony for something she'd said or done, or indeed just for her very presence, as he added, "But pray pardon me! My manners fail! It's likewise a fair long while since I last gazed upon one of your kind, so forgive me if my overall conduct has fallen short of common decency. And so, my Jewel, by all means: I apologise again without restraint, if my words have left you offended or unduly ill-touched - it was but a little harmless fun to test your mettle. I assure you it will not happen again."

Punctuating his small speech, the sailor offered her a courteous nod - the slant of change that brought new serenity to his golden features, both refined and unnerving. The man twisted as though to leave, yet something unseen held him then, for he did not turn from her as anticipated. Instead, pursing his lips briefly, Iambre watched him contemplate something she could only stab a guess at. Then the charming smile was back. Like a mask. "Lady Jewel, perhaps I offend again, but...? Well, since we have been so candid with each other, before we part ways, why not answer my initial question honestly? Why not tell me of your thoughts, as I enquired?"

Iambre gaped, her feelings bunching with confusion. *Harmless fun? Candid? The sailor was strange beyond belief. Maybe it was not she who was wrong in the head, but he?*

"My thoughts on what exactly?" she croaked with effort, in spite all, goaded by curiosity.

The sailor's shoulders visibly rose and lowered as he drew a breath and swung his stare aft across the length of his ship, seemingly... *seemingly fortifying himself?!*

"I enquired about your disposition towards this vessel. The Insandar? My ship? The Eikyr?" Chin held high, sounding for all the realm as though he was partly elsewhere – *distant* - the golden-haired man paused, his attention once more seemingly split between her and the need to peruse something of unknown interest in the distance. "See most people are drawn like flies to a carcass. I believe they consider themselves ... how do you say..? *Charmed?* So I wondered: are you?

Iambre reddened. Suddenly she felt daft all over again.

The ship. The Insandar. But of course! Amidst her own moment of enlightenment, she thought she'd detected a bitter cast to the words, but he was turned from her and the wild wind was perhaps making her hear things that were not there, even if his voice seemed to carry just fine. Then he turned a little to look back at her and she let it go.

"I am informed that the figurehead tends to instil some measure of awe that I personally never understood when the image is nothing but dead wood and paint, but still... I hope you have not felt inspired to stand before me disappointed?"

The sailor offered her a peculiar half-smile.

"It is a 'Clipper'; 'a fast traveller', probably even one of the fastest in these lands," he continued in a voice void of infliction or sentiment: a neutral lecturer of facts. "I wonder: would it help you to know that I approve of your show of good fortitude just now? Would it help to offer you my condolences? Because in truth you will undoubtedly need it - and so, I would reward my lady for her good sport tonight, by assuring her that the Insandar will serve very well the purpose of evading the fiends. Indeed, cloak yourself in that fortitude, my Jewel, for there is a truth riding these winds tonight, yet you will be safe. You will."

Fast traveller? Jewel? Lady? Fiends? Safe? A peculiar feeling stealing over her, Iambre found she was no longer remotely attracted to the man. She truly was slow off the mark today but still there could no avoiding the fact that this sailor was pervasively odd. For mercy, she had no idea how a sailor *should* speak, but somehow she hadn't imagined this. But perhaps sailors were just odd people? All that water and wind and rocking – she'd maybe be inclined to feel a little odd too, wouldn't she? And if the ship was his, one might understand his keenness to receive flattery – particularly if that commonly happened. *The Insandar? It was a beautiful name to be sure, and as for the ship...*

"Your ship is... It's magnificent."

Iambre hadn't realised she was going to speak in such complimentary terms, yet nevertheless, once spoken, she knew it just praise. Almost she was waiting for the sailor to reply, to thank her for the kind remark, or to mock her even – *either, really* - but the man simply nodded once as though some dispute had been settled.

On a sudden whim, she inquired, "Innsahndaarh? What does that mean?"

Unbelievably, the sailor's lips twitched with amusement.

"The Insandar," he corrected, mild infliction drawing on the vowels, Kheltian harshness wrapping 'h' sounds around the structure of each syllable, "I believe there is no translation for this abbreviation. 'The Insandar'? In essence, I suppose you'd call it a simple endearment. It is the shortened version of the word 'Act'lin-Insahndaar'marahn' – an Elvern word, which Humans hold to mean 'The One Born, Arisen From Fire' – though, in truth, there is lot more nuance to the concept than what I have patience to spend time on explaining today."

Iambre blinked, freakishly inspired to think herself in need of a fool's hat again. Staring at the man, she was getting used to 'speechless', though; again he had spoken with almost charming rudeness, but he kept distracting her with his words. *Who the fleck was 'Elhvaarrn'? Or what? A long-dead poet? A region of the Realm lost to the Chaos Wars, like the Armearan?*

Razing her eyes across the quayside, mind spinning and picking answers, weighing and dismissing, she looked back on the ship, ready to question, but again she blinked.

The sailor was gone.

The ghost of her pent-back breath escaped her. Flustered and frustrated, Iambre surveyed the bowsprit and the railings, but nothing! The man had disappeared. Swallowed by the deck, or the water, or...?

Almost she spun on her heels to check her surroundings, but rational thought prevented the superstitious move. *What...?*

Iambre found herself still watching the point where the man had paused to relay his final words. She did not believe in spirits. This would have a logical explanation. The sailor had gone back on deck. He might have been smoking something unsavoury and she might have caught the backdraft of the effect on the strong win, or maybe...?

Confused royally about the feelings churning like some unsavoury soup within her, Iambre tried to shake off all his odd comments and strangely familiar behaviour. A part of her resented him disappearing like that, a part felt only relief, but still...! He'd demanded to know what she felt about his blooming ship, only to bolt on the back of strange words, relating his disenchantment with the idea of further clarification. *Was her ignorance that offensive?*

A 'harrumph' escaped her and then she was stomping away from the water's edge raking the loose tangles of stray hair from her face as the wind seemed to synchronise with her mood to push her along in a sweeping gush of skirts and cloak. *Half-dressed, stuck up loon of a half-wit sailor... propositioning her like some common-*

Iambre wrenched the thought in half. She could not bring herself to even think the word!

And what was his to-do with that accent? It sounded as old-fashioned as some of his phrases! It was all most irregular – but worst of all, she'd become distracted from her purpose; wasted her precious time, and all for nothing. She'd not even asked for help, had not even mentioned Bilan's plight!

Iambre shook her head. With all her running and the strong wind, her cowl had come off her head. For now she didn't care though and pushed the nuisance that was a long escaped strand of hair out of her eyes to hook it behind one ear. If she let herself linger she'd go mad. Most likely Bilan would already be waiting for her at the Keep. *Most likely...*

Focussing on the braziers as she walked straight towards the strip beyond the gate-less old arch she suspected might be named Roshar's Run, it was hard to believe what she was doing, or indeed where. The two enormous braziers looked welcoming: imbued with the unvoiced promise of what might be encountered once you stepped from the quay-side into the space beyond and she walked a little faster, slightly night-blind now as the growing light invaded her vision. Shelter, company and merriment; the street beyond looked a mere road, but it was lit-up like on a festival day, the long sloping hill offering the guest a steep climb towards the inner walls. Luckily the visitors' path looked to be broken by several choices of entertainment that seemed to centre around the tavern variety, though maybe by the time one had navigated the various alehouses and theatre-inns, there was maybe more on offer between these walls than what was first envisioned.

Sound filtered down now. *Loud Voices. Gaiety. Normality. Well... after a fashion.*

She wished Bilan had still been here. *She hoped; nay, she prayed-*

Iambre decided she could not think like that again and in place of Bilandro Metavo, the sailor popped straight back into front row consideration.

She huffed. *If she never laid eyes on that blue-eyed man again, it would be a very good thing indeed! She could deal with peculiar courtiers, obnoxious local traditions, yes she could even usually see through fingers with personal insult, but that sailor!*

She realised it bothered she hadn't been able to read him, nor his intentions. Rather than it being her in control, he'd somehow played upon something within her, and the result...

She shivered with embarrassment. If ever asked to recount any of this she was suddenly not so sure that she would be able to - and not simply because she decided herself *unwilling* either. The details of her strange encounter felt unexpectedly 'wishy-washy'; the conversation - such as it had been – blurred. And since she'd much rather not think too much about it anyway, Iambre tried to rekindle the tricks taught her by Queen Ishjah and let the wind cushion and bolster her as she drew up to the old arch before Roshar's Run.

Doing the Right Thing!

IT FELT FOR A MOMENT as though she was looking past the threshold of some magical gate into another world. The braziers that had led her here were old, both bowls dented, the thick rims blackened with soot, and the stilts attaching to the wall, bowed as though bent by angry giants. Yet the flames were hot on her face – something more than charcoal to burn with such vigour – and she coughed as smoky air laced with the wind to enter her nostrils.

Still, though the arch suffered peeling plaster and heat damage, the scars of cracked neglect perhaps worrying, the overwhelming effect on the visitor was still one of welcoming – a concept enhanced by the gaiety painted by the awaiting taverns and guesthouses already candle lit through the fluttering reams of bunting, flanking doors and windows.

She realised the latter must have been hung in her honour, the strung-up triangles of assorted cloth lifting barely-flayed edges, too-new to have suffered the extensive damage of the abrasive elements that their cheap make would soon sustain. It was oddly heart-warming to see the care gone into making these small trivial things, yet she wasted no time gawping at the colourful assortment.

Aware that she still carried a certain unattractive riff about her person, and that it was mostly due to the tanner's robes, Iambre shrugged from her over-cloak and discarded it to one side. The tabard and smock underneath were hardly much better, but they hadn't been part of the original tanner's garb and though the malicious odour might linger a tad, she'd not been dressed in these clothes for long enough for the effects to be permanent and the wind would air the rest enough to diminish the effect. *She hoped...*

Unable to do much more about her appearances, she smoothed down her hair and re-positioned the drab hooded capelet over the top once more. For good measure she pulled the stiff fabric as far forward as possible, sheltering her face in shadow just as promised Bilan.

It did not mean that she was not suddenly filled with doubt. The street rising steeply before her was protected by cobbles hollowed by centuries of foot traffic, packed right up to the carved-out six inch gutters, channelled out and lined by river rocks to flank the roadside like two unbroken canals left and right. Looking up the challenging incline, the path between the two- and three-storied ale houses and taprooms appeared hemmed in, without the possibility for her or anyone else to deviate before the first intercepting crossroads, a good fifty paces ahead. It was oddly assuring. *Only one way forward...*

She turned her face momentarily to breathe new energy into her body, the subdued song and bustle of sound meandering forth as she caught a fresh taste of briny air. She'd figured as much but apparently the establishments of Roshar's Run were already well-frequented. A lilting mix of indistinguishable human voices made dents in the night with the same press of variety she'd often heard upon entering a banquet hall where for half a blink, unconcerned, uncensored merriment would continue to roll around the large gathering before everyone was made aware of her presence and the blanketed effect fell over the room. The usual hush of demand would not greet her here though and she was cheered a little by the prospect of not being the one on display for a change.

Strange sensations writhing in the pit of her belly, Iambre touched the old wall - cool, damp plasterwork feeling both solid and gritty under her fingers. The arch might be one of the oldest in Zanzier, but there was no evidence of a gate to protect against invasion or even ruckus sailors – not even a bent bracket, not even a rusted nail. Still perhaps it was long gone? The thick layers of plaster had cracked, the hairline fractures peeling into wider grooves - in some places sporadically exposing large patches of the original dark brick, raising ideas of blight now rotting and scarring the wall as it was allowed to continue eating past mortar and stone unhindered, untreated, but for sure it did not alter the charm of what lay beyond. Not even if it was a kind of charm she'd never dare to fully embrace.

Staring ahead, letting her fingers trail off, she started walking. There were not many people about outside – maybe it was the weather, maybe not – but she was grateful. A pale-eyed older man, cloaked against the elements and securing his broad-brimmed hat with one hand, offered only a brief glance and a subtle incline of the chin in greeting as he passed, walking out the gate, and though it meant little, the cheer within rose a notch. *She was going back to the Keep. As promised. And then...*

Eying her surroundings, some of her stress seeping from her core like a staggered breath, Iambre had a feeling of calm descend over her the more steps she put between herself and the quays. Strangely, for the sombre Zanzierian preferences, wherever she looked, colours ruled, and unlike the harbour wall, the old plaster-work of these buildings carried proof of repair. It was an illusion of sorts, yet whatever might be said for the manner of entertainment found within, it made everything look pretty, the alternative of red, green or blue, drawing the attention as it was surely meant to, the warped flawed panes of double-casement windows somehow breaking the garish effect by emitting an enticingly warm glow. Unsurprisingly, against the deepening evening, it served well to reveal snap-shots of interiors and the patrons already resident: gambling, drinking, singing... *other.*

Iambre recalled the Charmstress in her mind's eye. *She didn't want to; they had pleasure lounges for a reason: so that decent people could avoid having their eyes burned by such kink notions and need.* However, sadly she also recalled the woman they'd passed entering the market square, and the way the strumpet had so easily caught Bilan's attention...

An acidy burst of something reeking of jealousy raced through her, upsetting her heartbeat, but she was being daft. Bilan had just saved her petals. More than once. She owed him thanks. *And more.* If only he'd take it. *But he wouldn't.* And so she'd be sending him home...

In a strange flash of insight, Iambre evaluated herself, staring directly into her possessive strain that seemed to pollute, and mercy... there it was. The root of her jealousy. The pain of all pains. The regret that other women could elicit such easy interest from him, simply because of who they were *not* - and that she couldn't, simply because of who she was!

Suddenly bitter, she chewed on her lip, hemmed by the usual burst of irritation towards life, imagining for one taunting moment, the faces of all the woman Bilan could play more than 'nice' with, providing... *providing he was all right. Providing he was still-*

Rolling her useless emotions into a ball and throwing it away, she sourly acknowledged that she could not demand any more of the man no matter what. What did she expect him to do? Remain celibate till the day they nailed the final offering to the top of his coffin?

Pish-posh!

She was a fool! Such an utterly deluded fool!

Randomly, she began to read the signs of the places she passed to replace the incessant wondering about whether or not Bilan was alright; if Lancei were?

The Merry Minstrel; The Tree and Trunk; The Blue Siren; Kira'Cha's Cup; A Captain's Log; the Captains Coc-

Iambre blushed and hastily averted her mind. Would it not be ironic though, if she were to come across The Golden Ball here; if, after all this disastrous activity, she was suddenly thrown eye to eye with the very place she'd come searching for? As she vaguely recalled, had the Chief not said the place was located near the deep quays?

Circumventing a pair of women in skirts too short to be considered more than oversized tunics, Iambre silently admitted to herself that feared to find the place now.

Was Roshar's Run a place the Chief would come? Sadly, she did not know the answer, but if it involved 'in the name of duty'; if it involved Solancei; she needn't guess to know facts. The names were plentiful and inventive, the signs sometimes as alarmingly colourful as the alehouses they represented – *Gods, in one foul swoop, her idea of an anchor was forever sharply altered* – but there was decidedly no 'Golden Ball' amongst the crude or the rude. *It was a relief, but also not!*

Roshar's Run was not wide, but it went as straight as an Etruian Boulevard, all the way up-up-up, now beginning to bisects other roads – and hence, *'opportunities'* - in a grid-work of developments that were probably as old as the Declaration of Unity itself. If she strayed she'd probably get lost, but fortunately she wouldn't have to go off route so her luck was turning peachy. *Well... sort of...*

Again she wasn't sure about her own feeling. She should have been crystal clear with relief but found herself riddled by a case of guilt too. *Which made no sense...*

It cheered her of course that in as far as she could see, the hill did not level out until it reached the narrow plateau of central Zanzier - situated just below the Keep - and at least this meant that she had been right in trusting her instincts; it meant that Bilan had been right.

It also cheered her that if she pushed for it - even up-hill - she would be able to get back behind those walls within the turn of the coming quarter! *And she wanted to! Gods, did she ever! Yet...*

'And yet, what if you did find The Golden Ball? What if you did?' sanity toyed, *'What would you do? You promised Bilan! You promised yourself! Straight back, but what would you do?'*

Though no one would ever hear her admit it, she felt drained, but if she found The Golden Ball, she also knew she couldn't simply walk past.

Marrow-deep desperation, spidery worry and cloying thoughts, decaying hope... together it all stacked high. As Crown Princess, for the love of everything, she ought to be able to simply point her finger and order the entire garrison out in search of her handmaiden, but of course not. Still... with every breath, she genuinely tried to take heart from the knowledge that this was not Solancei's first 'joust' so to speak; she tried to recall her cousin's wily wit and early years refusal to be hemmed in by walls - or indeed rules. *It had never ended too badly. It wouldn't now!*

In fact, at a stretch, she might compare this to other episodes. Some that happened a few years ago. Somewhere she and Lancei had sneaked out of Servangar on occasion so trawl round Etruia City, only the third time they'd been found out, hence ending their daring joint adventures from furthering, but Lancei hadn't listened before then. Her mother had once said that Lancei was not made for a rocking chair by the fire, nor five small heirs pulling at her laces for attention. It might be so, but Iambre actually hoped for del'Draventar's sake this wasn't accurate.

Her mother also used to say that Lancei was like a cat. That she'd come and go - maybe stay for a while if you treated her nicely - but that she had no true loyalty; no sense of family. It was a remark dropped after her cousin had been gone for two days straight, only to turn up like a ragged stray, without remorse or apology. Iambre had always known her mother had been wrong. She had to be!

Hating the seeds of doubt sown by the recent events, Iambre raked her gaze over everyone and everything as she went - *just in case* - now secretly feeling just a little more forgiving towards Chief Eso after seeing the sights of Zanzier for herself.

Gods but there were so many places to check; some evident, large and bold, some so small they appeared just like an afterthought – often little more than a sliver of a house between two others sunk-in as though hiding; as though uncertain of right or purpose, yet each little crevice had an open door, straw-covered floors, and a trellis serving both as bar and... well other! The Chief had told her that The Golden Ball was near the deep quays, but really... *that could mean anything!*

Iambre glanced up, wondering at the hour, but too much light and too many roofs obscured the rising stars and low moon. It bothered her there was no comfortable way of finding out how much time she'd spend chasing Eso, nor how long it had been since she'd split from Bilan. *By now the Chief might already have met with Natusse: she might have news or she might have none...*

She scratched at an itch on her arm. Bilan had told her he'd been shadowing her for the better part of an hour – perhaps another had passed since then and now, so she surmised the hour still early, however, what did she know, really? Without the tanner's bewitching stench to put people off, she realised she was being noticed for other reasons now - not by everyone, and for now it was little more than a curious look here and there, but it was enough to unnerve her. *Oddly she'd felt safer back in the old town, but...*

Harsh laughter pulled her attention. *Not the first time.* A quick glance left showed her an outdoor table by one of the larger establishments where an impromptu stage consisting of five large ale barrels - upended to create a makeshift performance area - was currently occupied by two older ladies dressed as men telling filthy stories to the delight and disgust of the assembled audience. One clump of men who looked to be sailors by their plaited queues and odd attire, were trying their hardest to set the lowest standard possible for their night in port, their language of all accents and none, comingling in harsh jests and already-drunken insults as they heckled the hapless performers in a way that that might explode from banter into worse at any moment.

Iambre kept her nose forward but felt momentarily blessed that the boisterous men had laid their interest in 'female company' with a couple of serving maids who did not look too much like 'maids' to regret the 'wanting' conduct.

Without looking left or right, she drew a little further into the middle of the uneven cobbles, not willing to get drawn in anywhere, whether by accident or demand. She was not completely green: as drinks continued to flow, and as arguments and disagreements erupted as they were wont to do, she could predict how this entire strip of road might soon turn rowdy. It was perhaps an unkind observation - yet Ina had told her stories, and she'd not been entirely deaf to the tales told by the soldiers of her retinue when camping on a quiet evening either.

Clutching her hard-won red parcel tighter, Iambre swallowed her nerves but tasted her own unease like a perfume in the back of her throat. She'd semi-forgotten the parcel, but as she looked at it now, her fingers intertwined so tightly around that bit of string, she could barely feel them. *She didn't care about that. She cared that Bilan was unhurt. She cared that Lancei was gone for a better reason than the idea of her mother's 'stray-cat syndrome', yet she was prepared to accept this, if only it meant Zulavi was not involved. If only...*

She looked down at the parcel and felt odd.

This night had been one of the strangest in her life! Aware of the parcel again, she suddenly recalled that other strange incident too: the one that had happened back before she and Bilan were attacked; the one involving that runner...

Her mind flickered with the memory. *Gods, but with everything that had happened, she'd near forgotten about that runner! Bilan had been quick to disassociate with the whole thing, but the runner had nearly trawled directly into them, and Gods...*

As she recalled the incident for a too-long moment, Iambre twirled her fingers further into the twine, semi-forgetting her surroundings.

Now Bilan might have thought nothing of it, but not she. Because she'd seen the face hidden within that deep cowl; for a split heartbeat, she'd actually looked the runner in the eye and-

But no!

Iambre shook her head. *She must have been mistaken! She could not possibly have seen what she thought she'd seen, because such a thing... NO!*

She pushed the mental image from her mind, as she did the runner's bizarre comment in regards to her purchase. *It made no sense! She was just tired: seeing things; hearing things!*

Sidestepping a pair of merry-sounding women and a slightly-keeling trio of men, Iambre judged by their slurred voices and sun-bleached linen clothes that they might need all the help they could get, not to land themselves shoulder, or knee, or... *well-anything*... head-first into the Mesatitan as they tried to clamper back on-board what-ever ship they'd taken leave from. One man winked at her as they passed, his furrowed face tanned and goodly-natured as he comment-ed something to his comrades, which in turn lifted their voices in laughter and sent Iambre scurrying with embarrassment, but it killed her thoughts about the runner. *Ruddy people, these sailors! Another wink?! Did they all possess such bad manners, or was it simply something she did?*

Iambre strangled the still mentally-striking image of 'Captain Breeches', her entire face turning stern and ten years older just thinking of the figure on the bowsprit.

That whole 'thing' had been a strange experience too - only her mother called her Jewel. Only her ruddy mother! And she hated this half-cut translation of her name with a vengeance. It must be something she did then. It had to be...

Iambre steered nimbly round a couple of brightly-clad lasses – not Charm-stresses by the looks of them, but in her book they might as well have been, with their low-cut Iddian-like bust lines and ringlets of hair piled loosely high in a strangely seductive, yet 'messy' style that she *most definitely* did not consider even the least bit endearing!

The girls went arm in arm, heads bowed and gossiping fast, and though she did not want to, Iambre caught herself doing a double-glance at the way they moved and the way they seemed to catch the men's eye with little more than a coquettish flicker of long eyelashes. *Something for her to try one day perhaps?*

No!

No. No. No!

Iambre could have cried at her own thoughts. *Definitely No! And she did definitely not like the way that blonde girl's hair seemed just about to join the loos-ened bits of curly ringlets that had already artfully 'escaped' her precarious ensem-ble! But Bilan might... Oh, midnight raffle!*

Iambre snatched her eyes back, keeping them solidly on the ground now. The wind flicked around her like a tiny tempestuous spirit and she let out a sigh of pent-up breath. *You did not bargain with the Gods, nor did you ever try to play them at each other, but still-*

A rumble on the edge of hearing half-registered with her ears. It wasn't really something she'd pay attention to, yet an urgency in the air flowed forth just blinks before an unpredicted string of indignant yelps and brute shouts of anger arose like a swarm of birds forced to leave their nests.

It was the only warning she got of the danger bearing down. Semi-dazed with her own thoughts, head rising to the alarm just in time to join others taken unawares, Iambre zeroed in on a carriage and its team of four foam-flecked sorrels careening directly towards her. A man to her left cussed hard and flailed to spin away in good time, yet somehow dumbstruck with surprise, the vision froze Iambre's muscles in place. Vaguely, she condemned the action; the sheer stupidity. *Gods, who was indeed stupid enough to canter a large carriage down an incline like this?*

Then the driver's cracking whip and his hard shouts to make the team go faster suddenly registered and the sense of danger spiked. *Midnight raffle! He was not even going to pretend at slowing down!*

Feeling her heart becoming a thumping lump in her throat, Iambre stared at the aberration as it came at her with thunderous speed, sending men and women jumping for their lives as it came on - yet for her, the world seemed to slow, leaving her time to observe the details with too much clarity that could only end in disaster...

The springs too soft, the carriage wobbled and bounced, a grotesque show that nearly unseated the driver as its elegant frame of black and blue lacquer shook and quivered like a thing alive; the sorrels had identical markings: white foreheads, long white socks on all front legs - markings that thumped up and down, over and over, so fast that the action looked a blur. The nosebands carried golden knots: expensive. The fast clatter of hooves, accompanied by a crazy jingle of harnesses and a rumble of wheels was all she heard. *Part of her knew there was no way she was going to move fast enough to avoid them; no way-*

Jostled sideways suddenly by a small group of madly scrambling people seeking to push their way out of the path of the elegant but deadly battering ram, Iambre was caught and shoved aside just a heartbeat before the mad driver brought his vehicle thundering past with unwavering intent. Iron-bound, gilt-trimmed wheels ran across the stone she'd only just occupied, leaving her with an odd assortment of impressions: some fine scroll work on the corner panels;

swaying tassels on the tightly drawn curtains; a flash of some finely drawn heraldry on one polished door... *two crossed spears and a plume of feathers?*

The carriage was away before she was sure and her breath - which had been
stuck in her chest - exploded past her lips. *Death and daffodils! What a mad
man!*

The two women who'd inadvertently been a part of the rescuing group,
shook their fist and shouted choice words of filth Iambre had never heard before but the carriage showed no signs of stopping as it continued its mad charge
down the street under repeated uproar as people looked up, spotted danger, and
parted like waters before the bow of a fast sailing ship in fear of its unforgiving
approach.

"Fleck!"

The profanity was out, but Iambre's indignant ire lasted only a heartbeat.
Completely in shock, the feeling was slow to abate and her knees nearly buck-
led then as her muscles seemed to release to become jelly; only a firm, steadying
hand to the elbow stayed her.

Iambre gasped, nodding her thanks to the women who'd just rescued her
again and the woman returned the nod as she let go, her gaze following Iambre's
as they watched the back of the elegant vehicle race on.

"I hope the river takes the snaff-box fool" the woman muttered, her
Zanzierian accent as flat as her angry stare as she spat out a black gob of thick
spittle, then turned away. Iambre swallowed nausea.

"Yeah," she heard herself agree, the shock lessening but sucking the energy
from her as it went. Finding strength from some reserve she didn't even know
she possessed, she locked her knees, determined not to wilt. The collection of
on-lookers and near-misses was already dispersing but Iambre watched the carriage for a heartbeat longer, whilst she collected herself - rather inclined now,
to wishing the driver away to the pepper fields of Carlundula for his neglect to
care! It seemed that her heart would not slow down – not even as the carriage
reached the arch, flew along through, to finally disappear from view.

She swallowed, working sliver back into her mouth. To force a team of
highly-strung horses through a populated street at such break-neck speed was
down-right irresponsible and she silently berated the passenger who'd asked his
driver for such. *People died in carriage crashes! Solancei's parents had died. It*

was just sheer good fortune that people had escaped with nothing more than a few bruised knees or the disaster didn't bear thinking about!

Doubly weary of everything, Iambre shook herself, feeling an inner coldness slowly spreading. *If she'd been involved in an accident no one would've known who she were; she could have died, and no one would've known what had become of her.* The fact that she could've disappeared just as easily as Lancei, was not lost on her: there was little or no equation between the vision she currently portrayed and the elegant Crown Princess with curled-high plaits of hair, draped in Dragon Silver ornaments. She'd already known as much of course, but the near-hit was yet another harsh reminder of her utter idiocy in coming out tonight. *The runner, the attack, the horribly attractive sailor, and now the carriage...*

It was more unhealthy excitement than she'd had for years. She needed sleep. Lots of sleep!

Picking up her feet she pushed on, but felt broken and tired. This had indeed been Eso's business all along. Every single thing that had happened so far seemed a painful testament to this and the realisation stung. *To be so reliant upon others and never realise...!*

But that was being Crown Heiress, wasn't it? That was part of her 'privilege': to have others ever do her hard work, be it dirty or complicated; anything!

Iambre shook herself and for some reason, saw 'Captain Breeches' face in her mind's eye in that moment of madness where she'd imagined herself able to sail away and-

No! This was straw hat-worthy, and she was not about to go there either! Her reality was already cast in solid steel; she'd always be filled with the need to 'do the right thing' regardless of her small personal 'wobbles' but today it was just very hard to admit that doing the right thing, would have been to do nothing!

The Keep was waiting, as was Ina and Palea with dresses to discuss and powders and jewellery to consider. There were occasions to attend, introductions to be made and people to see and food to be eaten and toasts to be spoken – sincere or half-hearted – and it was the world she must return to. Reluctantly or willingly. Gods, and so she did. But everything just seemed so wrong. And doing 'the right thing'...

Well, doing the right thing had never ever been quite so hard indeed...

Solancei's Memoirs

The Province of Tarléon.
Ivanor Fortress.
Winter of 780 P. C. W.

I spent the better part of that first morning trying to get Rainan alone so that I could plead my case. He was busy with our visitors as well as the general run of things, of course, and whenever I tried to wheedle myself past whatever councillor or soldier or petitioner he was due to see next, I was told by his aide to go braid my hair, or feed the dogs, or practice my arts skills, or play the harp.

The harp? I mean: really? *The harp?* I don't play the harp: never have, never will. I dabbled, of course, but mother banned me the fourth time I broke the strings, so...

Still, discounting that sadistic idea, normally I would have jumped to do any of the other things suggested, but not today! I had genuine cause to have my grievance heard, and I reminded them of this, but evidently even a Lord's daughter can only push her luck so far - for when they ignored me in favour of an ongoing conversation about blight hitting four more ice fields near the Kheltian border, then shut the oaken door to the council chamber in my face, I finally realised that my appeal against Lady Chief Mehadja's purpose was going to take some serious planning in order to get noticed.

So I retreated to the stables, snuck into Vaalar's corner, and climbed atop his silver-grey back. The nearness and warmth of my father's prime stallion calmed me and we had an affinity, Vaalar and I, in that I always brought him the gnarled, misshapen carrots no one wanted, and in return he always allowed me to lie back along the black eel of his spine without him trying to dislodge me as he would any other person bold enough to sit astride him, including my late father.

Jolting my father thus, was a trick that had nearly ended the splendid horse in one of the cook's pies, however, with Afhpar blood in his equine veins, and a stallion at that, my father could not allow himself the loss of such a valuable asset, so Vaalar had been kept for breeding little cute foals and nothing more. My luck, I guess. I don't know why Vaalar let me near him. Mother had been petrified that the 'wicked' creature would trample me when she'd first learned of my visits, but perhaps one rouge streak senses a kindred spirit in another, for that horse was never anything but a gentle lord with me.

But anyway, I often came here when I needed the comfort of another simple being. The horse provided me a good ear, and I would whisper to him in my mind, about all my fears and feelings and it often helped to straighten my thoughts and settle my heart. And so I told him about the strange lady who sought to take me to somewhere far away because some Queen had deemed it. I was vaguely aware of course, of my late mother's kinship with said Queen Ishjah but I didn't want to think about that. My mother had only been a Duchess and that had spelt trouble aplenty for me. What would not a Queen spell?

No, what I needed, was to stay in Ivanor. But how? I turned my limited knowledge of the situation upside down and inside out, and Vaalar listened – or maybe he did not, but I had found my happy place to reflect upon my dilemma – so whilst the horse chewed carrots and straw harvested and imported from the Plains of Pendrosa, I plotted.

Hmm... I say plotted...

The idea is laughable, of course. I didn't as much plot as I reacted, emotionally, to string my thoughts into the semblance of order I needed to formulate my arguments against going, as well as how and when to do so, which (crucially) was where I'd so far failed. If people would not let me get to Rainan in the day-time hours, then I'd go to him after dark: after the day was done and he was alone in his chambers. He'd have to listen. He owed me this, I figured, and though unfair I toyed with the idea of throwing the fault of my parents' demise in his face. I would then add how I thought he'd already failed them once (in not finding the guilty perpetrators already), so would he really wish to fail them again by denying me my birthright, which when all was said and done meant staying in Ivanor to learn how to run the place in preparation of my eventual coming of age. It was a similar tack I'd tried once before of course, but this time I'd throw in the words, 'birthright' and 'coming of age' – two concepts that had been dear to both my mother and father, and had also on occasion occupied their minds to what I'd hitherto considered 'unhealthy distraction'.

I hadn't cared overly much up till now. Those days where I'd need to consider such aspects of my life had been far away – indeed they still were – however, if it meant me staying in my home and sending this Chief Mehadja packing on her own, I'd promise any and all Gods listening, that I'd take an interest from now on.

Though it might not work, for now this avenue would be my most preferred way forward, for I did not relish the idea of trying my luck once the fierce lady in question officially got her claws on me. Her promises of woe and wishing myself back on the tower, had not seemed empty and I was used to adults following through on their assurances, good and bad. That woman would not jest about something like this - so if my only other option was to run away until the danger had passed, I'd need to make it a damned good effort for I'd only have one shot. And if I budged it... well...

But for all of my bravado, I'd rather not run away, of course. Apart from the cold itself, there were plenty of things that could kill a person outside these walls and a few handfuls within them too, and since I'd much rather not face any such horrors if I could avoid it, appealing to Rainan would be my best, most constructive way forward. *If only I could catch him alone.*

Lulled by Vaalar's heat and his quiet but powerful presence, I let my thoughts wander then. In my mind, a winged shadow brushed against my thoughts just as I almost connected with sleep, but the fear stirred me awake. Vaalar snorted under me and stomped as if disturbed by my mental images too, and it almost toppled me into the straw as I flung myself upright with blurry-eyed alarm, clutching the stallion's golden mane in both hands.

Rigid, I stared at my own fingers.

I don't know how I realised this only now, but sitting there, suddenly the horrendous idea stuck me that my dreams would never get any better. *Was this my punishment for surviving my parents and Taliana?*

Though often taunted by my imagination, I did not really put any scope in the notion that I should have died instead of them, did I? Rainan had assured me that my dreams were just a twisted amalgamation of my unhealthy love of wicked tales and my own soaring imagination, combined with some sort of misplaced guilt that seemed to grip most the Tarléonin people in the wake of the disaster, but what if it were not?

My head was full of tangled vines and prickles. I was too tired but I couldn't find peace even here, caught as I appeared to be in the fear of surrendering to sleep and what awaited on the other side.

Heart galloping with the spike in my inner dread rising in droves whilst blades of ice began to release rivers of chill down my spine, I pulled myself inwards to escape the same way I'd done multiple times over. I had no will, but at least there was a chance I might flood my senses with my renegade 'escape trick'; with this strange 'seeking of the void'- which I still did not know was a bastardised form of Veranto that I'd cultivated and was finding myself drawing on more and more frequently.

As ever, my success rate was rather hit and miss though. Certain days, I could float above it all and others...

Well today, I was plagued by the dread in my belly. I just couldn't seem to connect with the semblance of peace I'd previously been able to raise. *It was bloody typical. When I most needed my little trick, it wouldn't comply!*

I think I panicked then. Something locked within my chest, restricting my breath, creating a knot...

I came to half-slumped over the Vaalar's withers, half-draped across his left shoulder with my fingers still entangled in his mane. Aware of little else, his heartbeat was like a steady drum in my ear, somehow summoning to my mind the peculiar parting words of Chief Mehadja's... *'You need to breathe. Focus on your centre and on the breath to even out the aches of your fears and the assault of your feelings. Focus on your core; on your presence in the now. It will calm you and aid your sleep. Once you can detach yourself, I will teach you more.'*

How did I realise she'd been talking about my 'trick'? How did I even remember the words in said small given moment?

I really don't know. Somehow something clicked. The Now, was now! The now was me and I was it! I was too damned exhausted to think, but the sensation was unrealised. The stallion's presence suffused me; I was unaware of the choice, but I think I simply let go then to drift and become nothing more than my next breath, and the next, and the next. I don't know how, it's hard to explain, but for once there was no real conscious action involved, I simply surrendered to my every breath, I think. I was everything and nothing; within my body and without; but most of all I was simply here and now without a past, without a future. There was nothing but the warmth of the stout horse beneath me and the timing of his heart, which my own seemed to mirror in a slow, deliberate rhythm, and for a blink it all went away: my fears, my hopes, my sense of loss, my exhausted state of mind, my strung out body...

Breathing with the horse still, I think I opened my eyes and sat upright as if my body was an afterthought of my presence, yet also so much more. An utterly blinding sense of calm and clarity bloomed within the core of me that I'd never been aware of before, and there was no compulsion to stay my need for sleep, because I was awake and hence in no need to rest. I had no fears because they no longer mattered in 'the now'. I felt neither cold nor warm; I existed in synchronicity. The present moment was all there was: the now, the smells of wood and horse, manure, and warmth, and straw, and with it the memory of dissipating summer which coloured the air with subtle dust, and further removed the tendrils of tack, leather oil and glycerine, damp grain and the cold, strident cleanliness of new snow. A waft of tobacco followed, sweet cherry, burned oak and vanilla, a tangy coppery metal and underpinning it all, the delicious fragrance of freshly baked bread, and (oddly) pale-haired Lady Michilla's deep, heady perfume!

As you might imagine, it was unreal. I became aware that I could hear better too. *Like at the funeral.* Like when I'd caught the whispers of truth about my parents in the corners - but also less diffuse, each snippet of conversation seemed to lock itself in my mind with zero margins for misunderstanding. It made me almost feel like some supernatural creature out of some story but I was so calm; so beyond the need to care at that particular time, but I heard men speaking of an evening banquet in honour of our visitors, I heard the chink of metal on metal and Smith instructing an apprentice to heat-treat a blade; I heard a surprised yelp of fright and learned a great new swear word as someone slid on a bit of black ice; then came Trinian's affable voice as he guided a visitor down the main stable corridor – apologising profusely for the mess though the place was spotless – and I caught the Lady Michilla's shrill voice which always seemed to match her upturned nose perfectly. *It was suddenly growing louder as she ignored Trinian's deferential explanations about smells that could floor an ox but would not cling to her skirts...*

I remember thinking it was obscene: Lady Michilla's acute voice sounded nearer with every beat of my heart... Lady Michilla's perfume, overshadowing that of warm equine flesh, seemed to sear my nose... *Lady Michilla-*

A sharp pang of insight hit me.

Fleck! Lady Michilla! Coming closer! Here? Fleck!

It spoiled the effect I'd wrought with so little effort out of a few advisory words and exhaustion. It collapsed my enlightened, heightened state of awareness in less than a blink, but I couldn't lament the loss now.

Michilla was one of the dwindling number of women who fancied herself my new chaperone since Taliana's death and she had a way of showing up at the strangest of times, for the weirdest of reasons. I did not dislike her, but I was weary of her presence. She had more than a streak of my deceased lady mother in her and this included ideas of what a young lady should and shouldn't get involved in. And for certain, loitering in a dirty stables were definitely not part of her carefully constructed list of sanctioned activities...

I flung myself off Vaalar, swinging one leg over his neck in a scissor-like move I'd perfected since a long time to land without mishap on both feet, facing the box door. Then I beat feet down the corridor just as the lady and Trinian cornered the far end of the straight run. I heard the woman screech as she spotted me, her voice rising several octaves in demand that poor Trinian should instantly raise pursuit. Something about a bath and hairbrush followed, the urgency clear, then the sound of their chasing me took over.

I did not dislike the idea of a bath, but the knowledge of the required attendance at the afore-mentioned banquet made me less than amenable. Of course, Trinian caught me before long. I'd forgotten I was escaping down a dead-end - and the realisation that I'd been able to apply the Chief's advice to engross myself in this new experience was enough to distract me with the amazement that was slowly sinking into me. As Trinian held me firmly by the wrist, marching me back to Lady Michilla whose perfect complexion now carried the purple-tinted edge of exertion, I found myself wondering if I could do what I'd just done, again tonight?

It intrigued me. *Disturbingly so.* As did the understanding that I'd somehow done something right for a change. See, for a moment I'd felt invincible; removed from my own skin, yet becoming one with something so powerful that I could somehow channel the benefits I half-recognised from all my other times of seeking the distance - but this time in such a perfect fashion that it promised me so much more than my shoddy achievement had produced thus far.

Discounting the fact that it was the Lady Chief Mehadja who'd given me the key to this perfection, I meekly followed Lady Michilla back to the main living quarters, utterly engrossed now in the new sensations remembered.

This was my first true unfiltered taste of what the State of Veranto could do, and already I craved to 'submerge myself' again!

'*To submerge myself*'. I named it thus at the time, but of course the proper term for this experience is to 'create a link' – this the Chief told me that very same evening. And Gods help me if she didn't smile again. And Gods help me if I did not want to know more.

And so I was split – for how to request of Rainan that I should stay in Ivanor, when also wanting to glean what I might about this peculiar trick otherwise known as the State of Veranto. For to learn more would require my interacting with the very person I did not want to speak to; the very person, who though she scared me, also remained my sole chance to find a way to put to pasture my hag-ridden dreams for good!

You can imagine, I'm sure, that I did not appreciate the spectrum of my limited choices one bit. You can imagine also, I'm sure, that I did proceed to do a number of inconsiderate, rebellious things during the next 6 days, for sometimes I am both stupid and tenacious, and so the hard-learnt lessons would come fast and strong, without mercy!

Yet it was not all bad. For one, I learnt that I should trust my guts, for it was with some regret that I discovered myself right in my assumptions that when Chief makes promises, she most emphatically means to keep them. I also learnt that a good bluff can buy you time but unless you have the luck of Kira'Cha stored in your back pack, or unless you know how to weave a good spell or two – you will most likely only succeed in prolonging the inevitable – something, which I remembered but tried very hard to repress when that bastard-lord Simarovien Zulavi had me chained, crippled, and worse, all in the name of lawful conduct, personal-gratification-masking-as-entitlement, and mad dreams.

Had I known what were to come, perhaps I would have taken a different tack back then, but then again maybe not.

Remember I said I was stupid? Well I've grown up now; I know when the odds are against me and then some, yet way back then; way back in Ivanor - it would take me almost killing myself before I finally understood that even if I could've persuaded the Gods to let me be, our good Queen of the Realm would absolutely and assuredly not allow any such thing – and nor, as it happened, would Chief Klaasinah Eso Mehadja. *Not once she'd seen exactly what I could do...*

Solancei

At the Library of Life

"IT IS UNSURPRISING that you remain unsuccessful."

Bent over a few dozen scrolls flung carelessly open across a vast oaken table, the sharp-faced Elvern with the moon-pale hair did not even bother to glance at them. A vague hint of arrogance and hostility was ever-noticeable in the way that he chose to speak each syllable - but at least he was still complying with Sinuhé's polite demands and, as the days had passed, the man's tone had gotten gradually less haughty in favour of his mounting exasperation.

Nefer'Kemnebit, Best-Loved Daughter of the Sabén-Heshep Watchéran, knew this - not because she was overly familiar with the particulars of adult emotions per se, nor because she was clever enough to differentiate the subtle nuisances – but simply because that was what her new teacher had told her when she'd worried about their situation. The other Elvern man and her tutor had... *well, she guessed one might say that they'd argued concepts and necessity, theory and possibilities, from the moment she'd first been introduced to Sinuhé's 'assistant' - and to say that the two men did not commonly agree on a single thing, was perhaps a polite understatement...*

With the thought of the heated conversations witnessed, Nefer pursed her lips, wishing she'd not been anywhere near the two men during these 'discussions'. Very much aware that the *Flight of Fire* also did not applaud being given the title of 'assistant', she wondered if he still begrudged the fact Sinu had introduced him as such?

If he did, she sort of understood.

There was something grossly wrong in naming the Flight of Fire a simple 'assistant', Nefer thought, because the pale Elvern Spell-Weaver was clearly anything but – *and still...*

The foreign Heirah-Noor Ancient did not want her here regardless of what title Sinuhé had ascribed him. She was very clear on the other man's 'reluctance' on this point; or maybe he did not mind her presence per se, she amended - only not in the capacity Sinuhé had currently asked her to serve. It was a disagreement, which had meant that a fair portion of the witnessed the arguments had mostly been about her.

Nefer cringed. *Well over her... and a few other things besides. Like the futility of the pale-haired Elvern's presence here, for example.*

The younger man was acid and blades: abrasive and cutting. Ancient or no, she wasn't sure what to make of the way he behaved towards her new Esteemed Tutor though. He seemed mostly thoroughly rude; yes, disrespectful even – and yet Sinuhé did not seem to bear him ill-judgement and she knew without anyone telling her that it was indeed a sign of a wise and patient tutor when the older man behaved so graciously. *And thank Alérathnar and the Watchéran for that!* This was not the first time since Nefer had met the two men that she'd found herself grateful her Sire had chosen Sinuhé and not this Rhindarhlar Mehand'Arun, this 'Flight of Fire', to instruct her. *Grateful... and secretly relieved!*

Not that she'd ever admit such a thing to either of their faces, of course, but the foreign Elvern sometimes scared her with his pale skin and even paler hair – indeed, had it not been for his gemstone eyes that seemed to merge somewhere between blue and green in a colour she had not a name for, she might not even have found anything remotely appealing about him. Sure, both men might be scholars, but the Flight of Fire was also a warrior and thereby a contradiction, because it felt odd seeing him here in one of the library studies, radiating the same aura as her Sire's Mkhai. The latter guarded their people and the Sabén-Heshep way of life and she owed them thanks, but all the same, they scared her – just as did this Mehand'Arun – for the exact same reasons, and yet also... *not.*

Nefer quenched the contradicting feelings she was experiencing. *The Mkhai were there to protect, but she wasn't so sure about this man.* Where Sinuhé was calm, Mehand'Arun seemed ever-fiery. The Avatar name *Flight of Fire* was well-suited and where Sinuhé would offer her words of encouragements or even praise, Mehand'Arun would simply direct a cool stare or a dismissive nod her way. In short, she'd never really know what he thought or how she might improve his opinion of her, and it was an oddly disturbing feeling that did not sit well with her peace of mind.

Nefer looked surreptitiously at the Ancient in question as he perused a passage of the Quondam Kuferi text laid out before him, his keen eyes flying, the ornamental braids of his long hair falling forward to obscure. She'd never actually experienced anyone not 'liking' her before – *for she was certain that Rhindarhlar Mehand'Arun did not!* – and it was a disconcerting feeling; one that she did not like hanging over her, but...

...*but at least he was not Sinuhé. At least he was not.*

"It is truly that obvious, then?" the esteemed Sinuhé enquired mildly in response to Mehand'Arun's pronouncement, catching her attention with his warm expression and the timbre of his voice, both which were totally in contrast to Mehand'Arun's. She hadn't thought Sinu about to honour the other man with a response but this was yet another difference between the two men: Sinuhé was ever courteous.

Nefer offered him a smile. Her tutor was shrugging free of the voluminous folds of his wool-lined silk cloak to reveal the equally vast folds of his toga underneath, and he was seemingly unconcerned as he cast a look towards Mehand'Arun. There was no challenge intended, she felt sure, but in response to her tutor's voice, Mehand'Arun paused his reading for a beat, the change in his attention evident only because of the manner in which he slightly caught himself amid an intake of air.

For a long moment, it seemed the caustic man might not extend his fellow Ancient an answer but then he appeared to relent. "Yes, it's obvious, Speaker. You trail-in an aura of frustration every time you return from a meeting with the Chief of Vectors and it interrupts my concentration as though you'd sent the thought directly into my mind."

"Verity?"

"Verily." Rhindarhlar Mehand'Arun shifted imperceptibly, a sign she knew, that he was back at the text and Sinuhé nodded to himself, saying nothing as he walked to hang the outer garment studiously on the rail already bearing Mehand'Arun's dark Spell-Weaver coat and several scarlet tabards belonging to the eight acolytes currently assisting: fetching and removing documents, books, scrolls – *whatever the two men requested* – in an ever-ceaseless flow of white pleated linen and brown skin.

Nefer shivered but tried to cover her reaction. It was not that the cloaks or other outer garments were normally necessary here in the Sabén-Heshep but they'd all worked through the night again and the hour was early - *barely sunrise yet* - and the morning air held a bitter bite.

Nefer suppressed another quiver, tiny goosebumps travelling up her arms. There was just something about the pale Elvern's choice inflictions that had made her feel the chill of the morning dew still on her bare legs, but then Sinuhé beckoned for her to come join him and she went to his side whilst he turned his gaze onto Mehand'Arun's bowed head with a seemingly patient mien.

"My dear Sheriti," he began as he helped her from her own cloak, "you will notice how my fellow Guardian appears of eternally ill manners, but it does not mean that the rest of us cannot be civil, now does it?"

Nefer-Kemnebit looked towards Mehand'Arun as Sinuhé turned to hang her cloak, but the man gave no outward sign to indicate whether he'd heard the comment or not, and for a few moments she chewed on the word 'Guardian'. *Saew-Nebdar'Hotep.* Sinuhé had given her the approximating word in *Kuferi* – the native language of her people. Up till now she'd only known of these Guardians as the Maker's Ancients, and could never have guessed that she'd one day look upon these Avatars in the flesh, let alone be called to serve with one. It made her feel as though she was walking in the shade of one of her own visions, yet she recognised this wasn't the case, even if recent events seemed too strange for words.

Amidst it all, she was secretly pleased that her understanding had held true though. It accounted for her Father's actions on the day she'd met Sinuhé, and explained her Mother's lacking interference. As she'd known, but not truly appreciated or understood till now, the title of 'Guardian' demanded honour and respect – even from the Watchéran Himself – and it seemed the two Ancients took the benefits for granted: another issue too strange for words.

Marmosets and mustard... she still struggled to comprehend that their presence came with a power of magic so deep that it was a part of the bond these two unlikely men seemed to share; a bond which had them linked and working together here, even though this Mehand'Arun seemed so unerringly... *reluctant.*

"Reluctant..." Nefer spun the word on her tongue. Yes, where *'Saew-Neb-dar'Hotep'* seemed an odd word to her, *'reluctant'* seemed just the opposite and a very fine word, indeed. *A good word to describe just how the Council and the Chief of Vectors continued to push them away; a good word to describe the Care-takers of Records; a good word to describe Mehand'Arun and his poor ability to dis-guise how this place seemed to 'irk' him.*

"To irk..." Nefer tasted that word, slowly too. 'Irk'.

Yes, now here was another excellent word: a new one the pale impatient Elvern had spat at her on the first day Sinuhé had brought her here to meet this 'fellow Guardian'. It was another word she'd never heard before that day but no one had needed to explain it to her: Rhindarhlar Mehand'Arun's every move, word, and action, had seemed to paint that translation quite clearly in her mind and it continued to do so still. "Irk... "

"Keep that odd girl away from me if she is determined to mutter words of random under her breath. It's disconcerting."

Nefer startled. Mehand'Arun had spoken to the page before him, though there was little question that the words were clearly directed through his aura towards the older man by her side. *Again he looked vexed.*

She signed. She hadn't realised she'd been speaking aloud and for a moment she felt herself crumble inwards with upset to be told off. She wanted to bolt from the chamber and hide away from this 'petty' meanness somewhere amongst the hundreds of floors and levels that made up the *Library of Life,* but even as Sinuhé totted disapproval behind her, Mehand'Arun looked up sudden-ly to catch them both with his luminous eyes. It stilled her on the spot and froze her breath in barely a heartbeat.

Much of the twenty-foot table lay between them: the other Elvern was a good many paces removed from them and on the far side at that – indeed, he'd barely moved, for he was already standing, hands splayed against the table on either side of a wide document - *and yet...*

As he leaned just a little forward, Nefer felt like shrinking back. Her tutor's garment seemed a very welcome place to hide behind suddenly, but then a hand steadied her and Sinuhé stepped forward with a loud sigh – *the closest thing he ever came to losing his aplomb, she'd discovered* – and gently shielded her.

"You are scaring my student with your uncouth behaviour, and I will not have it," her tutor scolded in that calm, reasonable manner of his, "She's had a testing hour already and the day is barely begun. Nefer-Kemnebit does not deserve this level of disregard and you best recall her Sire's kindness in allowing us access to her *and* the Library! Should *He* hear of your behaviour, I am not certain His hospitality will continue? You do see this, do you not Guardian?"

Sinuhé's voice carried mild reproach and she felt it clash with Mehand'Arun in a way that made the other Elvern's sorry mood instantly intensify. In response Sinuhé lifted a hand in gentle warning, a thing that usually worked - only today Mehand'Arun did not appear easy.

"Oh, by all means, let the Watchéran rescind his invitation," he told them both in dry tones as he straightened. "I can find no reason to remain here, anyway; no word out of place, no text; black hex, not even a whisper of irregularity! Good Speaker, we are wasting our time! *I am wasting my time!*"

Mehand'Arun let his stare burn into Sinuhé's one moment longer, then he flung out one hand towards the layers of documents with an exasperated breath. Ripping his eyes away, he reiterated, "Guardian Speaker there is nothing here. Nothing!"

"Maybe not '*here*'," her tutor allowed, seemingly unfazed, "but there is something amiss, somewhere... We just haven't found it yet."

"If I – *if we* – had an eternity to spare, we would not have time for this!" Mehand'Arun looked back at Sinuhé with an expression of building despair. "If you intend to have the girl help, then put her to good use. Now! Who knows: if she could prove her young talent here, she might also stand a better chance at persuading the Chief of Vectors of her mad dreams-"

"They are not mad dreams!" Nefer flung at him, surprising everyone in the large chamber - including the two silent acolytes who jumped and had to juggle armfuls of papers and scrolls in order not to unload the tall piles across the cedar floor instead of the table as intended - but Nefer did not care if they lost the entire historical account of the last two millennia right then. With a righteous frown, she continued, "I do see things! True things: events past; events still to come; and I am not a liar!"

Nefer sent her tutor a pleading look and saw his perturbed expression alter into one of understanding. *They'd been to see the Chief of Vectors a grand total of three times in this last week since He-Who-Is, Sheshem'Kufunar, her Sire, had offered her into the care of Guardian Sinuhé and yet the Council still refuted her credibility! She might just be a girl but she'd also almost had enough!*

Across the chamber, Mehand'Arun spoke up, though in kinder tones it seemed, "If you wish to be believed then you must compel the stuffy old fools with more than words, girl! I am surprised that your good tutor has not already told you this himself."

Mehand'Arun shot Sinuhé a levelling stare and Nefer stifled a sniffle and straightened up next to the tall man beside her. Glancing up to gauge his reaction to Mehand'Arun's advice, she found that he was simply looking at his fellow Guardian with a certain savvy gleam in his deep-blue eyes, and Nefer followed suit then, meeting Mehand'Arun's dark star pupils with the silver of her own. It sent a surprising ripple through her, as for the first time a certain kind of understanding seemed to echo between her and the pale Guardian. *She couldn't be sure, but she sensed she'd surprised him.*

Whatever the reason, she saw him narrow his gem-stone eyes – *not in malice, but in sudden contemplation it seemed, as if he'd spied something different, or new even* – then Mehand'Arun folded his arms across his chest and shook his head minutely. It seemed to dispose of the flicker of tepid warmth that had nearly reached his eyes to become something 'more'. *It was not much and yet...*

Gaze on her, he said, "It is unsurprising that you remain unsuccessful... *Nefer...* because the simple truth of it remains that they do not yet wish to believe you. Guardian Sinuhé's patronage ought to tell them otherwise, but they are scared: scared that we might uncover some unholy mistake; scared of what you might do or foresee, irrespective of the Tapestry Weave. Princess, they are scared of what this might mean for them, and for the future, and so they bury their sage minds in the sands.

"And so we are stuck here-" Mehand'Arun inclined his head towards her and Sinuhé with a slight musical clink of the dragon silver in his hair, -"him, you, I... all of us... stuck! However, the main question is: what will you two do about it? *What?* Guardian Speaker, if you want her to 'See' – *then by the Black Hex of Conarhven* – let her look where we need! Otherwise, let me-"

"Guardian Rhindarhlar Mehand'Arun..." Her mentor's voice held an edge of warning she'd never heard, "We both know it's too soon. The girl is not yet of age-"

Mehand'Arun threw his head back with a disgusted snort, reminding her of a spirited Eikyr as he interrupted, "Guardian, I grow weary in this room: with the dust of all ages surrounding me and the words of all that went before weighing down on me like a cloak of iron! I would rather be with my own kind - *as the Maker intended!* - not languish here with the cowards of our strayed people's descendants!

"Guardian Speaker, sooner rather than later, I would wish to go guard the realm and Boundary of the Elvern I am sworn to look after, but the Maker knows I cannot-"

"The First Guardian was right," Sinuhé interrupted, returning the other man's slight with a hint of sadness as he left her side and took a step forward. "He told me you would begrudge this task but that he made you go anyway because of your near-disregard for the peace within the Circle! I wonder how I could so easily have forgotten just how you've always felt about these 'strays' as you name them!"

Sinuhé shook his head as if to clear it of some cloaking disappointment. "Well, it matters not, but let me remind you, Guardian, that these so-called 'strays' are *my people* as well as they were once yours; let me remind you also, *Guardian,* that you swore an Oath and traded your name with Alérathnar in exchange for more than just the pleasure of protecting the Elvern of Heirah-Noor!"

Sinuhé paused to draw breath. The other Guardian was nodding dismissively and made as if to speak but Sinuhé was not yet done and overruled the attempt. "As a Guardian, you will care for and protect all the peoples of the Nine Realms equally! To do anything less, is against the Laws of Existence and this is regardless of whether you're present here due to Guardian Denarlin's order or not!"

Nefer saw Mehand'Arun's eyes flare, then turn flinty. "Guardian Sinuhé! You had better recognize that I am here *precisely* because I am following my Oath to Alérathnar to the word – not because Malandaar'Vahran Cor'Esardan told me that I had to, and I-"

"Guardian Denarlin, if you please," her tutor corrected, the interruption bearing a hint of his impatience now, "and I know why you are here, Guardian; no need to reiterate. Surely you must know that had the First Guardian not demanded your presence, I would have asked it regardless – after all, you do have a unique way of peeling back the layers and pursuing that which you need until you have it uncovered and cornered and we need that skill. No one is better than you."

It was flattery, Nefer'Kemnebit was sure, but Mehand'Arun looked anything but pleased. Somehow he hadn't liked what the other Guardian had said but she did not understand why. *So many new things...*

Sinuhé reached out and palmed a random collection of pages, then lifted his eyes back to Mehand'Arun. "It has been around a week, Guardian. A mere week! I did not expect us to find anything concrete so soon anyway and you are not alone in this,-" The tall older man waved his selection of pages in the air as if to remind his fellow Guardian of the fact he'd picked them up, "-oh, and if you think me negligent enough not to already have supplemented my work with Nefer'Kemnebit's aid then you are sorely out of touch. However, I will not subject her to the level or depths you'd have her perform at and that is that. The Council will believe her... it is only a question of choosing the right time."

Guardian Sinuhé looked at Nefer with a kind smile on his dark face and she came as he motioned, following him like a shadow as he gathered his layers of robes with an elegant swirl of fabric and started towards the door that connected with two additional but identical chambers, both laid out similarly with a seemingly random array of documents.

Behind her, she heard Mehand'Arun expel hissing sigh...

No, he did not like her - but maybe it was not just her, maybe it was her people? He certainly had not spoken in fond terms when he'd called them 'cowards' and 'strays'. She didn't understand his aversion but worried it must have something to do with the way her ancestors split from the Heirah-Noor. One day she'd have to ask her tutor; one day...

Nefer chanced a look over her shoulder as she passed an arriving acolyte - a Human boy - with his arms full, the pile of scrolls so tall he could barely look over the top of it, and she ignored the fact that he neglected to recognize her status. Her Mama would have scolded the boy – and then her - but the boy was barely older than herself and faltering under his heavy load besides, enough for her to feel sorry.

In place of the boy though, Mehand'Arun stole her interest again and as the acolyte wobbled past her, she saw the fair-skinned Elvern rub a hand across his face before turning back to the table to steady both palms firmly against its surface in a near perfect imitation of his earlier pose.

"Take back eleven, twelve and thirteen..." she heard him address the acolyte in an absent-minded tone, and as the boy hurriedly unloaded his wobbling load of manuscripts onto one corner of the table, Nefer'Kemnebit turned away. She did not like this Mehand'Arun either, she decided, and yet she could not help but to wish there'd be something she could do for him to think less harshly about her Sire's People. The Sabén-Heshep – whether Elvern or Human - were not bad. Just because they'd once chosen a divergent way of life to that of the Heirah-Noor, did not mean that they had somehow become something less. *On the contrary!* And besides, in that earlier moment of silent accord, she was sure the two of them had shared an understanding of something *more;* of something *important;* and there'd been something very appealing about that.

"Sheriti? Are you attending?"

Her tutor's voice made her blink and she realised she'd lacked behind, for he was already in the third chamber and she hastened to follow.

"Do not mind the man too much," he told her with an easy voice as she entered the room and saw him already busy perusing the stack of pages he'd brought. They were much like the stacks and stacks of other paper mounts that decked out the enormous table already and Nefer silenced a sigh of her own, secretly feeling just a sliver of kinship with Mehand'Arun as she eyed the columns. In a moment, Sinu would ask her to move around the various piles and touch them to see if she 'got a feeling' or 'an urge' flowing forth out of any of them - just like he had done for the last seven days now. It was not boring work as such: she felt a great many things when they did this exercise and for every stack she delved into, be it but a blink or an entire hour, she increased her already decent knowledge of the *Glorious Lands* as well as what she knew of the History that surrounded her Sire's people – but...

Well, if it wasn't a bad way to spend the day, it was still tedious. If only she could... could change something!

Nefer ran a slender hand across her naked, un-painted skull, secretly delighted that she was able to do so without incurring Ti-A'nakit-Suh's wrath. The tiny stubbles of hair that were slowly appearing now that her Mama's sorceress no longer administered a daily shaving, seemed to prickle and tickle and she wondered what it might be like to possess long hair like that pretty lady in her vision. *It might be nice... but also warm; Sinuhé had told her how he'd felt tempted to rid himself of his own white halo of hair but Nefer hoped he'd keep it. She liked hair.*

"Are you hungry?" Her Esteemed Tutor cut in, forcing her to forget about long or short hair, "I am sorry, we Guardians don't much think about the smaller things – the Maker's magic is enough – but if I neglect your care, you must speak up. I am still not familiar with the quantities nor qualities of food or drink that someone your size might need to ingest in order to thrive. I..."

Sinuhé shrugged apologetically. "I fear I am at a slight loss, my dear."

Nefer smiled as his honesty. "Thank you, but I am not yet hungry, Sinu my Esteemed Tutor, but... well, I think perhaps my cat is. She is crewing a hole through that pocket in my kilt as we speak and maybe...?"

Nefer veered off, to produce her small panther with relatively little trouble this time, and – quite as if it understood her intent - the tiny animal growled appreciatively at her and began to purr and rub against her fingers.

As she'd become accustomed, Sinuhé smiled at the sight. "Ah but of course! I keep forgetting about her... she is still so small... but yes: breakfast is in order. Porridge, fruit, chicken and ham?"

In spite her declining breakfast two blinks ago, Nefer still nodded eagerly.

Rubbing the small cat along its spine with the end of her pinkie, she felt her stomach roar just as Sinuhé closed his eyes for a heartbeat, now calling magic into Will and forming the Persuasion of choice.

She almost didn't notice the wonder of magic today though. Her small pet was such an attention seeker and would eagerly flop onto its side in sheer bliss whenever she groomed its tiny belly, which in turn delighted her every time.

For a beautiful wonder, she'd still not quite gotten over this amazing present, and if for nothing else than the fact that Sinu had been so kind, she wished to repay him. If this in turn meant working as tirelessly as he and Mehand'Arun in attempting to uncover these supposed mysteries within the documented history, then so be it! She did not know exactly what he was looking for: she'd enquired of course, but he'd told her nothing specific; supposedly *so that her mind would not be pre-empted into looking for only one thing'* but he'd warned her to give word immediately if she got the sense of 'wrongness', or of danger, or of disaster.

Nefer was not unlearned. She knew there'd been wars, despicable deeds and horrid disasters. Sinu clearly did not want her exposed to that kind of things if it might be avoided – and thank the Maker!

The blood and the dead she'd seen in her other vision had clearly been enough, *he'd told her with a serious light in those normally sage, kind eyes* - and she agreed. She'd kept it to herself, but that series of visions still horrified her and she wasn't about to disobey! His concern was pleasing to her: she was the student after all, but it was nice that he cared about *her* and not just her *Ability* and she wondered if this was what made him so different from Mehand'Arun?

By the sounds of it, she figured that the latter might not have thought to spare *her those impressions at all – but still... in her secret heart-of–hearts... maybe she* *might just have been alright with that. Maybe...*

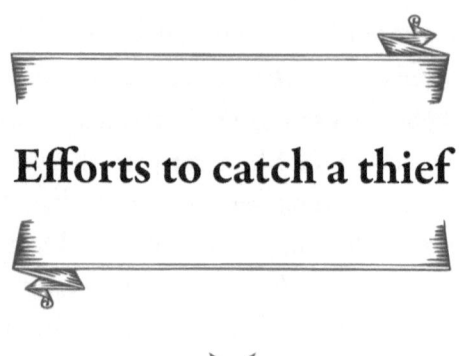

Efforts to catch a thief

IAMBRE WAS SOON SWEATING. *Actually sweating!* The wind was still cool, but for the final hundred yards or so, the incline had become a small mountain. Together with the last few hours, her somewhat bruised mental state and a bone-melting urge to sit down, the extended amount of exertion was dragging at her reserves like skeletal fingers clawing for the imaginary hem of her last stamina. It weighed down her feet. She felt heavier than a horse.

It was an analogy that made her grit her teeth in anger.

Okay, fine... so this was the sum of too much time spent in her ruddy coach these last months; the sum of too much wine and honeyed tea and cakes! And who'd have thought her ever about to admit such a thing, but she was badly out of breath, and thus, by default, out of shape. *Why had she not ridden her horse more often? Why had she not made herself walk the perimeter of all those campsites they'd struck up?* She had done so in the beginning but the 'attraction' had worn off these last three months! *Why had she not...?*

Of course, she knew perfectly well why she'd not done any of those usual things. The 'culprits' were Bilandro and Solancei. To ride would have meant listening to Lancei's lectures on duties and the pointless aspirations of people 'in love', and the idea of Lancei's escalating frustrations about Iambre's 'interests' in Captain Metavo had not seemed one bit enticing. *Gods, but whenever their conversations had started on an innocent topic, they'd soon taken a turn regardless!* In fact, it had sometimes felt as if the two of them had had this damned curse rammed down over them, where life had made it increasingly impossible for them to prevent the subject from cropping up. *And then? More arguments!*

She winched. *Well that had been the horse-back rides 'ticked off' as a non-viable pass time, hadn't it?!*

Iambre felt her spirit droop just thinking back on it, but her having continued taking even a general interest in the camp and the running of her retinue, would've meant spending time with Metavo – the man in charge, whom she'd also foolishly banned from sight in a fit of sheer spite. *It had left her in the carriage with Palea and said handmaiden's love for Deb'Aran sweets that she'd happily foisted on both Iambre and Ina. Was it any wonder if her waistline had suffered!*

It was a cause for regret – and not just for her sorry lack of condition or the softening swell of her hips. *When she had Lancei back, she'd listen! And she'd honour her word to Bilan: she'd hand him his discharge. On her life, she would!*

Something brushed against her skirts, bringing her internal rambling to a halt. Through fast movement to her right, she got the half-cut impression of scruffy, frayed sack-cloth, modified somehow into something that looked a tunic with too-short sleeves and 'matching' loose breeches. On closer inspection, the unlikely ensemble was worn by a skinny urchin of indeterminable age and gender.

It only mildly surprised. But, what did bring pause was the sight of the child who now just stood there... looking at her...

It was the same kid as before. That sort of surprised too!

Iambre actually couldn't have said when exactly she'd first become aware of the kid, but it couldn't have been long after the carriage incident - when for a handful of paces, it had looked to be deliberately following her whilst stuffing its face with something small and black from a crinkly bag that Iambre had really hoped wasn't full of dried insects. Then she'd lost sight of the kid and she'd hoped the poor mite gone home or something, but evidently it had not, and since it was really not appropriate for a child to be out at this time of night, she felt a streak of worry. *To imagine a kid here... cold and alone... without anyone...*

The true age of the small unfortunate creature eluded, but this was the first time she'd caught a good look and she made the incidental estimate of nine or ten, though there could be no arguing that the kid's direct gaze possessed something somewhat older within the black, knowing depths.

It felt not the eyes of a child as they focussed on her face, bringing to mind an image of *'need'*, and she didn't like it. *To allow a child to be wandering the streets alone at any time...?* Well, there ought to be a law against it! Whoever the parents, they were guilty of neglect as far as she was concerned – and that too struck a chord, but her efforts to spot someone willing to take charge of the urchin had failed before and it did so again.

As she glanced around, the child seemed to belong to no one or nowhere – but whilst it seemed a crime of sorts, she could also not make herself be distracted by the imagined scenario of a kid without parents! *Tonight had been horrendous enough already and it would not get easier if she let this touch her. So she wouldn't, but-*

Iambre started to speak, but the child darted from sight behind the growing throng of people. *Gone.*

Unable to help it, she stretched to catch a glimpse of the sack-cloth, and half-managed, but the short, narrow shape was away again, streaking in and around a small group of people to her left, thus obscuring her opportunity, only to re-appear from behind another set of pedestrians and cross directly in front of her path. Here the child fell into a comical sort of long gait behind a seemingly random man who did not appear to note the mockery and Iambre felt her mouth twitch.

The shape looked briefly over one tiny shoulder then, plastering a pair of wide eyes on her face - again tucking at her heart. *Those were jet-black eyes indeed: compellingly wide and slightly upturned at the corners, winter-born for sure, and though perhaps a little too large for the face, the child would undoubtedly age to grow into them, as they seemed a good match with what was still visible of the child's harshly cut jet-black hair.* As before she could not determine the gender – the night and that raggedly shorn hair saw to that – but the child was as skinny as a stray dog, and just as alone...

Gods but she could not allow herself to get drawn in! Not emotionally and not physically! She could not.

And still her gaze followed the child - observing every small gesture, every strange capering stride and wide-eyed look, allowed her. The narrow face was dirty – grimy smutches covering the slender bone structure, layering colour and complexity in such a way that Iambre felt certain that the poor thing had not seen water or soap for weeks, but... *but this was not her problem; she could not make it her problem!*

She hardened herself, deliberately looking to her feet. When she looked back up the child was sashaying fluidly back towards her...

An uncomfortable feeling washed over her.

The solemn look in those eyes was at odds with the child's seemingly playful strides. Bizarrely, she got the idea that it somehow wanted her to do something, but it seemed a ridiculous notion. *Walk. Just keep walking. Her intentions were clear, except...*

Emotions welling, Iambre shuddered and looked away, her deliberate pace dismissive and fast, her eyes focussing straight ahead. When after a handful of paces, she looked through the corner of her eye, the child had disappeared. It was shameful, but she was relieved. *Too relieved!*

She drew a careful breath and put extra vigour into her strides. *She was not unkind but-*

Something bumped into her, not hard enough to stagger her, but firmly enough nonetheless to make her look up in nuisance.

Not ten paces in front stood the child. Facing her boldly; unconcerned. Holding in both scruffy hands, a red parcel.

Her red parcel!

Unable to control herself, she did a double take, halting her advance mid-stride. The unexpected development quenched most of the affront she should have felt at discovering the small creature in sudden possession of her purchase. Quite naturally, her first instinct was even to disbelieve: she'd tied the parcel to a belt loop under her cloak after the twine had eventually cut into her fingers uncomfortably hard. *The parcel should still be there...*

She already knew it wasn't. A quick fumble was all it took for her to assure that it was decidedly not!

Iambre raised her brows at the child, unsure of her feelings. *She carried some coins inside the ripped lining of her right boot; if the kid wanted food, maybe-*

The child took a step backwards and shook her head - *uh... or should that perhaps be 'his' head? For a blink, she'd felt positive it was a girl after all, but it was truly hard to tell the gender!*

Nevertheless Iambre followed, now puzzled and abandoning her attempt to reach for her boot-shaft. Again the kid retreated to match. *Really!?*

She ignored a subsequent small stab of annoyance, drew a deep breath and let it whistle past her lips. She just about resisted the urge to leap forward in order to somehow catch the small thief by the scruff of its scrawny neck; it was tempting to try but something told her she'd never be fast enough, so she refrained. *But dear Gods! Why did everything seem to be testing her this evening? This kind of stuff never happened to her! Never! And yet, tonight...*

Well, tonight, nothing had been remotely easy or even slightly straightforward. Nothing!

Whatever the gender, the kid certainly knew how to vex a person, and thinking the situation ridiculous, Iambre pursed her lips and held out her hand.

"You should not take things that do not belong to you," she lectured, totting with disapproval.

What the parcel contained was not all that valuable, nor was it even all that important, and she toyed with leaving - however, the fact remained that children should not grow up thinking that stealing was alright! Parents or no, they should not! She was the adult here; she was going to get her purchase back, and atop of that, there was also a part of her – *just a small part mind, but a part all the same* – that most assuredly wanted to scare the kid into never doing such a thing again!

Iambre wasn't fooled about her chances of success here either, however. The same instinct that had tipped her off to the idea that she'd never be fast enough to snatch her parcel back, now also warned her not to be too hard, or else she might never see the kid for dust. *Different tactics then...*

"You can give that back and I will not be mad," she promised the child, loud enough to be heard over the whistling wind, a rumbling ox-cart loaded with barrels of what appeared to be ale, and the mournful tune streaming off a trio of fiddlers riding forth from a nearby establishment with green-lacquered window frames. *No reaction...*

"I might even be persuaded to offer you a few coins for the trade?" she tempted in a voice of lilting sweetness, adding, "Provided mind, you go straight home now and find your bed. So... how about it then? Can we trade?"

In response to her offer, the child shifted uncomfortably. The black eyes looked around. No one really seemed to pay them any notice, yet Iambre read *reluctance* all over the kid, right from the way those two hands of scruffy skin and black-rimmed nails cradled her box, to how the kid held itself, to the expression she spied beneath the layers of grime as it continued to look at her. *But what more could she do?*

The youngster suddenly pointed straight at her and made a beckoning motion with the opposite hand and Iambre stared, pulling a questioning face of disbelief. In response the child retreated another step, never taking those dark, dark eyes from hers.

"What are you-" Iambre caught the rest of her protest between her teeth as the urchin suddenly smiled at her: a wide, very good and very cheeky smile of white, even teeth that seemed to light up everything surrounding them.

For a wonder, this she hadn't expected! There was something slightly off about that smile, however – not in the sincerity of it, or anything like that – Iambre just couldn't seem to put her finger on it, yet no matter what, there was certainly also something very winning about that urchin, dirt and all.

The cheek of it made her want to stamp her foot in frustration, though instead, she couldn't help but smile back.

"This is all very nice, but-" Iambre began to scold, but got no further. With a twirl of cloth, the child turned and fled - dirty, naked feet flashing almost as dark as the old sack of burdock as it ran – and Iambre's emotions bunched with vexation. "Why you pesky, little... "

She did not know what possessed her to give pursuit. After all, the herbs in that parcel were *really* easily replaceable – *well, after a fashion, sort of* – and the theft of the red box certainly did not merit her chasing a dirty, half-naked kid through Zanzier Town, but...

Iambre hitched up her skirts. And ran.

Indignant disbelief coursed through her even as the urchin caught her eye with a rapid glance over one shoulder as if to lure her on. *Death and daffodils! Kids should not steal! It really would not do!*

Dodging around a slow-moving cart with an assortment of odd-looking cuts of meat, Iambre hopped to avoid the sunken strip of gutter and felt a little light-headed with relief that she did not plant a foot in another dubious-smelling mire; the kid was faster than a rat, scurrying here and there, in and out of view, but at no point did she truly really lose sight, since a bit of grime-covered skin, or one part or another of the sack-cloth outfit, kept flashing into view as though by design. *Which was good... because she intended to catch that little piece of vermin!*

Sensations swirled. Beneath the surface of determination, Iambre felt a bubble of laughter begin to worm its way to the fore and she had to suppress the urge to giggle. *By Gods and virtue, if her mother could only see her now. If only Solancei could...*

The kid measured the distance between them over one shoulder, and as though the charming pestilence knew exactly what she was thinking, it sent her another one of those brilliant smiles, only to intensify the pace. *Mercy...*

And so they went: at rapid speed in and out between people and whatnot, Iambre gasping for breath, yet determined to keep up with the fast *'thing'!* It seemed an illogical choice - *she was pointedly aware of that* - and at one time, as her pursuit led her over one of the large crossroad sections, diagonally dodging various vehicles and pedestrians, Iambre even managed to question her own decision to carry on.

It was ludicrous behaviour and she knew it! However, the clear-sighted reluctance did not last. She wanted to catch that kid – and that even if she was vaguely aware how she was no longer climbing straight towards the castle but rather seemed to be going along a semi-perpendicular route to Roshar's Run.

Just like she'd felt it with the Insandar, something seemed to draw her on. The way was open, the roads widening, and hence not as much of a problem to navigate as those that traversed Old Zanzier. She'd easily be able to back-track her steps - *once she'd caught the urchin that was!* Which, hate it as she might, certainly seemed a problem. The path she'd been forced on was levelling out, which could only mean that the chase had led her to a section of Zanzier where the topography was becoming less steep in favour of the gentle plateau that ultimately pointed towards the training grounds beyond town.

On a South-Western circuit then! A quick calculation in her mind, and Iambre knew that if this carried on much longer she'd be circling the entire hill upon which the main Keep was built - except she'd hit the garrison compound before that could happen. *Which would not be good!* The chances, however, that she'd make it that far, were not good either! Her lungs were burning. She was winded. *Too winded! This was really not the proper conduct for anyone of noble heritage! Death and daffodils! Why was that not obvious before? Why had she run this far? Again?*

Iambre slowed her run to a slow jog, then halted completely. Her breath was so laboured that for a moment she had no choice but to rest her hands on her knees and hang her head as she strove to recover enough to stop the fire in her chest and throat. *She'd run after that kid without minding danger or time. It was stupidly done, not like her at all! Not like her...*

Iambre looked up, but could not see the charming pestilence.

Her head sank down again and she heaved some more. *By now, surely the child would be long gone and for what?* Iambre sucked in a full breath, feeling her chest expand, finally with a little less urgency. Almost, she was too hung to care.

Huzzah... she'd expended herself. What utter lunacy! Gods but this evening had been nothing but one crazed disaster! And, she'd rarely run so much in her entire life – a few soft games of Falcon Rounder's back at Servangar, but... but never like this! *And never again! Never...*

Iambre looked up, relinquishing her pride in favour of steadying herself against a wall whilst taking stock. She was right on the corner of another cross-roads – and closer to the river again, if the somewhat stale smell of brine and tar was anything to go by, but at least that was a positive thing. At least she'd not ended back in the rat-tack labyrinth of lower Zanzier again and that was something. *She supposed.*

She drew another freeing breath. She was recovering quickly now, which was another good thing – but midnight raffle, if she hadn't come to her senses that kid might have run them right out of town!

Her eyes wandered. Stout, affluent-looking buildings butted up to the crossroad: three to four-stories tall, Zanzierian; pale and uniform in their de-sign, yet somehow also as individual as the dresses in her wardrobe trunk. And they were solid too, she noted - in a way that screamed 'this way lies money' - still, there was no town watch in sight here either, but maybe it was not needed. *Within streets like these, crime would not go unpunished, the affluent would not allow it. They never did.*

Calves cramping, she stooped to rub her sore legs. The houses and build-ings with their cool-washed, dark timber-framed walls and expensively tiled roofs – pale and thereby probably Kretorian-hewn - were of pristinely clean ap-pearances in comparison to everything she'd seen thus far. The more she got her bearings, the more she imagined this the quadrant where visiting nobles, dig-nitaries and tradesmen would do business – *it was an area too decent to merit anything less and in a town that seemed otherwise full of rot, it was a part the well-to-do would wish to keep intact!*

Iambre frowned, not quite sure about her own feelings on the matter. As illustrated before her very eyes, the gap between rich and poor was too steep. Why did Zulavi not distribute the Crown's money with more attention to detail? It made no sense. Clearly, there were several reputable inns to choose from here: enough to generate a certain kind of income, but where did the taxes go?

Thoughts hurting her head, she let go, acknowledging instead the sensation of relief that seemed to flow forth within her.

This was actually a good neighbourhood, and mercy: there was not as single Charmstress nor boardwalk in sight! The long even slabs of paving looked as solid and as uniformly correct as the white-washed neatness of the buildings they surrounded – *and Gods...* after everything she'd seen earlier – all the poverty and mud – no matter what her feelings, it was almost an unexpected surprise to find herself back inside a semblance of civilized normality.

Well, it was no wonder they'd given her south-facing accommodation back at the Keep. In truth, now that she looked at it, the area even felt slightly familiar: like she'd seen-

Out of nowhere an unexpected pang of understanding whipped through her. This was the district she'd come through upon their much-belated arrival into Zanzier; it had to be. *Midnight raffle! And what a botched-up experience that had been too!*

For a few blinks, Iambre felt black inside. *Word of her nearing the town had not been received in advance, nor had it travelled ahead as one might almost certainly have expected. Instead of a suitable welcoming party, her retinue had been greeted by the surprised, semi-disbelieving guards at the South Gate.* And that had just been the beginning...

A runner had eventually been sent to the Keep but by the time they'd begun to make their way into town, word had spread and the throngs had begun to gather, lining the streets thick with people from all walks of life.

The effect had been disorganised chaos, the sheer numbers soon forcing her procession into a slow near-crawl as the locals clamoured to catch a glimpse of her - and though Iambre willingly admitted that Zanzier Town was not big by some standards, it could also not be ignored that many people lived here: crammed in between the tall walls of the Snake and the grey depths of River Mesatitan.

Indeed, as she recalled with aching precision, on the night, the press of the curious had seemed to number in the thousands; she hadn't felt threatened per se, but all the same, it was an experience she'd rather not care to see repeated. Happily, however, she'd managed to swallow her own claustrophobic idiocy to be within touching distance of so many bodies after that lengthy stint of 'open' lands – but only because Solancei had ridden on one side or her carriage, and Bilan on the other, irrespective of her orders to stay himself away from her sight.

But no, it hadn't been pleasant. Solancei had somehow pushed South-Point so close to the side of the carriage that the horse's black-dabbled flanks had nudged the door on occasion, and though her friend's face had been veiled, Iambre recognized she'd been worried. Lieutenant del'Draventar flanking Lancei on his borrowed black Rayon, one high stepping pace behind, made even more sense now, but with 1st Horse Guard Benedron riding similarly to Bilan's right, and Sir Mortrat forming the stunted arrowhead of their procession, it had all seemed a strange blur. Still - with plenty of her own soldiers forming up front and back, Ina had soon suggested that they must all be safe enough for the Princes to pull down curtains and slide back the window-glass to make herself be seen.

So she had done. And it had been a popular choice with the crowds, if not with Solancei, but anyway...

No one would ever have been able to ram themselves between her Shield and the carriage door, and if they'd tried...

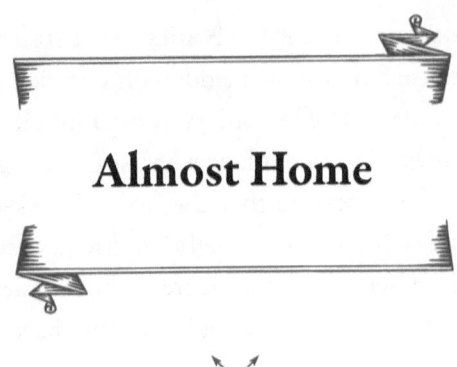

Almost Home

✕

IAMBRE SMILED THINLY to herself. *In verity, she couldn't have said what Lancei might have done if an eager spectator had somehow managed to push past the outer flank of guards, but maybe it was best not to speculate.* There'd been a vibration in the air – now lacking – for which she was grateful, but her mind recalled the slow progress with a sense of nervous flashback: an echo of her actual feelings on the eve itself. And she recalled Palea chewing sweets with too much gusto for comfort. She recalled Ina's obvious enjoyment of the buzz as she preened like a queen on the Princess' behalf, whilst Iambre herself had been rendered semi-blind by the endless flickering glare of torches and multiple flashing lanterns scattered amongst the spectators - ever in movement - as the undulating ranks of people clamoured to keep up like the massive roll of a shifting landmass.

With the nervous snort of horses, the then-almost-invasive-now-almost-familiar-stench of river brine, the ruckus calls, and shouts of good-will for her benefit, her belly also remembered the feeling of being utterly reliant upon others protecting her.

It hadn't been a comfortable sensation then. It wasn't one now.

By the time they'd finally been able to rendezvous with the mounted Zanzierian escort sent to greet her, a good hour had passed and they'd eventually trudged through the castle gate to face a less than welcoming Zulavi.

Clearly, the man had not been impressed; but then again: when was he ever?

She was aware that they'd served him poor notice, of course; that the Red Wing she'd sent had somehow never arrived; it was unfortunate! Zulavi had received word of their surprise arrival too late to serve up the traditional fanfare and pomp that usually heralded her presence in a new place and with the Zanzierians being such sticklers for tradition, it took no bright head to imagine how the Knights Commander's senses must still sting with the idea of this gross slight.

Still... there was no need for such pig eared stubbornness. Sir Mortrat, a most excellent diplomat, had accounted for their situation, of course; had offered very humble and thereby suitable apologies for the entire mishap; gifts of peace had been extended as were proper; the statements of apology had been made public, along with several singing praises for the Commander's quick and graceful dealings with the difficult circumstances surrounding her arrival...

What else could he possibly want?

Iambre caught herself before a curse on the man could escape her. *Zulavi was still 'off'; she couldn't pinpoint the exact thing, but she felt it. Indeed, fears about Lancei, and Bilan's assurances aside, it seemed to her there must be something else at play, but what?*

Gods, how could they have known that Red Wing had not arrived? In fact, if she chose to turn this on its head, might she not also feel entitled to offence over the lack of official welcome she'd received at the man's very town gate?

As it were she did not. Not even when they'd been stopped like a common merchant train and asked to await customs! Sir Mortrat had been a picture of frustration, and Bilan awash with cold anger, and only when the Captain had shoved the badge of his station in the commanding sergeant's face, and only after he had pointed out the royal crest upon her carriage, did the fool realise his mistake.

Iambre shivered. Her retinue had trudged through Zanzier on that day, travel-worn and weary because of her cruel determination to show Bilan his place – yet he'd still doggedly protected; championed her. Mercy, but even had she not been in love with the man, it was a humbling testament to his loyalty, and she prayed he'd managed to escape their attackers unscathed. *Prayed. Prayed. Prayed.*

Iambre shivered again and watched a stage carriage rumble past at a stately pace similar to her own when she travelled. It was a long vehicle - laden with luggage and pulled by a team of six, controlled from the front bench by two men in neat caps and dark coats. The clop-clop of shod hooves sounded unnaturally loud in the night and she could barely relate to the fact that her own ride-through had been slowed to a near-standstill. *Perhaps if the Knights Com-mander had had time to prepare, this would not have been the case? Perhaps he felt embarrassed that he had not provided better for the realm's future Queen? Per-haps...*

Iambre knew something deeper surrounded the man's behaviour but made a mental note to herself all the same, maybe to send two Red Wings next time? *There was a lot to be said for order, and that man-*

For a few heartbeats she stared idly at the single lantern lit outside the man-sion directly across from her. The three-story building was impressive. Shame that such wealth existed in a place where some children ran the streets without shoes at night, and an entire old town lay draped in destitution and filth. It was something she felt a need to address. Maybe once she'd arrived in Tuxama, where indeed she'd have oodles of time spare to get matters moving, to issue or-ders, and draw up proposals. Zulavi would simply have to co-operate, whether he saw the need or not, and-

Zulavi! Again!

Feeling angry with herself, Iambre looked up and down the street slightly exasperated. *Gods... Zulavi was the least of her problems! Why had she run like a lunatic to keep up with that child? She was parched. And tired.*

She looked toward the imposing inn that curved around the corner across from her position, stretching down the entire block. It made her wish for a mo-ment that she could just be 'normal' enough to walk in there and ask for wine. The white-washed walls were easily five stories tall and as straight and stout as any castle wall.

She might be daft, but it looked like the kind of establishment that had good wine, she mused.

Her chest rose and fell. *The Parthenon forgive her, but she could do with the fortification right about now, but it would not do either, though one could dream...*

Of an entirely different calibre than the other inns with their plain slate signs and modest size, this building was parading its superiority and age like a proud matron promenading in all her finery on a simple market day, but it did not seem grotesque; not in size, nor in presence. The lanterns on the outside were as welcoming and inviting as the soft light emitted through most of the pointed, mullioned windows, whilst the dark-stained timber-frame sparked no-tions of glory long-past as the eye wandered to the steep, but well-maintained, roof line of glazed pale tiles and decorative chimney-stacks. The latter arose like a veritable forest of two-tone brick and twisting spirals, leaking white streamers of smoke that spun like children's fascinators, all very much complimented by the single hexagonal tower seen jutting from the roof on the far-distant side.

The tower was in itself an interesting feature: an unapologetic ode to archaic architecture, adding both a certain level of character as well as charm to the overall building below – something which was helped by the tower's own steeply pointed roof and the addition of an obscure scrap-metal weathervane jutting straight up into the sky from at the very apex.

Contemplating the inn, of course, the tower seemed an odd addition, but then again: she had to recall that this was Zanzier. They could be terribly backwards, and the tower did look like an old structure from which the surrounding walls had sprung up – and the Zanzierians would never willing ruin any link to their illustrious past if they could help it - that much she knew: sticklers for protocol and nearly-forgotten history that they were! No such destruction would simply never sit right with them, and though she could not verify it in the dark, part of her suspected the tower-construct must pre-date the Chaos Wars!

Iambre let her gaze flow from the tower back down the main building just as a sedate rumble of hooves and metal-rimmed wheels tucked at her attention. It was another six-team coach, heading for the inn and slowing to a veritable crawl as it got closer, swinging wide in order to navigate the lengthy vehicle through the relatively narrow mouth of the arch that would commonly lead to an inner courtyard where travellers could disembark and retreat to the comforts within. It was getting late so they might even stay the night while the horses got watered and stabled, and for a moment she knew wistful regret that her party had never been fortunate enough to come upon one such behemoth during her tour of Ostravah. This inn here looked as though it could've easily swallowed the better half of her retinue and what she'd not sometimes give for a good bed and a chamber with a door rather than a pallet and a semi-draughty pavilion!

Still, she supposed that for now she should be pleased that she at least had a decent bed in the Keep above. Sure, it might be under Zulavi's roof, but – garish tapestries or not - at least it was comfortable.

As if on cue, a yawn escaped her. Vaguely she hoped the urchin would have a bed to climb into also. In spite of the thieving little beetle, she was still strangely horrified to think about the fact it had worn no shoes. *They were in the depths of autumn now, and-*

Iambre shook herself, strangling another pitiful yawn. She could not 'save' the realm. No matter what, there'd always be people with 'less'. The best thing she could do was to try and make things better. And thinking of which... though her muscles hurt and her chin ached, she could not really dawdle. Somehow she had to find a little more strength to force on. *She could not be far now and thinking of her bed...*

She yawned, and turned, and-

For a blink she could've sworn her eyes widened enough to bulge like a toad's...

There, on the ground, not two feet removed, the colour strangely garish even in the dark, sat her red parcel!

A tiny sound, barely audible, made her swing round. Head spinning, she felt her eyes widen again.

The kid was back! But there were no other people now. Only the two of them – no one to hide behind; no one to make a mockery of. Only the two of them... and the parcel.

Clearly awaiting her reaction, the child beheld her with a curiously guileless expression that to Iambre seemed to mask something deeper - yet on the surface and to the casual onlooker, the kid might seem tarnished only by the offensive dirt that seemed to cling to the pale skin like soot to a chimney sweep.

Iambre's eyes swept low. She couldn't help it.

No shoes. The small urchin stood before her, definitely minus shoes.

She returned her gaze to the narrow face, startled to find the child's irises suddenly impossibly huge. A trick of the light, it was nevertheless disconcerting to see only a nails worth of white within the near-black, appealing eyes, and for a heartbeat Iambre felt goose prickles travel down her back. The wide mouth and high cheekbones made the child seem both handsome and alien, the large eyes speaking solemnly at her spirit, and for blink Iambre no longer felt the adult here. *It was a good trick.* She shook herself. *There was not three pace between them now...*

A whim ghosting through her, almost she drew a step forward to clasp the urchin by a fold of cloth, but stopped herself when the child made no move to run or otherwise evade.

With a slow breath, she controlled the urge to pounce, yet chanced a tenuous step towards the child, now carefully voiding the distance between the two of them - but he/she – *Iambre could still not tell if she was looking at a boy or a girl* – only tilted their head to accommodate, and for a fey blink, she could've sworn she was staring into the heart of something larger and older.

The sensation made her gasp, but the feeling was already gone. The urchin barely reached past her waist. From the sweeping structure of the jawline, she had the sudden urge to believe it was a boy, but...

Gods, what was the kid's game? Iambre frowned and hoped she looked suitably stern. She was not going to play along anymore now, and with a shake of the head, she retreated, relinquishing the steps she'd just gained.

At her move, however, the boy only tilted that dirty face towards her and nodded with a certain satisfaction before pointing with persistent stabs of one finger over his shoulder. *The wrist was thin: the bones markedly noticeable through the icy-pale unblemished skin. Gods, how much food would a kid like that get to eat in a day...?*

Ill-touched Iambre followed the direction with a bemused glance to cover her true feelings and shrugged. The road with the single-lantern mansion was not the way to go; nor was the road she was on. The vast inn still looked inviting – there'd be no denying that - but she didn't really comprehend the significance of the child's random gesture and... *enough was enough.*

"I am sorry." She shook her head. "Not this time, little one. I'm afraid I'm am finished playing now."

She made as if to withdraw another step but the child's loud sigh gave her pause. In return, the child looked at her with a glimmer of impatience in the depths of the night-black eyes, the solemn expression now faltering slightly under the sudden stubborn tilt of his chin as he jabbed one finger defiantly towards that same point again. Beneath the grime, the nail looked shiny as though buffed; it was a finger too perfect for a child. *Defined. Elegant.* But Iambre could not think of this right now and snorted with disbelief over the child's persistent meddle.

"Well you are a funny thing for sure, but I must be going now." Shaking her head, turning very deliberately, she made an attempt to retrieve her parcel – *well she'd chased the kid for it, no sense in simply leaving it now, was there?* – only to shy to a stop when the child slinked around her to stand between her and the red prize. *What...?*

With a frown of displeasure, Iambre watched the child make a very adult gesture to indicate her clear lack-wit stupidity, and her displeasure would have turned to anger then, but for the quick smile the child sent her on the same breath. It somehow allayed the affront before true offence set in. *Another excellent trick.*

As the kid watched her, those jet-black eyes appeared to grow luminous – surely aided by the moon as it exited the clouds – but...

Gods! She might be a sob but-

"Fine!" She relented. "Tell me what you want then."

The boy smiled winningly – if it was indeed a boy – then proceeded to make a number of simple but effective hand gestures as though to communicate numerous pieces of information all in one go, and Iambre knew sudden suspicions turned-to-fact within a blink then.

Consternation followed. *Gods be good! The child could not speak!*

Iambre gnawed at her lip with a frown of concentration, everything falling into place as the kid completed the series of signals with a rapid gesture to his lips, following a curt negative nod.

"Oh my!" Feeling unexpectedly stupid and embarrassed all the same time, Iambre smoothed clammy hands down her old rags, not sure what to do suddenly. Because she felt the need, she said, "Verily... I am sorry – I get it now. You are... You cannot talk, can you?"

The kid puffed out a breath of air as though to show her she'd been slow on the uptake but now appeared to be catching up, and gave her an affirmative nod. Iambre smiled, her feelings of affront now cooling under a small influx of sadness. *What a clever little mouse. The kid might very well be a cast-away: rejected by unscrupulous parents or indeed forced into thievery, as a means to make up for his disability.* It drenched her in sadness, yet it still did not explain any of this. *Had he tried to rob her and felt it wrong? Had she somehow managed to appeal to his sense of right and been 'heard'?*

Unsure what to do, Iambre looked around feeling a little lost but the kid once more put on a very serious mien, then stabbed a finger at her chest and then towards the street. *It was bewildering! There was definitely-*

The kid tugged at her sleeve. Urgently. Once. It might have been a mistake, but Iambre looked him in the eye. *She was maybe going to regret this, but... but how could she not ask!*

"What?" She relented. "You think I want to go down that intersection there?"

An eager nod and a tug on her cloak assured her that she'd interpreted the child correctly but Iambre backed up a little, instantly waving her hands to indicate how she disagreed. "No. No. Now listen: you're very sweet and everything, but really... I have to be elsewhere. The only reason I came this far is that you stole my parcel - which is wrong by the way – and I am in a good mind to give you a good earf-"

Iambre cut off and closed her mouth so fast that her teeth actually clicked again. *Sweet Belanzia'Cha, Goddess of Clarity! But of course...*

"Why, you stole my box so that I'd follow you, didn't you." It was a statement, not a question, and the child's dirt-smirched face took on a very adult aspect as the kid nodded just once, affirming.

Taken aback with this candid admission, Iambre experienced a stab of unease. She was missing something here. But what? Absent-mindedly, she rubbed the heel of her palm against the centre of her forehead. It was beginning to throb but she ignored it as she tried to make out what to do next. This was way past silly but apparently the urchin shared much the same opinion, for the kid gave her an impatient look and huffed.

Then repeating the series of gestures rapidly, the small creature ended the 'tirade' with a quick stab of one hard finger against her shoulder, this time actually touching as though to punctuate and bring home some point of value and Iambre winched aloud, shifting from further contact though it never came. *For a small thing, the kid was surprisingly strong but she managed to repress the urge to rub the spot.*

Gritting her teeth, she finally crouched in front of him, displaying as much of an apologetic frown as she could muster.

"Fine little one! Fine. Let's try this again," she encouraged with more patience than she truly felt, the invisible mark where the kid had finger-stabbed her shoulder still competing for attention.

The kid did not take note. Instead, nodding just once, he carefully made a sort of cupping motion with both hands before pointing to Iambre's head and back down the apparent 'route of choice'. *It could mean anything. Gods, anything!*

It seemed daft. It all seemed terribly daft, but Iambre tried to be inventive. "So...? A piece of bread...? You're...hungry? Or... no, no – wait I got it: you need money!"

'No!' Mouthing the word, the kid looked close to exasperation. Running a hand rapidly through the silky black tufts of hair, he shook a finger, cloaked with ingrained dirt, in denial.

"Right then... " Iambre hesitated, casting her mind about for something else. Then copying the signals for herself, she haltingly spoke the ideas that came into her mind. "So this is a what? A bowl? A hat? A... *a well?*"

Iambre paused, knowing without looking at the kid that her interpretations were ridiculous. *Seemed that Osari'Chi had decided to interfere with her thoughts and once the God of Confusion and Veils did that...*

The urchin reached up - and without further ado, simply pulled back the tight cowl from her head to spill out her hair.

"Hey!" Iambre exclaimed in surprise. "What are you do-"

With an impertinent tug at one trailing strand, the child effective cut her off and nodded in approval. Then, keeping her eye for a moment as if to show her the importance of the action, the kid once more did the curious rounded motion with both hands.

Iambre was lost. "Hair? What about my hair? Are you saying head? No? Hair then? Yes – something about my hair?!" Following the urchin's eager nods, Iambre knew a moment of total confusion, then spat out the newest concoction, "Hair-balls? Is that it? Head with hair? What? No? But yes...?"

The kid hissed like an animal and actually hit her then. Not hard, but enough to shock her into silence. Sinking back on her haunches, Iambre sighed. *How had she ended up here? What was she doing? She should just take the parcel and go.*

Shaking her head disarmingly, she made as if to get up when it suddenly hit her like a mallet full-force on the head, staggering her balance. *Holy Fleck! But it could not be, could it?*

Ignoring the kid, her head flew up to look along the road towards the intersection as indicated by the child. The inn was there, flooding the pedestrian run and parts of the street in golden light, and...

As if drawn by an invisible string, Iambre let her eyes rise high, past the wide pewter gutters, across the tiled roof and twisting chimneys where the smoke off kitchens and fireplaces escaped in unbroken tendrils of haze: up-up-up, past that ancient tall tower, to the strange weathervane, and...

Looking at the Weathervane, again something clicked. It was surely too far-fetched, but-

She shivered hard as though someone had chosen that moment to suck the marrow from her bones and the fight from her heart. She'd never 'seen' this when she looked at the tower before, and midnight raffle... *without the boy, she would not have seen it now either, but...*

Iambre smiled. Just a little. Then a flash of trepidation claimed her.

This was of course just about as moon-shot as everything else that had happened this eve – perhaps worse because it could not be a co-incidence – yet rather than forgetting how to breathe, for the first time in a while, Iambre was suddenly breathing without a lump in her chest for the weathervane atop the tower might just look like mangled old brass, yet the shape of it was suddenly indisputably clear!

And so, far from being just any old mangled metal soldered together from long bending scraps to form any odd shape, the piece of precarious art had become indisputably circular.

Circular like a ball.

Circular like a bloody, bold-as-brass, stylised golden ball!

Thank you so much for reading!
The story will continue in Episode 8: All in a Day's Work
Available Summer 2019

Post Script from the author:

Hi there!

IF YOU ENJOYED THIS book (or any of the others ☺), I'd really love if you would take just two minutes to leave a review on your media of choice(s).

It matters because

   a. Feedback on my writing will help me learn and grow as an author. I care that my readers enjoy their experience so I'm always looking for ways to improve and expand.

   b. Feedback in the form of reviews may also often help other readers understand if this book is for them and – very importantly – that it's okay to take a chance on an indie publication.

   c. The world of books is super competitive! As an indie author it can be difficult to get noticed, or taken serious. Reviews offer the necessary stamps of approval that can help indie authors grow their visibility and brand.

So from the bottom of my soul, thank you so much for reading and reviewing! I hope to see you soon!

Linda
<3

And don't forget...

If you are curious about the world of Ostravah please visit my official web site

on **www.llthomsen.com**[1]

Here you may find lots of additional information,
including: glossaries, maps, character index, and much more...

---

1. http://www.llthomsen.com

Also – to stay up to date with the latest, for exclusive offers, re-ductions, competitions, give-aways, and much, much more, please sign up to my newsletter either via my web site
www.llthomsen.com[2]
or via
https://mailchi.mp/486a3a8674b0/themissingshield

For other social media – please 'Follow' and 'Like'
www.amazon.com/L.-L.-Thomsen/e/B07B8K4J6S[3]
twitter.com/LLThomsen1[4]
www.facebook.com/linda.thomsen.12979[5]
www.facebook.com/themissingshield/[6]
www.instagram.com/llthomsen/?hl=en[7]
www.bookbub.com/profile/l-l-thomsen-f2ca9717-7697-438c-909e-59b0332c0de3[8]
www.pinterest.co.uk/llthomsen7589/[9]

---

2. http://www.llthomsen.com

3. http://www.amazon.com/L.-L.-Thomsen/e/B07B8K4J6S

4. https://twitter.com/LLThomsen1

5. http://www.facebook.com/linda.thomsen.12979

6. http://www.facebook.com/themissingshield/

7. http://www.instagram.com/llthomsen/?hl=en

8. http://www.bookbub.com/profile/l-l-thomsen-f2ca9717-7697-438c-909e-59b0332c0de3

9. http://www.pinterest.co.uk/llthomsen7589/

THE MISSING SHIELD Series

THIS STORY BEGINS IN Episode 1 of The Missing Shield.
Below is the full list of books in the series in order of release.

> > A Change of Rules – Episode 1
> > Unexpected Bargain – Episode 2
> > A Perspective of Death –Episode 3
> > Running the Gauntlet – Episode 4
> > Notions of Risk – Episode 5
> > The Final Card - Episode 6
> > The Lure of an Ancient Fable – Episode 7

AND COMING UP SOON in 2019...

> All in a Day's Work – Episode 8
> The Way Star –Episode 9
> All Thieves' Honour – Episode 10
> The Neidar Ba'raie – Episode 11

This will complete The Missing Shield – Vol 1 of 'The Veil Keepers Quest'.

www.ingramcontent.com/pod-product-compliance
Lightning Source LLC
Chambersburg PA
CBHW022122170626
46808CB00002B/816